To,
PAUL

PENGUIN BOOKS
BANKERUPT

Ravi Subramanian, an alumnus of IIM Bangalore, has spent two decades working his way up the ladder of power in the amazingly exciting and adrenaline-pumping world of global banks in India. It is but natural that his stories are set against the backdrop of the financial services industry. He lives in Mumbai with his wife, Dharini, and daughter, Anusha. In 2008, his debut novel, *If God Was a Banker*, won the Golden Quill Readers' Choice Award. *The Incredible Banker* won him the Economist Crossword Book Award in 2012.

To know more about Ravi visit www.ravisubramanian.in or email him at info@ravisubramanian.in. To connect with him, log on to Facebook at www.facebook.com/authorravisubramanian or tweet to @subramanianravi.

FROM
YOSI & RASHIDA.

Also by Ravi Subramanian

FICTION

If God Was a Banker
Devil in Pinstripes
The Incredible Banker
The Bankster

NON-FICTION

I Bought the Monk's Ferrari

BANKERUPT

DESIRE. GREED. MURDER.

RAVI SUBRAMANIAN

PENGUIN BOOKS

PENGUIN BOOKS

Published by the Penguin Group

Penguin Books India Pvt. Ltd, 11 Community Centre, Panchsheel Park, New Delhi 110 017, India

Penguin Group (USA) Inc., 375 Hudson Street, New York, New York 10014, USA

Penguin Group (Canada), 90 Eglinton Avenue East, Suite 700, Toronto, Ontario, M4P 2Y3, Canada (a division of Pearson Penguin Canada Inc.)

Penguin Books Ltd, 80 Strand, London WC2R 0RL, England

Penguin Ireland, 25 St Stephen's Green, Dublin 2, Ireland (a division of Penguin Books Ltd)

Penguin Group (Australia), 707 Collins Street, Melbourne, Victoria 3008, Australia (a division of Pearson Australia Group Pty Ltd)

Penguin Group (NZ), 67 Apollo Drive, Rosedale, Auckland 0632, New Zealand (a division of Pearson New Zealand Ltd)

Penguin Books (South Africa) (Pty) Ltd, Block D, Rosebank Office Park, 181 Jan Smuts Avenue, Parktown North, Johannesburg 2193, South Africa

Penguin Books Ltd, Registered Offices: 80 Strand, London WC2R 0RL, England

First published by Penguin Books India 2013

Copyright © Ravi Subramanian 2013

ISBN 9780143421382

Typeset in Sabon by R. Ajith Kumar, New Delhi
Printed at Manipal Technologies Ltd, Manipal

To
Anusha, Meghna and Manya

1

21st April 1999

Washington

Bill Clinton, President of the United States of America, walked into the Central Rotunda, the large-domed circular room on the second floor of the Capitol Building in Washington. An impressive ninety-six feet in diameter and roughly double that in height, the Central Rotunda was the most imposing part of the seat of the US Congress.

The events of the previous day were playing on Clinton's mind. In a fatal attack on Columbine High School, Colorado, two high-school-going teenagers armed with assault guns walked the corridors firing indiscriminately at everything in sight. The result was mind-numbing: twelve students and one teacher dead, over twenty-five injured and hundreds scarred for life. That Tuesday, the ugly side of guns had reared its head once again.

Walking quietly around the room, a preoccupied Clinton revisited the Democratic Party's desperate attempt to curtail gun abuse in the USA. In 1992, when initially elected President, Clinton had become the first presidential candidate in over eight decades to have run his campaign on promises of stricter laws around gun control. He signed the Brady Bill, which introduced a five-day mandatory waiting period for a gun purchase and required local police to run background checks on buyers. He was also a signatory to an Assault Weapon Ban (AWB) in 1994, which banned most semi-automatic rifles and weapons. Why then did incidents like the

Columbine High School massacre take place? This was the thought running through Clinton's mind when he stopped.

In front of him hung a 12-foot by 18-foot eighteenth-century oil on canvas painting by John Trumbull. For a long time he stood there staring at it teary-eyed. 'You,' he said. 'You are the one responsible for this. Mr President. You. Thomas Jefferson. I blame you.'

The painting depicted Thomas Jefferson, the principal author of a committee of five, presenting the Declaration of Independence (DOI) to the then President John Hancock and the Second Continental Congress on the 28th of June 1776 at the Independence Hall in Philadelphia. Right next to the painting was a floor display unit, which held an image of the parchment on which the DOI was written:

> *We hold these Truths to be self-evident, that all Men are created equal, that they are endowed by their creator with certain unalienable Rights, that among these are Life, Liberty, and the Pursuit of Happiness—That to secure these Rights, Governments are instituted among Men, deriving their just Powers from the Consent of the Governed.*

Clinton was not wrong.

At the time the constitution was being debated, eleven years after the DOI, the fathers of the DOI were worried that a strong central government would trample upon the rights of the individual. A need was felt to protect the constitutional rights of the American citizen—rights that are guaranteed and are not at the whims and fancies of any government. This was seen to be in line with the DOI, which clearly said that governments must derive their just powers from the consent of the governed.

On 15th December 1791, ten amendments to the constitution were ratified. One of them was the Bill of Rights, commonly referred to as the Second Amendment:

A well-regulated militia being necessary to the security of a free state, the right of the people to keep and bear arms shall not be infringed.

The Second Amendment conferred on the Americans the right to keep and bear firearms. This made it very easy to own assault-grade firearms in most American states. Most of the Republicans and gun rights lobbyists argued that any alteration of this fundamental right could only be brought about by modifying the Second Amendment, and that was only possible through a change in the constitution. For which one needs to go back to the people. The last line in Jefferson's DOI came back to haunt independent America.

Clinton sighed as he walked away from the Central Rotunda. He was getting late for a meeting of the standing committee of the senate which had been formed to discuss changes to the Second Amendment.

A lot changed in America over the next few years. Clinton moved on in January 2001. Under George W. Bush, a Republican from Texas, gun rights took a significant step forward. Unsurprisingly, the Supreme Court struck down key parts of the Brady Bill calling them unconstitutional. Even the AWB was allowed to lapse into oblivion in 2004.

Guns were back in business.

2

5th June 2008, 9.25 a.m.

Boston Public Garden

There was a fair bit of commotion at the northern end of Boston Public Garden, right next to the weeping willows growing by the lagoons. There were quite a few people in the park, though the fifty-acre expanse made it appear sparsely populated at that hour. A few late morning joggers were hurriedly going through their routine, oblivious to the ruckus at one end of the garden.

The medic was doing his last few laps in a section of the park. Three more rounds and he would be done. He'd head home for a big breakfast, a few hours of sleep and be up and ready for the late evening shift. He was sweating through his Nike T-shirt. Cheap China-made earphones playing Metallica kept him company as he jogged. That's when he heard a woman shriek, loud enough to drown out Metallica for an instant. Pulling out his earphones, he ran rapidly in the direction of the shriek. The wails grew louder in the direction of the weeping willows. The incessant barking of a dog added to the noise.

When he cut through the crowd of twenty-odd onlookers and made his way ahead, he figured out what the commotion was all about.

He bent down and felt for the pulse. There was none. He pulled back the eyelids and looked for the dilation of the pupils. Desperately, he tried to listen for the heartbeat. Nothing. Absolutely no sign of life.

The person lying on the ground was dead. There were no physical injuries on the body to suggest murder. Probably a tired jogger who had suffered a cardiac arrest while jogging.

Someone from the crowd had already called 911. The cops arrived with the paramedics in the next seven minutes and the body was wheeled away to a nearby hospital.

3

Early March 2008

Boston

Cirisha Narayanan was alone in her cabin in the Academic Block, intently staring at the bright screen of her iMac. Petite-framed, Cirisha was an extremely attractive Tamilian, born and bred in Coimbatore. An assistant professor in Social Psychology, she had joined the Massachusetts Institute of Technology (MIT) a few years ago.

Her eyes were riveted on the screen in front as she ignored a steaming cup of black coffee on the table next to her. Two stories had caught her attention that day.

On the home page of *International Herald Tribune* was the tale of the spectacular collapse of Bear Stearns, a New York-based global investment bank and securities trading and broking firm. From the dizzying heights of a hundred and seventy-two dollars, its share price had plummeted to two dollars, which was the price at which it was picked up by J.P. Morgan Chase—a figure which was just 7 per cent of its price a few days before the collapse. It was a morbid tale of greed and lust for power which had led to the loss of livelihood and savings of hundreds of people.

'Hope someone pays for this mayhem,' she muttered to herself as she grudgingly moved on to the next story. Her mind stayed with Bear Stearns while her eyes moved on.

The second story was about two prominent American historians, who had had their research retracted over the past three months on account of conduct that was unbecoming of research faculty. Professor Hubert Didymus, who had won the National Book Award for his biography of Thomas Jefferson and even the Pulitzer for his book, *Brothers in Barracks*—the *Revolutionary Generation*, had been found guilty of lying about his experience in the Vietnam War and even referring to it in his books. Investigations conducted by the *Boston Globe* had revealed that he hadn't even gone beyond the East Coast of the United States in his entire life. The second, professor Stephanie Walsh, author of more than thirty-five books over forty years, had plagiarized entire passages from papers of authors whose works had been mentioned in the endnotes.

While the first incident shocked her about the greed of the nation she was working in, the latter left her distressed about the state of the profession that she had chosen to be in. How could people so reputed, so trusted in their professions, compromise the faith reposed in them by millions of people? More importantly, what were they thinking when they committed these professional indiscretions? Were they hoping never to be exposed?

So lost was she in these thoughts that it took her a while to realize that the phone on her table was ringing. It was Louisa.

'Michael wants to talk to you. Can you come to his room?'

'I'll be there in a minute.' And she walked out of her cabin, turned left and walked up to Michael Cardoza's enclosure, five rooms down the corridor.

'Yes, Michael. You wanted to see me.'

Cardoza, her supervisor, the one who had hired her at MIT, looked up and smiled. She liked him. Fifty-seven-year-old Cardoza couldn't stop the wrinkles from making an appearance on his face, but had maintained a physique that would put men fifteen years younger to shame. Probably a result of the discipline and training he received during his time with the US Army in the Vietnam War in the early 1970s.

He got up from his chair and walked around the table. His six-foot-two frame towered over the five-foot-two Cirisha.

'Are you ready?' he had a grin on his face.

'For?'

Cardoza laughed. He turned towards his table, picked out a folder from the pile of papers and stretched out his hand towards Cirisha. 'There you go.'

'Oh no! I completely forgot! It is that time of the year.' She opened the folder. It contained forty-two sheets of paper. Each of them had a photo of a student accompanied by a brief profile. 'How much time do I have?'

'You have time. They arrive in three weeks. The induction begins early next month.'

'So I have to memorize these names, their profiles and mentally match it with their appearances.'

'Yes, sweetheart. I know you don't like this, but Cirisha, at MIT, we believe in our faculty knowing the students even before they land here. Before you enter the class, you are expected to know each student by name. Background. Profile. Even country of origin. Faculty must address students only by their first names. This goes a long way in making them feel that they belong here.'

'When you hired me, Michael, you never told me that you would make me take an annual memory test.' Cirisha had a grin on her face. She hated memorizing the names of students. But she had to do it, because that's the way the institute operated.

'Time for memory booster pills,' said Cardoza. Cirisha smiled wider. If it had to be done, it had to be done. She took the folder from Cardoza and walked out of the room.

Back in her room she was flipping through the student profiles when her mobile phone rang. She picked it up. It was a call from India. After the initial courtesies, there was a long pause.

'When did this happen?'

A pause.

'And why?'

A longer pause.

'How could you even do this?' It was difficult to make out if she was angry or upset. 'Weren't you worried about the consequences? How could you?'

A pause.

'My return flight is next Wednesday. I will bring it forward. But when I get there, you better have all the answers ready.' And she abruptly hung up. She was extremely anguished by the call. Her entire world was beginning to crumble.

With Louisa's help, she changed the dates of her travel back to India and brought it forward to that night.

At the Boston Logan International Airport, she walked past security check and made herself comfortable in front of the departure gate number 12 and looked at her watch. Her flight would take off in an hour. She had time to kill. She glanced up towards the television that was tuned to a news channel. She could make out that the news anchor was discussing the collapse of Bear Stearns. Just then, a ticker at the bottom of the screen caught her eye. '*Staring Down the Barrel* in the eye of a storm. Democrat Senator Kristoveyich from Illinois casts serious doubts on its veracity.'

4

Summer of 2000

Greater Boston Global Bank, Mumbai

It was in the summer of 2000 that he had met her. Dressed in denims and a red semi-formal top, she had walked in with a team from Coimbatore.

She looked strikingly beautiful. Aditya, who was standing outside the CEO's room with a colleague, was smitten the moment he saw her. How could someone be so pretty, yet so innocent-looking? Twenty-five years old, at best, with an intensity in her deep brown eyes that Aditya had never seen before. Hair straight and combed neatly, held by a tiny band at the nape of her neck, this dusky beauty was straight out of his fantasies. There was a certain serenity about her, a calming, yet agitating influence. She strode to the conference room and took her seat along with the rest on one side of the table. The fact that the dark man next to her was her father, Aditya would only find out later.

The moment the door to the conference room closed, Aditya jumped. He ran to the reception on the fifth floor. 'Who are these guys? Who has brought them here? What are they here for?'

The receptionist was taken aback by this barrage of questions. Weren't investment bankers meant to be stylish and classy? 'I don't know. Saif brought them here.' After a teasing pause and a seductive look in her eyes, she added, 'To meet your boss.'

'My boss? Nalin?' Aditya was surprised. 'Really?'

'Hmm.' The receptionist nodded.

Aditya quickly snatched the visitors' register from her and peered into it. They had been ushered in as 'Saif + 4'. He frowned. 'Why don't you go in and ask for her name?' The receptionist smiled mischievously.

'Shut up.' Aditya darted back in. This time he went straight to the cabin of Nalin Sud—the head of investment banking of GB2. Nalin was extricating his jacket from behind his chair, presumably preparing to walk up to the conference room.

'Who are these guys, Nalin?'

'Who? The guys with Saif?' Aditya nodded. 'I don't know much. They came scouting for some loans. Fifty crores. Quite a large sum for us to consider lending to a new customer. Saif requested me to meet them and see if we could help raise some money through our network of investors.'

'Doable?' Aditya queried.

'I don't know. More importantly, it's not part of our target list of companies. No one knows them or has dealt with them in the past. So corporate bank is not interested. But it's too small for our business. Even if we help them arrange an investment of fifty crores, we will hardly make any money. At best a 2 per cent arranger's fee. Not worth the effort.' He rolled his eyes, took a deep breath. 'It's OK. Saif feels that if we help them now, he might be able to get some business from them at a later stage.'

'If that's what you think, Nalin, why do you want to waste your time? I will deal with them and let you know if it is genuinely worth your time and effort.' Aditya sensed an opportunity and moved in. Nalin fell for the bait. He didn't resist. 'Cool. Call me in if you need me.' The jacket went back to its original place on the chair. Within fifteen seconds, Aditya was at the door of the conference room. Standing outside, he drew a deep breath, calmed himself, opened the door nonchalantly and walked in.

'Good morning.'

'Hey Aditya! How are you?' Saif had a surprised look on his face.

He was expecting Nalin when the door opened.

'Nalin's not been able to make it. He's asked me to step in for him.'

'Oh! No problem.' Saif turned, looked at the visitors and said, 'Please meet Aditya Raisinghania, a senior member of the investment banking team.' A round of introductions followed. Saif introduced all the men and finally came to the girl in red. He seemed to have forgotten her name so he introduced her as the daughter of the dark man seated to her left. No names. Not wanting to make it too obvious, Aditya moved on. 'So gentlemen, how can we help you?'

'They have an interesting project proposal, Aditya,' Saif began.

'Emu. Have you heard of emu?' asked the father, looking at Aditya. Aditya shook his head. The electric trains in Delhi, where he had started off his career as a Xerox salesman over a decade ago, were called EMU (Electric Multiple Unit) trains.

'Not heard of emu? The bird. The big emu bird.'

'Australia? That one?' Aditya asked, raising the index finger of his right hand subconsciously, like a schoolkid.

'Yes, yes. Same thing. We want to get into emu farming.'

'OK,' Aditya acknowledged. It was more of a question. He had no clue what they were referring to.

'Emus are very popular in Australia for their eggs and meat. Even for their skin and oil.' Hardly had the father spoken when music started playing in Aditya's ears. 'Big birds. They can't fly. Are quite productive too. In one season, the emu hen lays about twenty to fifty eggs, and they are productive for over twenty-five years. The demand for emu meat is quite high. Supply is low. Guess that's because of its low-fat, low-cholesterol meat—contains less than 1.5 per cent fat. Whatever fat there is, is used to produce oil which goes into cosmetics, dietary supplements and therapeutic products.' For the first time the girl spoke. What a sweet voice! The nasal twang made it seductive to Aditya. It surely couldn't have been the result of her Coimbatore education. Her command over English was a cut above the others. 'An emu egg can feed many. It's large.

And at two thousand rupees an egg, it's very expensive too. Even the meat retails at two thousand one hundred rupees a kilogram,' she said.

'Sounds very interesting.' Aditya nodded his head.

'A year ago, we imported a few emu chicken from Australia and started rearing them. What started small has now grown to over two hundred and forty emus—all of them at our farm on the outskirts of Coimbatore. Emu farming is a great opportunity. Untapped potential. We want to grow that business now. That's why we need the money.'

'Fifty crores? Isn't that a bit too much for the kind of business you are talking about?'

'Sir, I'm not sure how much you know about emu farming. It's an expensive business to run. We need to acquire land to build these farms. These birds need space because of their size. Until we develop scale in this country, we will need to import chicken from Australia. To start with, even the feed needs to be imported. Poultry insurance costs are staggering. Overall they are high-maintenance birds, but the returns on them are very good.'

'Hmm.' Aditya nodded. The girl was irritatingly cute.

'That's not all,' the girl continued. 'We need to set up plants for extracting and storing oil and beauty products manufactured from the meat and eggs. All of which costs money.' The girl then stood up and extended a spiral-bound set of papers towards him. 'Here's the project report. It outlines the investment and the potential returns. If you give us some time, we would like to present this in detail to you.'

Regular poultry was always seen as a high-risk business by most banks on account of the susceptibility of livestock to diseases. But emu farming seemed to be something different. He skimmed through the pages. It was extremely detailed. The concept was beginning to fascinate him.

'Thank you. I will go through this and come back to you.'

'Thank you, Mr Raisinghania. When should we connect with

you again?' Aditya was very impressed with the finesse and class the girl oozed.

'I will call you back as soon as I am ready. Are your contact details in this docket?'

'They are on the last page.' Instinctively Aditya turned the page to check for her contact details. And there it was. He read the name twice. What a lovely name! Even the name was unique. There was clearly nothing run-of-the-mill about her.

'Thanks, Ms Narayanan,' he said and stretched out his right hand. Her extended arm hurriedly met his in a very feeble handshake. 'I will revert to you soon,' Aditya added.

'Sure. We'll wait.' With that, the entire team stepped out of the conference room, leaving Saif and Aditya behind. 'Does it look doable?' Saif asked.

'Saif. Oh my dear Saif.' Aditya sighed. His right hand moved up to cover his heart. 'If we don't do something for her, who will we do it for? I will discuss with Nalin and get back to you.'

That evening Aditya came to meet Saif in his cabin. 'Nalin feels it's a small business for us to take on. But I convinced him. We will take it up.'

'Wonderful!' Saif beamed. 'Now will you call them or should I let them know? In any case you were the one who seemed smitten by that girl.'

'Kirisha. Her name is Kirisha. She is pretty, isn't she?'

Saif just smiled. 'If you call her that, she will throw whatever she lays her hands on, at you. The name is spelt with a C, pronounced with an S . . . Cirisha Narayanan. It is Sirisha not Kirisha. She took pains to explain this to me but I forgot about it when making introductions. You will thank me one day.' Aditya bowed his head in gratitude, smiled and walked away mumbling something to himself.

'And by the way,' added Saif. Aditya turned back. 'They are in Mumbai until the day after tomorrow. You might want to meet them again to take this forward.' Aditya couldn't stop grinning.

~

It was seven in the evening when a freshly showered Aditya, smelling of Armani Acqua Di Gio, tossed his car keys to the valet at Taj Lands End Hotel in Bandra, Mumbai. Saturday was a day off for him. He had been sitting at home the whole day, waiting for this moment.

Cirisha had suggested that they meet at the hotel where she was staying. He saw her as he walked in. She was standing in a corner of the hotel lobby, waiting for him. Big eyes. Shapely lips. Perfect face. Her dress sense was subtle. Regular denims. The red top had given way to a purple shirt. An unpretentious handbag. She didn't look like the daughter of an affluent businessman. That said, every inch of her looked modest, unassuming and very pretty.

After the initial pleasantries, Aditya led her to the twenty-fifth floor, to Taj Chambers—the rooftop private lounge for members. Since it was only seven in the evening, the lounge was empty. They settled on the sofas in a cosy corner on the terrace. There was a slight chill in the air because of the soft cool breeze that wafted over from the Arabian Sea.

Cirisha was a teetotaller. She ordered an iced tea. Without sugar. It surprised Aditya—it's not like she had to watch her weight, he thought. Aditya picked out his favourite single malt. He also figured out the secret of Cirisha's accent. She had spent a significant portion of the last few years studying overseas. After completing her undergraduation in Coimbatore, she had pursued postgraduate studies at Oxford, specializing in Social Psychology. She even worked for a year at Oxford before a nearly fatal heart attack that struck Mr Narayanan made her return to India. Her mother had died of acute diabetes a year and a half ago.

'I am so sorry,' was all Aditya could say when he heard about her mother. 'Are you planning to give up your career in Social Psychology and be in India for good?'

'Never. It's my first love.' The answer was definitive. In line with the way she had behaved all along. Very confident and sure of herself. 'I came back because of my father's illness. Now that he is fully fit, I am considering going back. I've written to a few universities. Something will be finalized soon.'

'I am sure you will land a great job.'

'Well, I wish I do. I have decent references and have been interviewing at a few places too. Let's see.' She smiled. Her dimples became more pronounced. Aditya's heart sank even further. 'Anyway, Mr Raisinghania. Enough of my story. What do you have to offer? What do I tell Dad?'

Aditya was blank for a moment. What was she talking about?

Sensing his confused state, Cirisha added, 'About the funding. The fifty crores!'

'Oh yes. Yes. Emu farms!' Aditya had completely forgotten about it. Why did she have to bring the deal into all this? 'I wanted to speak to you about that too.' He lied. It showed on his face. Cirisha was smart enough to see through it. She smiled.

'Ms Narayanan,' Aditya began.

'Cirisha will be just fine.'

A mild laugh ensued. 'Cirisha. It's an interesting business. We will be putting this forward to a few people in our investor community. I'm hopeful that we will be able to generate interest.'

'That's nice to hear. How do we go ahead? As in, the next steps.'

'Give me three or four days. I will get back to you with a detailed plan. My intent today was to communicate to you that we are willing to help you raise funds.'

'How much will GB2 charge us for that, Mr Raisinghania?'

'Well . . .' Aditya hesitated. 'We can worry about that later.' This was at variance with his standard operating procedure. Commercials were always discussed upfront. This was a different deal—definitely not a commercial transaction for him.

The next round of single malt was ordered. Cirisha decided to go slow on her iced tea. Aditya was very curious. He wanted to know everything. 'Tell me, Cirisha, how did you get into this space?'

'As in?'

'Social Psychology. Now emus. Totally unrelated spheres. How come?'

'To be honest, I didn't know anything about emu birds. We are a family with an interest in textiles. We have mills in Tiruppur, the textile town neighbouring Coimbatore. Dad stumbled upon this emu idea on one of his trips to Australia. Since I am here, I am helping him with this project. He is a brilliant businessman. But he is more of a man of the street. He has never walked into a foreign bank. Its glitz and glamour intimidate him. So I decided to come with him to Mumbai to present the project to your business banking team. GB2's Coimbatore branch helped a lot.'

'Good you came.' And he paused. He was surprised at her candid approach. 'Otherwise how would I have met you?'

'Yes, of course. I'm glad we met.' It didn't seem like their second meeting. They kept chatting away like old friends. By the time he left the place, it was midnight.

Four days later, Aditya called Cirisha to give her a progress report. 'I spoke to a few private equity firms. They haven't shown too much interest. But I did speak to a few HNIs who are willing to invest small sums. Three of them are people who work in my bank, including my boss. I have commitments for about five crores. I am confident that over a period of time we will be able to raise the balance. You don't need the entire amount at one go, right?'

'Yes. Sounds good. I will inform Dad.' Cirisha didn't sound too interested in emus. 'I was in any case going to call you.'

'What happened?' Aditya was suddenly excited.

'I have been shortlisted for the post of adjunct faculty at MIT.'

'Oh wow! That's awesome.'

'That was not very convincing.' Cirisha had seen through his forced enthusiasm.

'Well, I don't know how to react. The first time I met you was five days ago, and now you are going away. So I'm not as thrilled as you are, I guess.' Aditya couldn't camouflage his thoughts any longer.

'Hmm . . . I'm in Mumbai tomorrow for my visa interview scheduled for the day after. I'll see you then.' And Cirisha hung up, leaving Aditya wondering if he had said anything inappropriate.

Aditya was travelling with Nalin the next day and couldn't meet Cirisha when she landed in Mumbai. He met her after the visa interview.

'When do you have to leave?'

'If all goes well, three weeks.'

'That's like . . . very soon.'

'Yes. I've already had three rounds of interviews through videoconferencing and now they have asked me to meet their head of the department in person. It's more of a formality. If I get the job, it will be wonderful. It will be the best of both worlds for me.'

'Why?'

'Because they need someone who can manage their research in India and the region.'

'As in? Where will you be based?'

'If they do give me a job, I will be contracted for ninety academic sessions in a year. Boston will be home.'

'That's it?' Aditya squealed. It didn't take too much math to figure out that ninety sessions a year meant seven and a half sessions a month.

'Yes. Only ninety classes. It's a well-known fact in academia—the focus is more on research than on teaching. In a month, I will be required to spend one week at MIT to take care of my academic commitments and the rest of my time I can be in India and carry out my research projects.'

'You can do that?'

'Of course. Almost all the overseas faculty members at MIT do that. And you know the best thing about this? I will have to fly in and out of Mumbai or Chennai.'

Aditya was suddenly excited at this proposition. 'At least I'll get to see you.'

'Yep!' nodded Cirisha. She was beaming. 'Come, let's celebrate today. Tomorrow I will be back to the depressing, voiceless emus in Coimbatore.' She held Aditya's hand and pulled him towards the car.

For the first time, she had held his hand. Aditya was over the moon. They partied the night away. From south Mumbai to Bandra, they covered all the pubs. What joy she, a teetotaller, got out of a pub, Aditya didn't bother to ask.

When he finally dropped her back, he felt like going up to her room, but controlled himself. Cirisha was honest. Honest to herself. It was not the fear of rejection as much as the feeling of impropriety which held him back. He didn't want to get carried away and do something which would lead to all the memories of the day being wiped out. He bade her goodbye and walked back to his car. His mobile phone beeped. It was a message. 'Thanks for the best day of my life. I have never laughed so much.'

A year later Cirisha and Aditya were married in a simple ceremony in Coimbatore. Cirisha was against extravagance of any kind and didn't want an elaborate wedding. It was a court marriage followed by dinner for a few close friends.

~

Early next morning, they left for Ooty for their honeymoon, a hundred kilometres from Coimbatore. They had planned a trip for a week. Hotel Savoy, the only five-star hotel in town, was running at full occupancy and hence they had to check in to Sterling Resorts, a timeshare holiday home.

Three days went by in a jiffy. They only stepped out of their room for lunch and dinner. After three days, on Cirisha's recommendation, they decided to do some sightseeing. 'If people ask us what we saw in Ooty, we at least need to give them some credible responses,' she said coyly one morning. Aditya smiled and agreed. A hectic day of sightseeing later, Aditya suggested that they stop somewhere for a drink.

'Have it in the room. Order it through room service.'

'The resort's selection of whisky is horrible. I can't drink any of those.'

'Drop me back and go and buy your drink. I am tired.'

Aditya dropped her at the hotel and went off to buy some alcohol. As luck would have it, it was a dry day. None of the wine stores was open. He went all around Ooty trying to find a shop that would give him a bottle of single malt. After half an hour of searching, he found a shop with its shutters half down. He walked up to the shutter, bent down and peered inside. An old man, sitting behind the counter reading a newspaper, looked up and smiled.

'Laphroaig?' Aditya asked.

'Dry day,' the old man replied. 'No sale.'

'Need one bottle.'

The old man waved his hands, indicating that he would not supply. 'If I sell today, I go to jail.'

Aditya reached into his shirt pocket and pulled out three hundred-rupee notes. 'Will this help?' By then he had entered the store.

'Make it five hundred. Then maybe it will. But I don't have Laphroaig. Only Chivas.' The wine shop owner was surprisingly candid.

Aditya smiled, pulled out five hundred-rupee notes and placed them on the counter. 'Seventeen hundred more for one bottle,' the shopkeeper demanded. Aditya paid the amount, picked up the bottle, hid it in his backpack and walked out of the shop.

Cirisha freaked when he told her about how he had managed to get a bottle of alcohol on a dry day by paying an additional five hundred rupees. 'How could you even do that? You bribed a shopkeeper for a bottle of alcohol! How can you be so cheap?' she ridiculed. 'I can't believe this.'

'It's OK. I am happy, he is happy. I got what I wanted, and he got more than what he wanted.'

'Getting what you desire at any cost is all that you crave for, Adi. Right?' Cirisha was livid. It was not about the five hundred rupees. It was about the fact that Aditya had broken a moral code of conduct that she had expected him to adhere to. He didn't understand what the fuss was all about. But seeing Cirisha go ballistic, and in the interest of peace, he apologized. The bottle of Chivas was consigned to a shelf in the room, with Aditya promising not to touch it on that trip.

It was for the first time that day that Cirisha was exposed to Aditya's tendency to focus on the ends more than the means. Shortcuts didn't matter to him as long as the objectives were achieved. This worried her. But in the euphoria of the honeymoon, the incident was forgotten. At least temporarily.

5

June 2004

Mumbai

Aditya and Nalin walked into the coffee shop of the Grand Hyatt. They were late for the meeting with Jigar Shah.

Hailing from Kolhapur, Jigar Shah had created Step Up Shoes, one of the most successful footwear brands in western India, from scratch. From a modest beginning twenty-six years ago, when he was hardly thirty, Jigar Shah had grown the company to clock a turnover of over four hundred crore rupees.

Somewhere along the line, handicapped by the lack of big-corporation finesse and hindered by his lack of pan-India selling and distribution skills, Jigar Shah had hired a CEO. A professional who came to him armed with an MBA from a premier business school with a decade's worth of expertise in managing businesses. Shivinder had been with him for over six years and it was under him that the company had really flourished. Of late, Step Up Shoes had even diversified into other products like belts and handbags. Jigar Shah maintained a small corporate office in Bandra Kurla Complex, while his manufacturing facility was located outside Mumbai on the Goa highway.

Nalin was distinctly uncomfortable. It was always a red flag when a promoter wanted to exit a business. He had mentioned this to the branch banking head of GB2 who had set up this meeting.

'I am told that he is a very finicky guy.'

'I've never met him.' Aditya said.

'For the first time, we are meeting someone without knowing his complete background.' They had heard about him. Everyone had. But no one from the investment banking community had ever met Jigar Shah. It was because Jigar Shah was not seen as someone who would ever sell his company. For Jigar Shah, Step Up Shoes was not just another business; it was a means to provide livelihood to the thousand people who worked for him.

Jigar Shah was in the coffee shop waiting for them. 'My apologies, Mr Shah. The traffic was horrible today.'

'I can understand, Mr Sud. My office is close by. So it wasn't a problem for me.' Jigar Shah turned out to be surprisingly warm and welcoming.

The pleasantries continued for a few more minutes. Nalin took the lead. 'Pardon my ignorance, sir, but I am not completely conversant with your business in terms of financials, scale and dynamics.'

'Oh yes. My CEO will take you through the details.' And he raised his hand, pointing in the direction from which Nalin and Aditya had entered. Both of them turned to see whom Jigar Shah was pointing towards.

'Shivinder?' Aditya exclaimed. 'What are you doing here?' The CEO had just walked into the meeting.

'So you know each other?' Jigar Shah was confused.

'Of course. We went to the same business school,' Shivinder Singh quickly responded. 'Good to see you here, Adi.' And he walked past Aditya's extended hand and hugged him. 'Didn't know you were with GB2. The last I met with you was when you were a photocopier salesman. Modi Xerox it was. Right?'

'Yes. Years ago.' Aditya nodded. 'You joined Step Up Shoes?'

'Shivinder is our CEO. He has been with us for six years. He is like family now,' Jigar Shah stepped in.

Nalin, who was just a spectator to this reunion of B-school alumni, was getting impatient. 'Let's begin.'

All of them settled into their respective chairs around the coffee table and Shivinder began. 'You must have read the profiling document that I had sent out.' Aditya and Nalin nodded. 'The company was started by Jigar Shahji over twenty-five years ago. A first-generation entrepreneur, he built this company to its current level. Last year we clocked a turnover of roughly four hundred crore rupees, out of which we made a profit of around eight crore rupees. Our growth trajectory has been fairly impressive.'

Nalin was listening intently. He held back his questions.

'Over 40 per cent of our turnover comes from the overseas market. We are suppliers to Puma and even Nike. We adhere to the latest CPSIA and ISO norms.' Nalin raised his eyebrows.

'CPSIA—Consumer Product Safety Improvement Act. It was implemented by the US government particularly with respect to children's products.' Nalin simply nodded. He had no clue what Shivinder was referring to.

'The remaining 60 per cent comes from the local market. Our margins here are quite reasonable. Better than exports. A shoe which costs only a hundred and twenty-five rupees to produce, retails for around six hundred rupees. We make roughly two hundred and fifty rupees a pair.'

'Interesting,' Aditya butted in.

'Yes, it's a good business to be in. I have built every bit of it with my own hands,' Jigar Shah finally spoke.

'Then why are you selling it?' It defied logic that a promoter would want to exit such a lucrative business. Nalin had obviously not been briefed about what prompted Jigar Shah's decision.

'I am physically not in a state to run it, Mr Sud. It has not been an easy decision. This business is my life. Last month, I had an open-heart surgery. I don't have any children who would take care of this business. Or, most importantly, the people who work with me. I want to make sure that after me, there is someone to take care of them.'

'OK. Fair enough.' There was no sign of emotion from Nalin.

Aditya looked at him. 'Never mix business and emotions. Else you will be in trouble,' Nalin had told him once.

For the next thirty minutes, Shivinder spoke uninterruptedly about the business, the challenges, their customers and their business model.

'What's the expectation?' Nalin asked Jigar Shah when Shivinder was finally done.

'Price?' Jigar Shah confirmed the question. Nalin nodded.

'Not sure. But I am not stuck up on the price. I only want to secure the future of my employees and their families. The buyer will have to be someone who commits to take care of these employees.'

'Emotional fool,' Nalin thought to himself. 'I presume you would value the company at roughly fifteen to twenty times its projected future earnings. Right?' Shivinder butted in, 'That's what we would expect.'

Nalin didn't respond.

The discussion ended in the next fifteen minutes. As they were walking towards the exit, Shivinder caught up with Aditya. Nalin and Jigar Shah were walking ahead. Nalin glanced back and, seeing Shivinder quite a distance away, whispered to Jigar Shah, 'Mr Shah, have you considered allowing Mr Shivinder Singh to take over the company? Obviously with funding from friendly private equity players. He has been around for some time and knows everything inside out.'

'I wouldn't want that to happen.' The response surprised Nalin. 'Shivinder is a fantastic salesman, but he is emotionally very cold with my employees. That's the reason why I have had to stay involved despite his presence. After me, if he is the only person running the company, I fear that the employees will have a tough time. I definitely don't want that to happen. If contractually he is bound to keep these employees intact, then I will be fine. Please do . . .' He stopped abruptly when he saw that Shivinder and Aditya had almost caught up with them.

'Understood,' Nalin acknowledged as he walked to the exit.

Aditya saw Nalin off at the porch and turned towards Shivinder. 'Where do you stay, dude?' Over six feet tall, he wore his slightly excess weight around the midriff well. Very articulate and clear in his thoughts, he sounded like a true-blue CEO.

'Santa Cruz. And you?'

'Bandra. Pali Hill. Are you heading home now?'

'Yes. Unless you're telling me there is some other plan.' Aditya smiled. Shivinder had always been a smart-ass. Never one to give direct answers.

'We can grab a drink if you are up to it.'

Shivinder looked at his watch, thought for a second and said, 'OK. Let's go.'

The two of them headed back into the hotel, to the bar, reminiscing about the old days and updating each other on what their batchmates were up to. They had a lot to catch up on. In any case, Cirisha was in Boston that day. Aditya didn't have much to do back home.

6

November 2004

Mumbai

Aditya was in his car, waiting for Shivinder in the porch of a suburban hotel, when his phone rang. Not wanting to pick it up, he let it ring for some time. He was in a foul mood. They had met a number of prospective buyers for Step Up Shoes and nothing had worked out. He had just got out of the seventh presentation and that too had not gone well. Four of the seven prospects found Step Up Shoes to be too small for them to evince any interest and three had found it to be too big. However, there was one thing in common: everyone had said that the profitability did not stack up to the valuations that GB2 was pitching it at.

The left-side door opened and Shivinder got in. 'Come, let's go somewhere and get a drink. I'm really pissed off. If this guy felt that we are demanding too steep a price, why did he even agree to meet us?'

'Shivinder.' Aditya cut him short. 'There is a problem. I am advising you not as your investment banker, but as a friend.'

'What's the problem? Don't we have a balanced and sustainable business model?'

'Yes, your model is fine. But your growth has been too slow for anyone's comfort. The valuation of two hundred and fifty crore rupees that we have demanded is not cheap by any yardstick. Our valuations are based on forecasted profitability of twenty crores, a profitability number that you expect to reach three years from now.'

'Yes. I am aware. We are asking for a valuation of Step Up Shoes at a multiple of twelve times the projected earnings. Which isn't excessive. I was initially hoping to get up to fifteen times the projected profitability, but we have climbed down from that stance. Don't people even go up to a valuation of twenty times the projected earnings?'

'Yes, they do. However, that's not the problem. The disconnect is not in the profit multiple that you are demanding, it's in your business plan. Your numbers have been projected to grow at 30 per cent for each of the next three years. However, you can't ignore the fact that your growth has been in single digits—nowhere close to what we are projecting. Our projections are sounding very fanciful.'

'So what are you saying?'

'Nothing. Come, let's talk over a drink.' And he turned into Turner Road en route to his house in Pali Hill.

Once they had reached home and after he had poured his first peg of Laphroaig, Aditya started off. 'Look, Shivinder, as the CEO, you own 3 per cent in this company.' Shivinder nodded.

'Your profit last year was roughly eight crores. How the hell will you get to twenty crores in three years? In 2007?'

'We have a business plan, a well-articulated strategy. If we execute it properly, we will get there.'

'Cut the crap, Shivinder. For meeting your planned numbers three years from now, you need to get to an annual turnover of over six hundred crores. You seem to be woefully short. Worse, in the first six months of this year, you have shown a de-growth.'

'OK. So?' There was a tinge of disappointment in Shivinder's voice. He didn't like Aditya showing him the mirror.

'If I take a multiple of fifteen times the earnings, instead of the twelve that we have demanded, the company, based on this year's financials, is worth a bit over a hundred and twenty-five crores.

Nothing more. And for the valuation to get to two hundred and fifty crores—the price we are asking for—we need to do something dramatic. Business as usual won't get you there.'

'So conjure up something dramatic. Who is stopping you?'

Aditya thought for a minute. 'I have a plan. It's not too difficult, if we figure out how to execute it.'

'What plan?'

'Look, there are two ways in which companies can build valuations. One, top-line growth, or, simply put, sales growth. Companies with higher sales figures are valued higher than companies with not-so-high sales. Two, profitability growth. In a country like India, most investors fall for top-line growth. The assumption is that if we grow the top line, the bottom line will automatically grow. If not now, then definitely at a later date. If not today, it will happen tomorrow.'

Shivinder had been in the trade long enough to know this. 'The challenge is, how to grow either of these.'

'It's possible.'

Shivinder looked at Aditya, surprised. 'Look, Aditya. Growing the bottom line is difficult. Growing the top line is a lot easier if we are willing to compromise on our margins.' And after a pause, he added, 'And compromising margins is something we have never done as a business strategy. Step Up Shoes has never been in the discounting game.'

'If your projections for the next three years are based on revenue growth, sales have to happen. Top-line growth has to come.' And then he walked closer to Shivinder, put an arm around his shoulder and spoke softly. 'By hook or by crook.'

'I have no idea what you are referring to.'

'Chill. There is a way out. But for that we need some help.'

'Like what?'

'Wait.' Aditya picked up the phone and dialled a number. 'Hi! Aditya here.' He walked into the next room, gesturing to Shivinder to get himself a refill. In a few minutes, he was back. 'OK. Deal done.' Seeing Shivinder's raised eyebrows, he explained, 'Look, your turnover needs to go from four hundred crores to six hundred crores in three years. This year, if you grow by seventy crores, it should be fine. You figure out a way to increase your turnover by fifty crores, I will get you another twenty crores.'

'When will you bankers stop talking in Greek and Latin?' Shivinder rolled his eyes and went back to his drink.

'See, dude. It's not as complicated as you make it out to be,' said Aditya and proceeded to outline the entire plan. By the time he was done, Shivinder's eyes were wide open. The effect of four Laphroaigs disappeared in a jiffy. He could never have thought of this plan. 'Is it safe to do this?'

'Shivinder, every company that we have dealt with does things to beef up valuations. What I am proposing is nothing compared to what others do.'

Shivinder walked up to the bar, pulled out a vintage 21-year-old Glenlivet bottle and smiled at Aditya. 'We must open a bottle for this momentous occasion.' And he poured out two large pegs.

~

It took them three months to put the plan into motion.

'The CFO is on our side now.' It was early February, and Shivinder and Aditya were having a mid-afternoon snack in the former's office. 'The billing and invoicing clerk is in place and so is the logistics manager. They are all guys who have worked with me for over a decade. I can trust them.' After digging into the samosa, Shivinder asked Aditya, 'Would you want to meet the CFO? Just to make sure that he is a guy we can back.'

Aditya thought for a moment. 'OK. Call him in.' After a pause, he added, 'One day you are going to get me into trouble.'

Within the next few minutes, a middle-aged man of medium build, about five foot seven, walked into the room. Most of the hair on his head had disappeared and his round Gandhian spectacles gave him a very down-to-earth, sober look. 'Meet Deven Khatri. Our new CFO,' announced Shivinder. 'He joined us two weeks ago.'

'Hello Deven. Good to see you.' Aditya welcomed him into the room. 'Shivinder has some really nice things to say about you.' The handshake was warm and firm. He took an instantaneous liking to the guy.

'Deven has been briefed, Aditya.'

Aditya looked at Deven. The latter didn't look too comfortable. The shifting of weight from one leg to the other was an indication. Was it a good idea to go ahead with their plan with a shaky and uncertain CFO?

7

February 2005

MIT, Boston

A spine-chilling cold had gripped the East Coast. There was a blanket of snow on the MIT campus. Everything looked and felt gloomy.

Cirisha was too busy to be bothered; she was in the final phase of her research project. Set in Vuyyuru, a small town thirty miles from the eastern coast of Andhra Pradesh, it was aimed at measuring the impact of the availability of credit on the choice of crops grown by farmers. She had spent months working with farmers in a belt that grew rice. A shift to sugarcane cultivation would mean more returns. However, it required more seed investment, a reason that prompted most of them to continue with rice cultivation. As part of the research, Cirisha had tied up with sugar manufacturers to offer financial assistance to farmers with a back-to-back captive arrangement for sugarcane purchase. The idea was to see whether farmers would shift to sugarcane if monies were easily available in their ecosystem.

She glanced out of her window. The sun was about to set. A few students were walking past the Academic Block towards the car park on their way to the dorm. To get there, one had to cross the car park and walk for half a mile. Straining her neck, she looked up. It was beginning to get dark. More snow had been forecast for later that night. She had better get going, else she would not be able to reach the parking lot without getting soaked. From the stiffened posture of people scurrying on the path below, she could make out that it was beginning to get really chilly.

A knock on the door distracted her. Even as she shifted her glance hurriedly towards the door, her brain registered something strange. Hadn't the person standing beneath the street light, pretending to talk on the phone, been waiting there for the last two hours? Was he a student? Another member of the faculty? Who was he? More importantly, what was he doing there, standing in the snow for so long? She ignored him and walked up to the door. It made her uneasy.

'Hi Richard! What's up with you? How come you are still at work?' Standing at the door was her colleague in the Social Psychology department. Richard Avendon had joined the institute a few years before her. Like her, Richard too was an assistant professor. At five foot three, he was only a little taller than Cirisha. However, his muscular gym-toned body made him a hit with most women around campus. With deep intriguing eyes, he was quite a Casanova, or so everyone thought. In the Academic Block, Richard's cabin was right above hers, on the second floor.

'I was finishing my research paper. Due for submission in three weeks.'

'Where are you getting it published? Have you started work on that front?'

'Yes. I'm trying for the *Journal of Personality and Social Psychology*. Looks like they will accept it.'

'Really?' Cirisha beamed. 'That would be wonderful. *PSP* is the best journal in its category. Is James helping you on that one?'

'He better! After all he is my mentor on this research. He was the one who raised the grants.'

Cirisha smiled. 'Helps to have a powerful mentor, doesn't it?'

'I just got lucky that I was picked by him. He was the one who brought me up from an adjunct faculty wanting to get tenured, to this tenure track position. Anyway, how's yours coming along?'

'Same story. Struggling with deadlines.' Cirisha did a mock-frown.

'How many papers more to go for you to be considered for your tenure?' Richard asked Cirisha casually.

'At least four research papers more.'

'Four more? That will take you another four years at the minimum, right? Assuming that you complete a research paper a year and each one of them gets accepted.'

'Guess so.'

'Are you willing to wait that long?'

'Do I have a choice?'

Richard thought for a moment. 'Yes, you do.' Cirisha was visibly excited to hear this.

Becoming a tenured faculty was the Holy Grail for most American academicians. In a way it guaranteed the right to academic freedom. The key benefit tenured professors got was permanency of appointment. It protected them against adverse action in case they openly advocated their opinion, which could be at variance with the institute's thought process. It also gave them the freedom and the ability to research topics that might not be interesting to the public at large, but were of significant impact for policymaking.

Tenures were normally granted on the basis of published research, demonstrated ability in raising research grants, academic visibility and teaching background. A tenured professor was clearly the upper caste in the polarized academic community in the United States of America. Granting of tenure, often a subject of intense political battle in any university, was a long-drawn-out process involving reviews by external parties, peers, department seniors, the dean and often the executive committee of the university.

'How would that be?' A conversation with Richard was always exciting, and when it was about her tenure, it was even better. She had been conscious about her tenure eligibility ever since she completed her doctoral research three years back. But she had never obsessed over it. When Richard said that she had a choice of not waiting another four years, it caught her attention.

'Can I come in and then discuss that, if it is OK with you, Madam

Cirisha?' Cirisha was embarrassed that she hadn't even moved away from the door to let him in.

'Sure, sure. I am so sorry!' She blushed as she turned and walked back to her desk. When she walked past the window, she instinctively glanced outside. The man below the lamp post was still there. The only difference was that this time around, he was looking up and his gaze was fixated on something that sent shivers down Cirisha's spine—he was looking in the direction of her room.

'Look, Cirisha,' Richard began, 'I have one research paper to go before I become eligible to be considered for a tenure.'

'Which you are publishing in the next three to four weeks. Right?'

'Yes. My tenure interview is coming up in the April–May cycle. However, there is a small problem. It is a bit of a risk going to the tenure granting committee after having completed just the bare minimum.'

'Why? Despite James Deahl's backing? I thought he was one of the most powerful guys on campus. The only other guy who is in the same league as Michael Cardoza.'

'Hmm . . .' Richard nodded. 'There is a deficiency in my research track record. Most of my research is centred on America. The cross-cultural touch is missing.'

'Oh. I didn't know it was that important.'

'It is. That's what James told me.'

'That's not something you can fix in a hurry. How are you planning to address it?'

'That's why I am here.'

'As in?' Cirisha's eyebrows went up. She had no clue what he was hinting at.

'Cirisha. Your research has a good Third World aspect. India, Asia and what not.'

'It suits me well that way. I don't need to stay away from my family for long.'

'If we collaborate, we can be of use to one another.'

'Sorry, I don't understand.' She was getting snappy and restless.

More so, because the man on the road had been staring unblinkingly in the direction of her room for the past fifteen minutes. It was beginning to worry her.

'Take me on as a co-author for your research paper.'

'What?' This was the first time anyone had said this to Cirisha. Though she knew that these adjustments happened regularly in the world of academic research, she had never been approached for such a thing in the past.

'Yes. It's simple. You add me on as a co-author when you publish your paper, and I will reciprocate. I will add your name as a co-author too. Which means that for you to become eligible for a tenured position, you will only need three more research papers and not four. We could agree to collaborate for our future projects too.'

Even though the proposal seemed interesting, it instinctively struck her as unethical. She didn't want to cheat the system. She had never done such a thing.

'I'll think about it,' was all that she could say. She was aware of the fact that Deahl and Cardoza would never see eye to eye on something like this. Richard and she were fond of each other, but the same could not be said of Cardoza and Deahl. They were sworn enemies.

In the field of faculty research, it was not about the pay packages: they never got paid that much to fret over. It was not about the car one drove, or the number of bedrooms in the house that one lived in. It was all about egos. The larger the project one did, the bigger the research one ran, the more the millions of dollars in one's research budget. Cardoza had a history of mobilizing large grants for his research projects for a long time until Deahl came from nowhere and upstaged him.

Cirisha considered, for a moment, that if Richard was suggesting something like this, would he have spoken to Deahl and sought his blessings? What about Cardoza? But then she dismissed the thought. Before worrying about Cardoza's point of view, she had to agree to it first. And as of now, she didn't.

The two of them spent twenty minutes together before they left.

On the way out of the block, Cirisha stopped and looked towards the lamp post. There was no one there. Where had he disappeared?

With brisk steps she walked towards the car park. Whether she was struggling to keep pace with Richard's longer steps or whether it was out of fear, it was impossible to tell.

As she got into her car and exited the parking lot, she saw someone peering from behind a large tree just outside it. It was the same man. Her heart skipped a few beats as she stepped on the accelerator and raced out of the parking lot towards her residence, not too far away.

8

February 2005

Mumbai

Aditya got up late the next day—it took the incessant ringing of his mobile phone to break his deep slumber.

'Hi Ciri,' he said as he picked up the phone.

'Sleeping? Still? It's well past ten there. Get up now. Not going to work?'

'Hmm . . . Overslept.'

'With whom?'

'Very funny. Shivinder was here. We had a few drinks. I slept at four, only after he left. Guess the alarm was not loud enough to wake me.'

'Oh, OK. I just got home some time back. Thought of calling you.'

'Reached so late?'

'The sponsors are on Michael's case. And pressure, like water, always flows from a higher to a lower level. Michael peacefully passed it on to his flunkies. So I stayed back to finish my work.'

'Oh. When are you flying back?'

'Next Thursday. You have a copy of the ticket with you. I had sent it to you.'

'Just asked.'

'You know, Aditya, I was very scared today. I felt I was being stalked. First time ever.'

'What nonsense!'

'Yes, Aditya. There was a guy standing below my block for two hours. And then when I drove out of the parking, I saw him hiding behind a tree.'

'Really?'

'I don't know if I'm overreacting.'

'Your instinct has more often than not been correct. Do you know who he was?'

'No. I've never seen him before. He had drawn his cap over his face. So I couldn't see it clearly.'

'This doesn't sound good at all.' Aditya was fully awake now. Nervous too.

'I know. But it is OK. I will manage.'

'Do you really have to do this?'

'Do what?'

'Do you really have to keep working there? Why can't you be here for good? You have fabulous colleges here where you can teach. Why struggle like this?'

'You know fully well it's not only about the teaching.'

'OK. You can pursue your academic career here. There are enough institutions. And in any case I earn enough for both of us.' For Cirisha, a career in academia was about more than just teaching.

'It's not about the money, Aditya. I have my own career. I have to establish myself. The research culture here is far stronger than in India. The respect that academicians command here is far higher than you can ever imagine. Unless you want me to come back and stay at home and make breakfast and coffee for you every morning.'

Aditya was in no mood to carry on that conversation. The two of them had had the same discussion many times before, and each time it had ended the same way. With Aditya backing off.

'Anyway. Don't go out alone. Take care. And if you see the guy again, please tell Michael or at least call the police. And by the way, the gun is functioning properly, right?'

'Yes, it is. I tested it at the firing range just last week. Don't worry. You take care.'

The moment she disconnected, she felt that she should not have told him about the stalker. He would unnecessarily get paranoid. It would give him one more reason to push for her to return to India for good. She opened her laptop and started working on her project. Her deadline was near.

9

May 2005

Mumbai

The boardroom at Step Up Shoes was packed. Jigar Shah, Shivinder Singh and Deven Khatri were present, all looking dapper in their well-tailored suits. A couple of private equity players who were considering investing in the company were also there. Three of their bankers had turned up too.

Aditya was standing in a corner watching the fun. A board meeting was a regular statutory affair at Step Up Shoes, though never had it been done on this scale, where everyone involved with the company had been invited as observers. It was important to showcase the achievement and the tremendous growth of the organization. A big splash was important in order to get noticed by the market makers. A few journalists had come in for a press conference which was to be held after the board meeting.

The annual result of Step Up Shoes was a delight in itself. The sales turnover had increased by about 35 per cent, while the expense line was up by only 20 per cent. Profitability had jumped by over 60 per cent. The small crowd was ecstatic. The applause refused to die down. Everything was progressing like a fairy tale, until one reporter raised his hand.

'But sir, your receivables position is quite precarious.'

'Precarious?' Deven Khatri ridiculed. 'What's precarious about it?'

'Yes. Precarious. Last year, when your turnover was four hundred crores, you had outstanding payment receivables of sixty crores. Today, on a turnover of five hundred and twenty-five crores, you have outstanding amounts of a hundred and ten crores. Isn't that too high?' There was silence in the room. Not because anybody suspected foul play, but because no one knew from where the answer would come.

'That's because a significant portion of our sales jump has come in the winter and festive season. Which is the period from November 2004 to March 2005 or, in other words, the last five months of the previous financial year. And we offer a hundred and eighty days' credit to our dealers. Hence those amounts have not even become due from the dealers. That explains why most of these monies have not come in by 31st March and are still showing as outstanding in our books as at the end of the financial year.' Aditya was impressed. Never had he seen Deven so confident.

'So you feel that's not an item to worry about?'

'Not at all. This cash will eventually come in. They are definitely not bad debts,' Shivinder stepped in nonchalantly. The journalist was convinced, more by the confidence with which Shivinder said those words than by what he actually said. He went back to his seat and started scribbling something on his notepad. Shivinder looked at Aditya from the corner of his eye. Aditya was smiling. They had handled it well.

The event went off brilliantly. Sales growth. Profitability growth. Expansion of the dealer network. Step Up Shoes looked good on all the matrices. So what if forty crores of the total turnover had been cooked up? No one would ever know.

'Well, the plan worked,' Aditya said to Shivinder when they met after the board meeting.

'Your idea to beef up sales numbers was brilliant, Aditya. I would never have conjured up this plan. This is why it helps to have an investment banker on our side,' Shivinder gloated. 'I was talking to Nalin on the sidelines. He congratulated me and said that we will now command a great premium. He even said that no one can prevent us from closing this deal now. If Nalin, being the expert that he is, couldn't see through it, nobody will ever be able to.'

Aditya smiled. Wasn't all of it Nalin's plan in the first place? Aditya was just an able lieutenant. He wanted to tell Shivinder to get real, but held back. The entire orchestration of the plan came floating before his eyes.

His thoughts went back to the day when, armed with Nalin's instructions, he had been introduced to Deven Khatri. That day he had coached Deven on what had to be done. Deven hadn't seemed too convinced. It had taken some effort to bring him on board. 'Our true sales will not change, Deven. However, in our books we will show an increased sales figure. Take our Delhi franchisee, Regalia Shoes, for instance. In the normal course, Regalia would buy shoes worth five crores every year. Now as per our plan, we will raise fictitious invoices for an additional two crores and show in our books that we have sold them stock worth seven crores. So our actual turnover, which should have been five crores, will show up as seven crores in our financials. A 40 per cent increase in turnover.

'These fictitious invoices won't be sent to Regalia. They will remain with you. Our recovery team that follows up with dealers for outstanding payments will be given a list, which will show the real outstanding amount collectible from Regalia as five crores only. Deven, you will have to manage this. You will have to make sure that the amount invoiced over and above the true order is removed from the overdue amount when the reports go to the recovery team.

'Once we raise an invoice, we will recognize it as a sale. We will ship shoes worth seven crores out of our factory. Shoes worth five crores will go to Regalia, while shoes worth two crores will go to our warehouse in Coimbatore—a warehouse that we will create only for these over-invoiced shoes. Our production unit manager will manage this. He has been briefed.'

A confused Deven had just uttered one word in the entire conversation, 'Understood'.

'Our costs remain the same. This fake sale wouldn't cost us anything incremental, except the cost of production of the shoes, which is very low. Net–net, we would have increased revenue and kept costs flat. And all this leads to . . . leads to . . . ?' and he looked expectantly at Deven.

'Increased profitability,' Deven responded to the prompt, even as he and Aditya nodded their heads in sync.

'Bang on. And increased profitability means increased company valuation. If we manage to increase the profitability by five crores, the company value goes up by roughly fifteen times, that is, seventy-five crores.'

'Over-invoicing of this kind on twenty to thirty big dealers across India will give us over fifty crores of excess sales. Isn't that easy?' It was at that moment that he had decided to cook up much more than the initially planned twenty crores. Twenty was the number he had decided on when they set out on the journey. By March, however, they had run up fraudulent sales of forty crores. And that had helped.

A tap on his shoulder brought Aditya back to the present. He smiled again. 'I was thinking about the conversation with Deven.' The smile showed no signs of going away. 'This guy needs to be managed. He is a bit low on the top floor,' Aditya told Shivinder.

'I will keep an eagle eye on him.'

'Yes.' Aditya stretched, let out a deep sigh and got up from his chair. 'OK. So we have to figure out how to pump forty crores of excess invoicing back into the system.'

'Yes. That's the amount of sales that we have fabricated. If we don't pump in that money, it will continue to show as receivables outstanding.'

'Anyway, these become due only in a few months. Dealers are supposed to get six months' credit. So let's worry about it later. If we have a good year, then we will adjust it against receivables this year.'

'How do you plan to do that?'

'Let's take the same Regalia Shoes example. If in the current year, they do exceedingly well and pick up stocks worth ten crores instead of the regular five crores, we will show it as a sale of around seven crores and adjust the balance three crores that they will pay us, against last year's overdues. If they don't do well this year, we will be in trouble. Bottom line: this year, you have to ramp up genuine sales so that the fraudulent sales of last year can be masked.'

'Worst-case scenario, we will have to manage the auditors and make sure they don't ask too many questions. They must take us at face value and report what we want them to.'

'That's not a problem,' Aditya interjected. 'We can get one of our own to audit the firm and overlook minor improprieties.'

'At a cost. We can manage that. What are auditors for? To write what we want them to.' Shivinder smiled.

That night Aditya and Nalin were at Jigar Shah's residence to celebrate the fabulous results of Step Up Shoes, when Aditya's phone rang. It was Narayanan.

'Yes, Dad,' Aditya said.

'Aditya, I need to see you. Is it possible for you to come to Coimbatore for a day?' There was a touch of concern in his voice. An urgency which wasn't normal.

'What happened, Dad? Is everything OK?' It was a very strange request from Narayanan and it worried Aditya.

'I'm stuck, Aditya. Need some advice.'

'About what, Dad?'

'Not on the phone, Aditya.'

'OK, Dad.' He was in no mood to debate. 'I'll come over the next weekend. By then Cirisha will also be back. I'll bring her along.'

'She is back next weekend?'

'Next Thursday.'

'Is it possible to come before that? I want to meet you alone.' Aditya found this strange. 'If for some reason you can't make it, I will come over.'

'No problem. I'll try to come this weekend.'

'That will be nice. Let me know and I will come to pick you up.' And the call ended, leaving Aditya worried and concerned.

The next morning, the *Economic Times* carried an interesting headline on the front page. 'The birth of an Indian Reebok.' A quarter-page article dedicated to Step Up Shoes and its financial results. This was unprecedented press coverage for Step Up Shoes. The article waxed eloquent on the management and leadership team at Step Up Shoes. Shivinder Singh had arrived in style.

10

End-May 2005
MIT, Boston

Cirisha was in the MIT Faculty Dining lounge that day. She had just finished lunch with a colleague and was about to pay up and leave when she saw a rather sullen-looking Richard walking towards them.

'I need to talk to you urgently.' Richard didn't even wait till he reached their table.

Cirisha looked at her colleague and said a hasty goodbye. 'Catch you later. Let me see what our friend here wants.'

Richard waited for her colleague to leave and handed her an envelope. 'What is this?' Cirisha asked him even as she opened the envelope and looked at the paper inside. It was an internal memo.

Dear Mr Avendon

The Faculty Evaluation Committee of MIT thanks you for your application for the post of Associate Professor and for appearing before the FEC for an interview on May 4th.

We regret to inform you that the FEC has declined your application. This is not any indication of your academic or research skills. The Institute would be happy to have you continue in your role of Assistant Professor. You will be free to apply for a similar post twelve months from now.

Your chair has been advised, and he will be in a position to

47

*address your queries. Should any remain, please feel free to write
in to us.*

> *Warmest regards*
> *Henry Liddell*
> *Dean*

Richard's application for consideration for the tenured position of
an Associate Professor had been declined. After reading the letter,
Cirisha looked up. Tears had formed in Richard's eyes. She knew how
much the tenure meant to Richard. He had been banking on this to
come through. 'Cirisha, don't you think I have the bloody brains,
skills, guts, initiative and self-awareness to get a tenured position?'

In a bid to console him, Cirisha held his hand tightly. She was
aware that not everyone on the tenure track ended up getting a
tenured position. It was public knowledge, often unstated, that it had
a lot to do with one's popularity amongst one's peers and the ability
to raise grants rather than pure research potential and academic
credentials. Richard's biggest strength was his biggest weakness too.
James Deahl. People in Deahl's team were never able to rise above
his aura, above the halo that he had around himself, and create an
identity for themselves. If a Deahl-friendly person was the provost,
all his people would end up getting their tenures. If Deahl didn't
have a friendly provost in chair, then all the people reporting to
him would suffer. That's the way it had been for years. The current
provost, Gordon Meier, was not particularly fond of Deahl.

'It's OK, Richard. You are much better than what this letter says.'

'Bullshit, Cirisha! Everyone's been saying the same thing. If I am
much better than the rest, why didn't I get promoted to the tenured
post? And you know what, there were four faculty members in the
tenure review committee. And they all approved of my tenure. It
got declined at the level of the dean. Why? Why did they do this to
me?' The tears were streaming freely now. She hugged even more
tightly, trying to settle him.

'Come, let's go,' she said when she realized that people around them couldn't help but stare. Richard's tantrum was becoming a spectacle.

'No, it is OK. I will be fine. I have to meet someone. And in thirty minutes I have to be at the duPont Center.'

Inaugurated only a few months back, the duPont Center was an Olympics-standard sports complex with every conceivable facility for students, faculty, employees and their families. Richard had been appointed as the faculty coordinator for the fencing classes. A brilliant game and a friendly demeanour made him the obvious choice. Despite being in his late thirties, on his day, Richard held the potential to beat even the university student champion at the game. It was this love for the game that made him join academia a few years later than usual. A failed attempt at becoming a professional sportsman had robbed him of a few years of an academic career.

'Fencing classes?' she asked.

'Yes,' Richard nodded. 'Need to take my mind off this crap.'

'Do you want to meet up after your classes? We can go out for a drink.' Cirisha wanted to humour him. He was intense and impulsive; Cirisha didn't want him to be alone. He would brood over it for a long time if he did not have anything else to keep himself engaged.

'It's OK, Cirisha. In any case you don't drink.' He put an arm around her shoulder and smiled. He knew that Cirisha was doing it for him. 'I am meeting someone else in the evening. Thanks for being there for me. Despite that boss of yours.'

'Haha,' Cirisha laughed out loud, hoping to cheer him up. 'It's not my boss. It's your boss who is a pain. And by the way, who are you meeting in the evening? Anyone interesting?' She winked.

'No, Cirisha. No one interesting. But I wish there were someone who would take an interest in me.' He turned and walked away, leaving Cirisha wondering if the cryptic comment was directed at her. 'Naah. He meant that he wished someone would take professional interest in him and fast-track him to a tenured position,' she thought to herself as she watched him walk down the pathway.

Just before he turned right towards the duPont Center, he was joined by someone who gave him a long hug. Cirisha looked at them and smiled. She had seen the other person somewhere but couldn't remember where.

11

May 2005

Coimbatore

Coimbatore airport was a small but quaint one. Ten flights took off from the airport on any given day. Aditya's flight from Mumbai to Coimbatore took a little less than two hours. This was only the third time Aditya was coming to visit his father-in-law.

Narayanan picked him up at the airport. A couple of minutes into the drive, Aditya realized that they were not headed home.

'Where are we going, Dad?' a curious Aditya queried.

'Nilgiris Hotel. I have booked a room for you.'

'I'm going back on the afternoon flight, Dad.'

'Yes, I know. We can peacefully sit and chat there.'

Aditya didn't want to argue with him. After all, if Narayanan had decided on something, he would have thought it through. 'Can we grab a quick coffee somewhere? Before we head to the hotel?'

'Nilgiris has a café on the ground floor.'

'Do you have a Barista Lavazza in Coimbatore?' Aditya hadn't particularly enjoyed the last time he had had coffee in the Nilgiris café and wanted to go to a better place. More so because the early morning flight had made him miss his morning dose of coffee. He hadn't even had time to grab one at the Mumbai airport.

'Of course we have Barista in Coimbatore. It's all over the place.' And Narayanan turned his car towards the closest Barista outlet.

Within minutes, they were at the swanky new Barista outlet

at the northern end of the upmarket Race Course Road. Since it was early in the morning, there were very few people in the café. Narayanan was happy. It meant fewer people eavesdropping on their conversation.

Finally, when they were settled in the farthest corner of Barista, Narayanan looked at Aditya and began to explain. 'Aditya, you must be wondering why I wanted you to come.' Aditya nodded. 'I wanted to talk to you without anyone else sneaking in on the conversation.'

'You are making it sound a bit strange, Dad. What's it about?' Aditya looked around. There was a young couple in the café, apart from the two of them. But they seemed too busy with each other to listen to their conversation. He turned back and looked at Narayanan.

'It's about my business, Adi.'

'Is there a problem, Dad?'

'No, Aditya. Absolutely not! When you guys couldn't help me raise funds, I was pushed to a business model which helped me grow exponentially.'

Aditya nodded.

'We decided to raise money from the public. We launched a scheme wherein people could raise emus on our behalf. For around one lakh rupees we would give them three emu eggs. They would rear the emus on their own plots of land, which would be sufficiently barricaded. We would, for a monthly fee, even supply the emu feed. After eighteen to twenty-four months, we would buy back the emus at a specific price and harvest their meat, skin, oil and so on. In the case of emu hens, we would hold on to them longer and make money on their eggs too. What we paid the customers was far less than what we would end up making on the birds.'

The coffee arrived, a cappuccino for Narayanan and a macchiato for Aditya. Aditya waited till the person serving the coffee was out of earshot.

'And did you make the kind of margins you were intending to make?'

'That and more. The initial phase was phenomenally successful. Almost everyone who came to us and started an emu farm made money. Initially people were very apprehensive. But once the first lot of people who invested started making their returns, the buzz started to intensify. More and more people began queuing up to open emu farms. In fact, the second wave was so intense that farmers started selling off part of their land to raise the deposit money and started converting their balance land into emu farms. We were loaded with cash, not knowing what to do.'

'Are there any rules around emu farming?'

'None whatsoever.'

'Then what is bothering you, Dad?'

'Adi, the problem is that the business has grown. And almost everyone pays in cash. The farmers, for instance, who have enrolled with us under this scheme, don't even have a bank account.'

'Dad, you don't need to get defensive about it. Almost everyone we meet these days deals with cash. What would you expect in a country where hardly 6 per cent of the population files income tax returns? That's hardly a problem. What's the issue?'

Narayanan leaned forward, elbows on the table, and whispered, 'The accumulated cash is becoming a problem.'

'That is not a bad problem to have. I would rather be rich and have excess cash to play with than be poor.'

'I know. I am not complaining. The problem is slightly different.'

Aditya just sat there listening.

'A month back, Gopal Krishna, the income tax commissioner of Coimbatore was transferred and a north Indian fellow has come in. Last week, he raided the offices of one of the largest emu farms in Mettupalayam—Rajah Emu Farms.'

That's when Aditya understood what the crux of the problem was. 'So you are worried that they will raid you. And if they lay their hands on your cash, you will be in a soup.'

'Yes. And they are likely to do so anytime. Temporarily, I have managed to get rid of all the cash. There are intermediaries who will manage it for me for the time being. But I don't want to leave it with them for long. They are not very dependable. Will it be possible for you to help me move the cash? Can you keep a part of it with you in Mumbai?'

'How much cash are we talking here?'

Narayanan looked around. He pulled out a tissue from the stand on the table, scribbled something on it and turned it towards Aditya. When Aditya saw it, his eyes popped out. He looked at Narayanan, then back at the tissue paper again, and whispered, 'Forty crores?'

Narayanan nodded.

'How the hell will I keep so much cash in Mumbai? And what will I tell Cirisha?'

'I don't know. I have to get rid of ninety.' He pointed to the paper napkin and said, 'CR.' Aditya understood that he meant crores and nodded. Narayanan continued, 'And there is nobody else that I can trust. And I obviously can't keep this in a bank.'

Aditya's palms started bleeding sweat. The very thought of so much of cash in his control worried him. He wasn't unfamiliar with massive amounts of cash but this was the first time that family was involved.

'Dad, I don't think I will be able to stash away so much in Mumbai and keep it under my watch. But . . .' and he paused.

'But what?'

'There could be a way out. We have done that for a few big customers in the past. A few businessmen and politicians. I can try and see if we can do that for you. But before that let's get out of here.' Both of them got up; Aditya walked up to the counter, dropped a five-hundred rupee note and walked out, without even waiting for change.

Once they were in the safe confines of the car, Aditya said, 'Look, Dad, what I am telling you can't be discussed with anyone. In Mumbai, we have a team of global relationship managers. These RMs, even though they are based in Mumbai, can help you open an account in any country. They operate below the radar. Even within GB2, not many know about these RMs. Not only will they help you open an account in countries with reasonably softer tax and extremely stringent privacy laws, they will also move your funds there. I recommend that you open an account in Geneva, Switzerland, and move your money there.'

'Will it be safe?'

'Much safer than here, for sure. The Swiss have very tough confidentiality and secrecy laws. No one will ever find out.'

'What if I need access to the funds?'

'Call the RMs and they will deliver the cash to your doorstep.'

'Oh? Is that possible?'

'Yes. The only catch is that these guys do not get involved if the amounts involved are less than fifteen million dollars.'

'Brilliant! Aditya, this is just brilliant! This gets rid of a big headache for me,' Narayanan exclaimed.

'Let me recheck the process. I'll talk to them when I get back to Mumbai. Once I have the information, I will call you.'

Narayanan was happy. Finally he had found a solution to his problem. After driving around for an hour more, Narayanan dropped off Aditya at the airport. Just before Aditya got off the car, he asked Narayanan, 'Dad, that warehouse? Shivinder and I would like to come visit it sometime next month.'

'Sure. Anytime. It's yours, Adi.' And he smiled. 'But just to give you a heads-up, the warehouse is nearly full. We need to look for a new one in case you are planning to store more stock there.'

'How long will it take for you to operationalize one?'

'At best sixty days.'

'That would be awesome. Thanks, Dad,' said Aditya as he stepped out of the car.

'Please do not discuss any of this with Cirisha,' Narayanan reminded him. Aditya nodded as he shut the door. He did not need to be told that Cirisha would never approve of what Narayanan was doing.

12

May 2005

Coimbatore

The process of opening an account in GB2 Geneva was laughably simple. Two well-dressed, deodorant-drenched young men in their late twenties landed up at Narayanan's residence. It took them exactly thirty minutes to complete all the formalities. An account opening form was filled up, photographs clicked, fingerprints taken and telephone numbers exchanged. Narayanan couldn't help noticing that they had a telephone number with a Swiss code prefixed to it.

'What's the amount you would want to transfer into this new account in Geneva, Mr Narayanan?' This question from one of the RMs made Narayanan uncomfortable. But Aditya had told him to be completely open and transparent with the guys from GB2.

'About ninety crores.'

'Hmm. Over twenty million dollars. Thanks. I need to sensitize the bank.'

'When will you pick up the cash?'

'A different team manages cash. They will get in touch with you, pick up your cash and give you credit into your GB2 Geneva account within the next forty-eight hours.' Narayanan was relieved.

Everything done, the two RMs got up, picked up the bunch of papers and put it into their briefcase.

'Can I get a copy of these papers?' Narayanan asked.

'You won't need them, sir. Within three days, you will get a call with your account details, using which you can access your account over the internet. That should suffice. Thank you, sir.' And they turned to leave.

As promised, within the next seventy-two hours he was called and given an account number and a password. He was also given a number to call in case he wanted to transact on the account. 'Of course, if you ever visit Geneva you are free to walk into our branch, sir,' the caller said before he disconnected.

'Aditya, they gave me a number to call to transfer funds. Is it safe?' Narayanan called Aditya within five minutes of having received the call from the bank.

'Yes, Dad. Call them and they will pick up the cash from you. Leave the rest to them. Don't ask them questions, answers to which might confuse you.'

The next day, around midnight, an armoured van pulled into the driveway of a ramshackle farmhouse on the outskirts of Coimbatore. A few men stepped out and Indian currency worth ninety crores was picked up from the farmhouse and loaded into the van. After the cash was loaded, the van stayed in his driveway for a couple of hours. Narayanan guessed that it had a currency-counting machine in it. His blood pressure went up a few notches when they left. He had no document to show for having given them the cash. Worried stiff, for the next forty-eight hours he sat by the computer, logging into his account, hoping to see if the money had been credited. Finally when he saw a credit of approximately twenty million dollars in his account, he breathed a sigh of relief. It was working.

He picked up his phone and called Aditya.

'The first lot has been transferred, Aditya. Thanks for getting this done for me.'

'No problem, Dad.'

'I was worried since I didn't know these guys.'

'Dad, it's a regular thing these guys do. You are transferring only twenty million. These guys manage ten times that amount and more for politicians and big industrialists. Relax. Your money is safe.'

13

July 2005

Boston

Deahl drove the Ford SUV into his parking slot. Though it was not a reserved slot, no one else parked there because everyone knew it was where Deahl parked his car. He got off and walked towards his block. The look on his face was tense. He had been summoned by the provost to be part of an ad hoc committee formed to review a decision taken by the Faculty Evaluation Committee (FEC) at MIT.

MIT guidelines were very clear on the process to be followed once the tenure application was denied:

> *'An individual can submit a written request for a formal review to the Provost within 60 days after being notified in writing of the decision not to promote or award tenure. If filed subsequently, the Provost may deny the review request as untimely. The review requester must identify any and all grounds for the request for a review since there is one single review of such a decision.*
>
> *The Provost will decide if a review will be undertaken after making a preliminary review of the request to determine whether the request provides one or more appropriate grounds for review. In making that decision, the Provost may consult with whomever the Provost decides is appropriate.*
>
> *After consulting with the Chair of the Faculty to the extent the Provost determines appropriate, the Provost will appoint an*

> *ad hoc faculty committee of three senior faculty (naming one as chair) and notify the review requester of the names. If the review requestor believes that any of the ad hoc committee members could not participate as an objective fact finder, he or she should timely write to the Provost explaining his or her reasons, and the Provost, in his discretion, will decide if there is a need for an alternate appointment.'*

Richard filed the review petition with the provost, challenging the earlier decision of not granting him his tenure. He was in his late thirties and close to completing nine years as a non-tenured assistant professor. To hit the late thirties without a tenured role was akin to putting an end to even a remote chance of building an academic career. More importantly, the university rules stipulated that anyone who was denied tenure at MIT twice had to leave within twelve months. Hence every shot at getting tenure was a matter of life and death. Being rejected twice certainly meant professional death.

The provost, after considering Richard's petition, had formed an ad hoc team of three members. Michael Cardoza, who was on the initial panel that had declined Richard's tenure application, Ahmed Siddiqui, the legal head at MIT, and James Deahl, the Chair sponsoring the granting of a tenure to Richard.

'It's been nine years that I have been a member of the faculty at MIT. Initially an adjunct professor and now an assistant professor. I applied for tenure a few months ago, as in my view, I had the required credentials—research publications, proven grant-raising skills, teaching assignments, student mentoring and even sporting duties. I have met the required criteria on every single parameter. Yet my application was turned down. The peer evaluation committee rated me highly and recommended me. I am at a loss to understand the reasons for the FEC turning me down. Your letter does not state it. I couldn't get a valid explanation from my Chair, Dr Deahl. That's why I decided to appeal to you, to reconsider the decision of the previous committee. The judgement has been unfair, to say the least.'

Ahmed Siddiqui waited for Richard to finish. He was from Pakistan and spoke in an accent he attempted to but failed to camouflage. 'Mr Avendon, I have reviewed the entire evaluation process from the standpoint of adherence to guidelines. The laid-out procedure has been followed. The decision of the earlier committee has been found to be appropriate. There have in fact been certain glaring acts of omission on your part, Mr Avendon, which cannot be ignored.'

'I'm not aware of what you are referring to, sir.'

'It has been alleged that you have approached two assistant professors with offers of co-authoring their research papers, just to fulfil the criteria for the minimum number of papers published. They have deposed in front of the academic subcommittee.'

'That deposition could have been motivated. It is also presumptuous to assume that as research guides, we will allow such accommodations,' Deahl sprung to Richard's defence.

Cardoza argued, 'Well, yes. But in instances like these, the university's stance is that such contested works will not be included in the list of eligible publications to be considered for granting tenure. The issue will be investigated, and if need be, corrective action will be taken. Till that is done, according the status of a tenured associate professor to you, Mr Avendon, will be in contravention of university norms.' Deahl was upset at the way this was panning out.

'For a minute, even if I agree to this stance, then isn't it appropriate that the committee place his appointment in abeyance till the issue of ghostwriting of a research paper is resolved? Declining Mr Avendon his tenure would mean that he cannot reapply for the next one year. Placing it in abeyance would mean that should he be found to be on the right side of the law, then there is hope that he will be accorded his rightful status once the clouds clear.'

'The laws don't permit that, James,' Siddiqui butted in. Richard was getting very fidgety and nervous.

'The law is silent on this, Ahmed. It's open to interpretation and that's why we, as seniors, are here,' Deahl retorted. While his tone was soft, his body language was aggressive.

'He is right,' said Cardoza. 'The law is silent. It might be appropriate to place it in abeyance till this entire issue is resolved.' He looked at Richard and asked him, 'Mr Avendon, did you proposition assistant professors Charles Boon and Obuza Gele that you would include their respective names in papers published by you, in exchange for them accommodating you as a co-author in their papers?'

'I deny it.'

Deahl was getting very restless. 'It's their word against his, Michael.'

'I agree. However, when different people talk about the same problem, it is impossible to ignore. But, as agreed, let's place Mr Avendon's application in abeyance and move forward.'

'Well, Michael, that was the only point of contention. On every other parameter, Mr Avendon scores. So I would recommend that we purge the earlier committee's recommendation and reconvene after your investigation into the allegations are complete. And instead of declining Mr Avendon's candidature, agree that we will re-evaluate it.'

At that instant the door opened and someone walked in. 'Mr Siddiqui,' he addressed Ahmed Siddiqui, who hurriedly got up and walked towards him. He led him out, embarrassed that the outsider had walked into the room directly. When Richard saw him, he was shocked. The look on his face was one of anxiety interspersed with fear. He had seen the person earlier. What was he doing in the interview room and that too with Ahmed Siddiqui?

'Why are you so late? You were supposed to have been here an hour ago,' Siddiqui said to him the moment they stepped out of the room.

'My car broke down. Fixing it took a while.' The visitor was very curt. 'I brought this for you.' He handed over a small brown envelope to Siddiqui and walked away.

Siddiqui headed back to the room, pulling something out of

the envelope and sliding it back in. The look in his eyes changed to a curious mix of distress and anger. He had been in academia for over twenty years. And now the very pillars on which he had built his career, the foundations on which the entire academic discipline had grown, were beginning to flounder. He wouldn't allow that to happen. At least not while he was alive.

'Ahmed! Where did you disappear? We are all waiting for you,' Deahl began the moment Siddiqui re-entered the room. 'Should we call it a day, or do you think we have more business to conclude?' Cardoza nodded his head in agreement as if indicating that for once he agreed with Deahl.

'You might just want to spend a few more minutes on what I have just received.' Both Cardoza and Deahl looked up at Siddiqui. He was waving at them the brown envelope that the visitor had handed to him. His face had gone red with anger. 'I would like to inform the group that allegations of certain improprieties by Mr Richard Avendon were raised by a few members of the student community, following which we conducted an investigation. I need to table these papers before the committee. Basis this fresh set of evidence, there is no need to defer anything. We can put an end to this discussion right here.'

'What allegations?' Cardoza was the first to jump.

'Here you go.' Siddiqui extended his right hand towards Cardoza to hand him the brown envelope. Just as Cardoza was about to accept the documents, Deahl butted in and snatched the papers. 'What is this about?'

'See for yourself.'

'It'll be unfair if I or anyone else does. Before we accept a fresh set of information or investigation report, I would like the committee to take note of the fact that university rules prohibit any information which was not available as on date when the first decision regarding Mr Richard Avendon's candidature was taken from being presented in front of the ad hoc committee constituted to review the earlier decision.' And then he paused. 'Am I not right, Ahmed?'

Siddiqui's eyebrows went up, his eyes focused on something in the distance. After thinking for a few seconds, he looked at Cardoza, and then at Deahl. 'Yes, you are right. This needs to be presented separately to the core group and then, if need be, a discussion held. But it is not entirely inappropriate to discuss it right now.'

'Incorrect.' Deahl spoke with a fair degree of authority and confidence. 'That's not right, Ahmed. As per law, you have to first discuss it with Mr Richard Avendon, give him a chance to explain and respond, and in case you find his explanation unsatisfactory, you can then take action or present it to this committee.' Then he got up. 'Thank you, gentlemen, for your time.' He looked at Richard and said. 'That will be it, Mr Avendon. We will be in touch with you.'

As he was walking out of the room, Deahl turned. He lifted his right hand, extended his index finger and pointed it towards Siddiqui. 'Ahmed, if this information, whatever you claim to have, is made public, you will be answerable. You don't need me to tell you that you will be liable for charges to be filed against you for wilful defamation of Mr Richard Avendon. I'm stating it just in case you intend to share it with Michael before you let Mr Avendon take a look at it.'

'Thanks, James. I wouldn't have been sitting here had I not known my job. And of course the laws of academia.'

'Well, from what I saw today, I have my doubts.' Deahl always had to have the last word. He left the room. The door swayed on its hinges a few times before it settled into its state of inertia, shutting out the room in the process. Cardoza and Siddiqui too left almost immediately.

It was windy outside. Instinctively Cardoza pulled the lapels of his coat tightly across his chest. Siddiqui was walking a couple of steps ahead. The two of them walked briskly to the parking lot. Deahl was ahead of them. He would have already reached the parking lot.

'Ahmed, wait!' Cardoza called out to his colleague. When he turned back, Cardoza pointed to the pavement slightly ahead of him. Ahmed walked back towards Cardoza, who bent down, picked up the papers that had slipped out of Ahmed's hands and passed them back to him.

'Oh. Thanks.' He took the papers and hurried towards the parking lot. Theirs were the only two cars there. A car crossed them as they made their way in. They knew it was Deahl's. Siddiqui waved at him, even though the tinted windows of the Ford SUV blocked out anyone inside the car from being seen. In the next two minutes both of them were on their way home. Darkness was setting in, and the street lights were starting to come on.

Siddiqui stayed in a six-bedroom ranch, forty miles from the MIT campus. A luxury most academicians couldn't have afforded. He was a legal professional who had made his money fighting lawsuits and compensation cases prior to joining the university, albeit on the administration side. He belonged to a wealthy family; his father owned a mid-sized moneylending business way back in the 1960s and 1970s, and that helped him get through two divorces miraculously without going bankrupt. He lived alone. It was public knowledge that he was dating someone, a cute twenty-seven-year-old lawyer who had interned with him once. Remarrying was not on his mind. He needed companionship and the young lawyer provided that in abundance. He would be home in the next sixty minutes, into the waiting arms of his young lover.

~

Early next morning, office-goers driving on Interstate 90 were witness to screeching sirens and an ambulance racing hurriedly past them towards Kingsley Park. In precisely six minutes from the time the call went out, an ambulance from Lincoln Hospital and three police cars screeched to a halt almost simultaneously near a cluster of cars parked by the side of the road. Cars normally don't halt on that lonely stretch. Seeing a car with shattered windows parked there at 5.45 in the morning, a woman passenger driving by had called 911.

Local transport office checks on the car ownership, fingerprints of the deceased and the permission sticker on the car all pointed to one fact: the body in the car was that of someone working at MIT, someone called Ahmed Siddiqui. There were no fingerprints, the car had been wiped clean. Siddiqui had been stabbed ten times all over his torso and neck. It seemed like a crime of passion. There were no CCTVs because Massachusetts state law prevents monitoring of roads through CCTV cameras. It invades privacy, some would say. The place where the murder happened was also a blind stretch and one with low traffic. No clues. No witnesses.

14

July 2005

Mumbai

Nalin's long-awaited move out of GB2's India business finally happened. Chosen to head the wealth management strategy unit at the global HQ in Boston, he was to move in three months. A farewell befitting his stature was organized. After all, hadn't he been one of the stalwarts of the leadership team, who had delivered for over seven years as the head of investment banking?

Aditya was given the responsibility of organizing the farewell. While deciding on the date, he had only two considerations in mind: Nalin's availability and Cirisha's presence in India. Cirisha was to land the night before the farewell.

Aditya was at home that night, preparing to go to sleep when his phone rang. Cirisha normally called either at this time or early in the morning.

'Hi Ciri.'

'Hi Adi. What are you up to? At home?'

'I was out with Shivinder. Just got back home.'

'Shivinder again!'

'Yes. Why?'

'He gives me the creeps.' Shivinder was not the kind of guy she was comfortable associating with even if it was through her husband.

'Haha! He is a decent chap. Don't worry, I'm not turning gay.'

'Rubbish!' she yelled into the phone. 'He is a rich guy, Adi, but to me he comes across as a con artist. You need to make a distinction between people who have a conscience and people who make con-a-science, Aditya. Mark my words, he will land you in trouble one day.' Her instincts about people were very strong and often correct. She hadn't liked Shivinder from day one.

'Oww! Wow . . . wow. Someone is in a crazy mood today.'

Cirisha realized she was being rude. 'Sorry, Adi. I don't know what's wrong with me today.'

'PMSing.'

'Shut up, Adi.' The long drag on the words told Aditya that something was not right.

'OK! OK! Peace. But what happened? You don't sound good at all.'

'I'm extremely tired. Just couldn't sleep last night.'

'I figured that out. What happened?'

'Lots of things. The MIT Police were all over the place. They were searching all our desks and workstations. A last-ditch effort to see if they find something incriminating. They have been doing this from the time Ahmed was murdered. We couldn't get any work done.'

'Now? So many days after Ahmed died? Looks like the cops there are quite similar to the cops here.'

'We had a report due tomorrow. And now that's been delayed because of these cops. I am going mad.'

'Be careful, Ciri. Don't get into any kind of trouble. You also have a flight to catch.'

There was a prolonged silence at the other end.

'Ciri. You there?' Aditya reaffirmed. 'Hello. Can you hear me?'

'Yes, Adi. I can.'

'What time is your flight, Ciri? Are you done packing?'

'I'm sorry, I don't think I will be able to make it to the flight today, Adi. Too much to finish. I'll have to extend my stay by a couple of days at the very least.'

There was silence at the other end. Cirisha could hear the silent hum of the air conditioner. 'What about Nalin's farewell?'

'Could you please manage it without me? In any case he is moving to Boston. I will throw a welcome party for him when he settles down here. I really need to finish my pending work, Adi.'

'Everything except your husband needs and gets your attention. Right, Cirisha?' Aditya had never been so cold.

'The cops screwed up our day yesterday. Today also seems like a washout. I have my work to finish. It has dependencies. There are other people who work together with me on a project. I can't just dump everything and come. You know that.'

'If only you show the same commitment towards home and me . . . Life will be so much better. But what can I say?' Cirisha didn't know how to respond. She kept quiet. After a long pause, Aditya spoke again, this time just murmuring, 'I gave you the dates three months in advance so that you could plan to be here. Nalin has done so much for me. But, it clearly was not to be.'

'I am sorry, my love. I wanted to be there. But . . .' She had not even finished her sentence when Aditya interrupted her. 'Forget it. Come whenever you want to. I'm feeling sleepy. Let's talk later.' And he hung up on her. Cirisha was surprised. A bit shocked too. Aditya had of late started getting worked up at her prolonged absence from India. She called him back. Aditya didn't pick up her call. After trying thrice she decided to let it cool down before calling him again.

Three days later, Aditya was at the airport to pick her up as usual. The drive from the airport back home was deafening in its silence. Cirisha had never seen Aditya like this. She tried her best to get him to talk. But he didn't go beyond monosyllabic responses. After parking the car in the basement, he quietly followed Cirisha up to their apartment. Cirisha had a spare key with which she opened the door. The moment she opened the door she was in for a shock. The living room was full of bouquets. Dry wilting flowers that were beginning to rot. She looked at Aditya. He had crossed the living room and stepped out into the balcony.

'What's all this, Aditya?' She found the rotting bouquets a bit strange. The place was beginning to stink. Her emotions were a strange cocktail of anger, frustration and curiosity. She turned to Aditya. 'Flowers? So many of them? And why are they here?'

No response.

She walked up to the closest bouquet and picked out the card attached to it. 'Dear Aditya, congratulations! May this be the beginning of a long and successful journey.' What did that mean? Not able to fathom what that message meant, she walked up to the next bouquet. 'Hey Adi. Congrats on your promotion to the head of investment banking.' It was Nalin.

'Adi!' she yelled. 'When did this happen? Why didn't you tell me?'

Adi was in the balcony staring vacantly into the darkness. 'Adi!' screamed Cirisha. She ran towards the balcony, knocking over a few of the bouquets in the process. Hugging him from behind, she stood in silence for a minute. 'Why didn't you tell me?'

'Had you been here, I would have told you.'

'When did you know?'

'A week back. More than the farewell, I wanted you to be here when they announced it at Nalin's farewell.'

'Why didn't you tell me? I would have made sure I was here.'

'Let it be.' And he turned.

'Adi!' Cirisha exclaimed. His eyes were red. They had fought often since their courtship days, but this was the first time she had seen him like this. She hugged him tightly in an attempt to calm him down.

'It's not about you not being here on this big day, when I received the most important promotion of my life.'

'Then what is this about, Adi? This was one of the few trips where I have been away for three weeks. Else I always come back in a week, maximum two.'

'What kind of life are we leading, Cirisha? Either you are getting over your jet lag, or you are preparing to leave. Even when you are here, you are travelling to interior Andhra Pradesh or some other godforsaken place. Is this the life we signed up for when we got married? We have been married for close to five years now and we live like nomads. I have been to the airport to pick you up more times than we have been to a movie together. We have not even thought about when we are going to start a family. We are not getting any younger. We are just living our lives independently, Cirisha. And somewhere our paths overlap, so we end up being together. This worries me.'

The party for Nalin's farewell and Aditya's promotion was just a manifestation of a deep-rooted problem that had crept into their relationship. In such situations, Cirisha knew, it was best to keep quiet. And let Aditya vent his frustrations. There was no point rationalizing. She tightened her hug. Aditya hugged her back. 'I am sorry, my baby. Really sorry,' Cirisha mumbled, her voice barely audible through the folds of his Tommy Hilfiger shirt.

15

August 2005

Boston

Law enforcement on campus was the responsibility of MIT Police. The chief of MIT Police and his team took care of routine issues. Even though they functioned largely independently, at the highest level they reported to the Boston Police Department.

A homicide team from the Boston Police Department working with the chief of MIT for well over sixty days had checked out all potential suspects. They met with the president of MIT, the dean, members of Siddiqui's team, the various departments and people whom Siddiqui interacted with on a regular basis, like Deahl and Cardoza. Outside the university, they investigated Siddiqui's girlfriend, her immediate family, his ex-wife and every conceivable suspect. Everyone had a foolproof alibi.

The cops finally put it down to an isolated incident of robbery on a lonely stretch of road, which had gone horribly wrong.

Three months later, Siddiqui's death was forgotten. No one was interested in holding the baby. The institute was happy pushing it away and laying the blame on an external party, the ex-wife and girlfriend were not pursuing it as they were worried they'd get embroiled in a legal tangle. Ahmed Siddiqui, a man who fought the battle for many individuals and organizations, died a very lonely death.

16

October 2005

Mumbai–Coimbatore

'Dad, can you please check if you have received a credit of roughly two crore rupees in your GB2 account? An amount of four hundred thousand dollars was supposed to have come in today.'

Narayanan called Aditya back in fifteen minutes. 'Yes, Aditya. Credited. They've deducted fifty-two dollars as service charge. Remitted by Snuggles Inc.'

'Great. Thanks, Dad. We'll figure out what to do with the money later. I just wanted to know if the money has come. We are signing tomorrow.'

On a pleasant Friday afternoon, Snuggles Inc., a global footwear giant, announced that it was buying Step Up Shoes. Aditya was the one who had convinced Snuggles about the relevance of Step Up Shoes to their plan to set up a shoe manufacturing and retailing base in India. Apart from the fees that GB2 made in seeing this transaction through, Aditya negotiated a four-hundred-thousand-dollar payout from Snuggles as lobbying fees for helping them jumpstart their business. Nalin's moving to Boston had definitely helped close the deal with the Boston-headquartered Snuggles.

As per the terms of negotiation, control of Step Up Shoes was to pass to Snuggles Inc. Anyone who had spent more than two years in the company would not be laid off at least for a period of three years. Shivinder would be retained as CEO with a 5 per cent stake in the company, provided he stayed with the company for the next five years. There was an obvious performance clause linked to it.

It was a win–win deal for everyone. Snuggles had spent thirty crores less than what they had budgeted for. Jigar Shah had got twenty crores more than what he had mentally settled for. Aditya got his payment. Shivinder got to keep his job as well as his equity in the new company. And the employees were secure. Overall, everyone was happy.

Until the first audit committee meeting six months later.

17

March 2006

Tennessee

Gary Barnard listened on. Horror mixed with anger was evident on his face when Christina Friggs told him what she had just seen. Friggs was the section-in-charge of seventh-grade students at the County High School in Jacksboro, Tennessee. Barnard, the principal, was a strict disciplinarian and had set very high standards for his school.

Walking to the side door of his huge, imperialistic principal's room, he called out to his assistant. 'Ask Ken Bruce and Jim Lander to come to my room. NOW!' he yelled. In no time, the two gentlemen were in his room. Both were promptly dispatched to fetch Nicholas Klingman, a seventh-grader from Ms Friggs's class.

Displaying arrogance unbecoming of someone his age, a supremely confident Nicholas strode into Barnard's room. The two assistant principals followed.

'Nicholas Klingman,' Barnard began, 'I need to inspect your bag. Is there anything there that you should not be in possession of?'

'No,' Nicholas replied smugly.

Barnard looked at Lander and instructed, 'Can you please take the bag into your custody and do a thorough check?'

'Is there anything in particular that you are looking for, sir?' Nicholas was suddenly cagey.

'Well, yes. Let Mr Lander search your bag and see if what we suspect is true.'

'Do you mean something like this?' Nicholas pulled out a small .22 handgun from the bag. From a distance it looked like a toy.

'Nicholas, please hand over the toy to Mr Lander.'

'It's not a toy. It's real,' Nicholas growled.

'OK, Nicholas. Hand over the gun to Mr Lander,' said Barnard, taking a step towards Nicholas.

'Wait!' yelled Nicholas. He pointed the gun towards Barnard and said in a menacing tone, 'I never liked you anyway.' He ordered everyone present in the room to line up with their backs against the principal's table. Then, taking aim at Barnard's head, he fired the gun. The bullet missed, but the carnage had begun.

By the time it ended and Nicholas was overpowered, Barnard had been hit twice, on his groin and thigh; Bruce was hit below the armpit, the bullet piercing both his lungs and heart. Lander was shot in the back as he tried to wrestle the gun away from Nicholas—the bullet grazed Nicholas's hand before penetrating Lander's lung.

The gunshots had by then sparked off chaos in the school. Nobody knew what was going on. Was it a terrorist attack? Was it the security guard's gun going off? Moments later, an intercom announcement confirmed everyone's fears. A badly wounded Barnard stumbled up to the intercom, blood dripping from his wounds on the freshly laid carpet. 'Attention students and teachers! We are now on lockdown.'

Someone called 911, while someone else made a call to the Junior Reserve Officers' Training Corps (JROTC) instructors. All four wounded, including Nicholas, were taken by helicopter to the Tennessee medical and research centre, where Bruce succumbed to his injuries.

This incident brought alive the debate on America's gun control, the Second Amendment and its relevance in the current state.

18

April 2006

Mumbai

The audit committee meeting at Step Up Shoes (now renamed Snuggles India) was to be chaired by Rohit Lal, a quintessential chartered accountant. With an eye for detail, he had built quite a fearsome reputation in the realms of audit, financial and regulatory compliance. Lal had been associated with Step Up Shoes for a long time.

A fortnight before the audit committee meeting, Shivinder was a worried man. For two reasons. One, the fudged sales numbers for the previous year showed up as receivables not collected—amounts overdue from retailers for over a year—and that was not a good sign. And two, this year too, they had fudged over twenty-five crores in sales receivables to meet top-line and profitability numbers. Snuggles was a global corporate, these amounts were small. Sixty-five crore Indian rupees—forty crores the previous year and twenty-five crores this year—added up to roughly fifteen million dollars: petty cash compared to the global financials. However, any adverse comment by the audit committee would seriously dent the credibility of the Indian team.

'You don't need to worry,' Aditya declared when Shivinder shared his apprehension. 'As of now, our stated position is that all the receivables are recoverable. Last year we showed fudged sales figures of forty crores from the large retailers. All of them have bought huge quantities from us this year too. So they would have paid us in the normal course this year too. Adjust those payments against last year's dues and show this year's dues as outstanding. That way we will be able to show recovery of the previous year's outstanding. Your CFO should be telling you all this. What is he there for?'

'Sometimes hiring idiots in these roles has its own negative impact, Aditya. But how do we handle Rohit Lal?'

'I know Lal. I will handle him,' Aditya reassured.

'But how?'

'Every individual, however upright he might be, has one weak point, an Achilles' heel. We just have to find Lal's whoring price. A price above which he will bend. I have a fair idea of it. I will manage. Lal won't be a threat to you.'

The audit committee meeting for the quarter passed off peacefully, much to Shivinder's surprise. Lal did not raise any adverse query on the receivables issue. Just before the meeting ended, Lal stood up and began his concluding remarks. 'This is the first annual audit committee meeting for Snuggles after its Indian acquisition. I have been associated with the Step Up Shoes group and Mr Jigar Shah for over seven years. It has been a very fruitful association. Now, as I sign off the eighth annual audit report for the group, I would like to request Snuggles India that, for the sake of propriety, they should empanel the services of someone else to head the audit committee. I thank everyone for their assistance and support in helping me deliver. With that, I herewith tender my resignation from the audit committee. A new head will chair the next meeting. Thank you.' He took his seat at the head of the table for one last time to the sound of thunderous applause.

Aditya, who was also on the board of Snuggles as the bank's representative, looked at Shivinder from the corner of his eye. A sinister smile played on his lips. Shivinder too smiled. The problem had been addressed for now. But in the next six months they had to find a way out of this self-created web of deceit.

19

Mid-2006

MIT, Boston

Cardoza was peering into his laptop, studying the latest research results from India, when a knock on the door broke his concentration. 'Mr Etienne Lucier is here to see you. Says he has an appointment, but it's not in my diary.' It was his secretary, Louisa.

'I don't remember having granted an audience. What does he want?'

'He won't say.'

'Can you check my diary and give him another appointment if you think it is OK for me to meet him? Use your discretion. I am a bit tied up right now. I also have to prepare for class tomorrow. Haven't even rehearsed the anecdotes for my session yet.' Cardoza, like every other academician, loved things to be planned and organized. So much so that he even rehearsed the jokes he would crack in class.

'OK, Michael,' she said with a smile. Realizing that it was not a good time to disturb him, she turned to walk back to her workstation.

'Oops. I'm sorry!' The moment Louisa turned back, she ran into Lucier who had followed her into the room and was standing right behind her. Six foot four, well built and broad-shouldered, Lucier would surely have been a basketball player in his youth. Age had made his shoulders droop and skin sag. The bags under his eyes indicated excessive drinking. Louisa could tell the age-related and sleep-deprived eyebags from the alcohol-induced ones.

'You might want to hear me out before you ask me to come back again, Dr Cardoza. It won't take too long, I promise.' Without waiting for an invitation, he headed for the lounge chairs in the corner and made himself comfortable. Cardoza was initially taken aback, but was quick to recover. He waved off Louisa, who was standing at the door, and walked up to the visitor.

'This better be good. The last thing I tolerate is someone infringing on my privacy. Mr . . .' and he stopped. He didn't remember the man's name.

'Lucier. My name is Lucier.' Without waiting for any reaction, he continued, 'Pardon my rudeness, Dr Cardoza. But it is important.'

Cardoza nodded. 'I am sure it is. Going by the way you barged in.'

'Surely you've read about the incident in Tennessee where a fourteen-year-old shot the assistant principal of his school? This was a couple of months ago.'

'Nicholas Klingman? More than a couple of months, in fact.'

'Yes. In March,' confirmed Lucier.

'What about him?'

'Our investigations show that it was a drug-related killing, but the school is concealing facts so that its reputation isn't impacted. We found out that Nicholas Klingman had brought in the .22 calibre semi-automatic gun to trade it in for two OxyContin pills. Unknown to his parents, he had smuggled out the gun from his father's vault and hidden it in his bag, amongst his books.'

'And this is relevant because?'

'This incident has restarted the debate on gun rights, Dr Cardoza. As a consequence, there has been a fair bit of public outrage over the Second Amendment in the past few months. Many pro-gun-control lobbyists have been using the media and this incident to whip up mass hysteria against guns.'

Cardoza nodded. 'Go on. I am listening.'

'The Democrats too seem to be interested in keeping this alive and fresh in public memory. It will help them as we get into election mode eighteen months from now.'

'So?'

'All of us know and acknowledge that the crime rate in the USA is higher than in most other countries in the developed world. That's not because the US has liberal gun-control laws and consequently a higher proliferation of weapons. On the contrary, the crime rate is high because the US has more poverty than many other developed nations. It's this poverty which leads to crime and violence. Gun control will achieve nothing. It will just make it difficult for decent, law-abiding citizens to possess guns.'

'Mr Lucier, I have a research paper due for submission to a journal by tomorrow. I have a class for which I need to prepare. I'd be grateful if you could stop going around in circles and tell me what you are talking about. And I am finding it difficult to comprehend what your interest in this entire matter is.'

'Well, Mr Cardoza, I represent the NRA.'

'Aah . . . the National Rifles Association. You guys are leading all the lobbying against any amendment to the gun rights. You don't want any of this gun-control bullshit. I should have guessed.'

'We want you to research human behaviour. Behaviour that leads to crime. Research that adequately demonstrates that gun violence has nothing to do with gun rights. Or for that matter, lack of gun control. The NRA will be happy to make sure that the institute gets funded appropriately for the research.'

Cardoza smiled sarcastically. 'So you want to presuppose the end result before the research itself?'

'Well. No . . . but . . . you see, Dr Cardoza . . .' Lucier began stammering.

'A single incident of gun violence in a school in Tennessee gives the NRA the jitters and it wants MIT to give authenticity to its presupposition that gun control is unnecessary. So that all your gun shops can make a killing, pun unintended. It is common knowledge, Mr Lucier, that you and your organization have opposed even basic regulations which would make things like introduction of child locks in guns, monitoring of gun shops, background checks on gun buyers and so on mandatory. Buying a gun today has become as easy as buying a Barbie doll because of you.'

'You misunderstand, Dr Cardoza.'

'Rubbish!' Cardoza shouted at the top of his voice. 'You want me to lend credibility to the research so that you can use it as one of your tools in driving public opinion against the Democratic Party's presidential candidates who have vowed to put an end to your misdeeds. I am not naive, Mr Lucier.'

'That is not a completely correct representation, Dr Cardoza. But on the right track, I must confess.' Lucier was calm and composed. Cardoza was getting worked up. 'Nevertheless,' continued Lucier, 'we are willing to fund this project and its chair with a grant of ten million dollars. Of which, should you be interested, you will not be asked to account for two million.'

Cardoza got up from his chair. 'Thank you, Mr Lucier. The offer is surely a generous one. But I am constrained to decline it. It is against my grain to take up a project which clashes with my moral values. I am fundamentally in favour of gun control and for me to take up a research assignment which is in conflict with that value system will not be appropriate. I'm not even going into the offer of personal gratification that you referred to.'

Lucier got up and walked towards the door. He had just opened the door and stepped outside when Cardoza called him back. 'On a related note, MIT never accepts grants of any kind from parties which may have a vested interest in the research findings.'

'Good day, Mr Lucier. You might want to call in advance whenever you decide to come in next,' Cardoza's secretary taunted him as he walked out.

20

Mid-2006

Mumbai

Aditya had managed to keep Lal and the audit committee quiet. Lal's daughter had secured admission to Yale for a postgraduate degree in management and her fees had to be paid. It was no surprise that the amount was transferred from GB2's Geneva branch.

In return, Shivinder and Deven Khatri had approved a corporate social responsibility programme for a similar amount, to be spent for the upliftment of textile workers in Tiruppur. As expected, the money was paid to an NGO run by Narayanan in the area.

In the corridors of the Snuggles HQ in Boston, Shivinder was a rising star. The growth in the last two years had been quite impressive too, at least on paper. Shivinder was given a fair bit of leeway in running the company. By mid-2006, he was inducted into the Asia-Pacific Board of Snuggles. After all, wasn't India one of the largest markets? There was only one restriction imposed on him: any expansion in the distribution and franchisee network had to be approved by the board. Unknown to the India management, a team at Snuggles in Boston was working on an acquisition which would give them access to a large franchisee network in Asia. This was the rationale behind the curtailment of franchisee expansion.

Despite all this, Shivinder was worried. The receivables position was unnerving. They didn't have any solution in sight. There was one, but Shivinder was not in favour of it. They could sell the stock which they had piled up in Narayanan's Coimbatore warehouse to regular retailers and use the payments those retailers would make against that to offset the outstanding amounts. But the problem was that a given retailer would only buy a certain quantity. If they supplied most of that from the warehouse, supply from the genuine production line would come down considerably. It would eat into their regular sales, and consequently, the sales volumes that they would show in their regular financials would dip. They would again be forced to resort to fraudulently beefing up sales using the same method that they had used in the past. He was stuck with a problem that he didn't know how to fix.

It was a rainy day in August. Shivinder and Deven Khatri were on a market visit. Strange for a CFO to go on a market visit, but Deven was seen as Shivinder's shadow. Wherever Shivinder went, he took him along. This time they had come to the Snuggles store on Linking Road in Bandra—one of the first stores to be rebranded with the Snuggles logo and signage after the acquisition. Shivinder spent some time there talking to the staff. The franchisee owner was also present.

'Mr Singh, when are you giving me the approval to open another store? I have just bought a commercial complex about half a mile down this road. Nike and Adidas have three stores each on the entire stretch of Linking Road, and we have only one. We are losing business.'

'I know. As of now, we are not opening any more stores.' Shivinder lamented the fact that they were not allowed to open new stores without the approval of the board. He had tried a couple of times, but the board had declined. Globally they were trying to acquire another footwear major. If that went through, it would give them access to another two hundred exclusive stores in India. Till that was finalized, the board did not want to go down the franchisee expansion route.

'In fact, if you have that kind of liquidity, why don't you pick up some more stock? The sales team can work out very good discounts for you,' Deven added as an afterthought.

'The store is right in front of your eyes. Show me an inch of space where I can stock more shoes. This store is maxed out. If you give me some more stores, I'll be able to do better.'

'It is difficult as of now,' said Shivinder. 'But I'll keep it in mind.' And he got into his waiting Mercedes with Deven and headed back to their office.

They were now passing through a crowded part of Linking Road—a half-mile stretch that had made it a popular shopping destination. The small 4-foot by 5-foot shops on the pavement sold every conceivable piece of clothing, jewellery, chappals and shoes, and catered to a wide female audience. There wasn't a time of the day that could be called a lean period. Shivinder passed that stretch wondering how women are able to shop at almost any time of the day, and how they manage to find something to buy in almost any shop they enter. 'Retail whores!' he exclaimed to himself as he left Linking Road and entered S.V. Road on his way to his office in the Bandra Kurla Complex.

He was lost in deep thought about the receivables problem. Sixty-five crores of receivables had been cooked up. How was he going to plough the money back? A Nike store went by on the right. The store displays were brilliant. 'That's how we should do it,' he pointed out to Deven. A little ahead, they crossed an Adidas store. He looked at it and said to himself, 'How nice it would be if we could have multiple stores on this stretch.'

As if he was reading his mind, Deven commented, 'Wish it was our store! Fabulous location.'

Shivinder smiled. Slowly the smile became wider. He looked at Deven, excitement palpable on his face. 'It will be. Soon.' And he turned away, his gaze firmly set on the shops which were speeding by.

He dropped Deven off at his office and drove straight to GB2. Aditya was in his room.

'I need to talk to you.'

'Dude, you should at least have called me. I am just heading for a meeting.'

'Cancel it. We need to talk.' He turned back, shut the door to Aditya's cabin and added, 'Now!'

Aditya knew that this was not just another meeting. He called his secretary and told her to reschedule his meetings and sat down on his chair. 'Shoot!'

Shivinder started talking. He spoke non-stop for fifteen minutes. Finally, when he was done, Aditya stretched back, closed his eyes and rested his head on the headrest of his seat. It was beginning to fall into place.

'Only if you help me through this will we be able to pull this off, Adi.'

~

Two weeks later

Deven dashed into Shivinder's room with a big smile on his face. 'Over twenty-five calls since morning.'

'Only twenty-five?' There was a hint of disappointment in Shivinder's voice. 'Twenty-five is not going to help.'

'Shivinder, it's 12.30 p.m. And we dispatched the letters only last evening. I didn't expect even a single call today.'

'Let's see how many come our way.'

The previous evening, following Shivinder's plan, Snuggles had invited applications for fresh franchisees. This was a closed-group invitation, sent out to four hundred existing franchisees of Snuggles, who were earlier with Step Up Shoes. But there was one change from the earlier times that Step Up Shoes had called for franchisee applications. This time around every franchisee application was to be accompanied by a non-refundable demand draft of ten lakh rupees—an amount which would be refunded only in case the application was turned down. Step Up Shoes had never done this. In the scheme document, it was mentioned as a Snuggles worldwide practice.

Shivinder had carefully planned it all. The franchisee enrolment scheme was sent out only to those retailers with whom Shivinder had a long history. They were people he had dealt with in the past and there was trust on both sides. Shivinder was doing this despite the fact that he had been prohibited from expanding distribution without board approval.

By the end of the week, they had received three hundred applications for opening up new franchisee stores. A ten-lakh-rupee deposit from each applicant meant a total collection of thirty crores.

Within the next three days, a new account was opened in GB2 for Snuggles. The Snuggles board had authorized Shivinder and Deven to open a bank account wherever they deemed fit. That board resolution came in handy. In any case, when the head of investment banking wants an account to be opened, there is little that anyone can do. All the franchisee application cheques were deposited into that account. GB2 was happy. It had acquired a current account with a huge balance.

'It is all falling into place,' Aditya told Shivinder one evening.

Shivinder smiled and cheerfully slapped him on the back. 'I have signed off the appointment letters. We have approved these three hundred franchisees. No one in Snuggles will know that they exist. These franchisees will not exist in our global IT systems. Deven will track them separately.'

'This was a brilliant one from you, Shivinder.'

'Getting the sales head and logistics head to be on our side always helps. Right?'

'Absolutely.'

'Once we have recovered our sixty-five crore rupees from them, we will slowly regularize these franchisee appointments and bring them into the mainstream.'

'We have already recovered thirty crores through franchisee fees. Only thirty-five more to go.'

Shivinder laughed. It was so loud that Aditya quickly looked around to see if anyone noticed. 'Are you kidding me, Aditya? That money lying in GB2 is our money. Why would I ever use it to settle the shortfall in receivables.' There was a glint in his eyes. A shine which told Aditya that there was more to it.

Aditya raised his right eyebrow. 'What's the plan?' He knew Shivinder's body language very well by now. Shivinder got up from his chair, turned around and walked towards the window. Aditya continued, 'We have to offset the receivables, dude. Snuggles needs to get sixty-five crores for the shoes it was supposed to have sold.'

'Snuggles will receive the entire money for the shoes it sold, Aditya. Now chill.'

'But how?'

'Aditya, for the last year or so, sixty to seventy crores' worth of stock of Snuggles is lying in your father-in-law's warehouses. This is the stock we falsely invoiced and shipped out of our factories but instead of sending them to stores, we sent them to your father-in-law's warehouse. The stock left the factories and our vendors also got paid for having manufactured those shoes. Now they are just lying there rotting. When will that come in handy? We will just repackage that stock in new boxes.' Shivinder continued, 'Re-sticker them with current dates and supply them to these new franchisees. They will pay us for those and we will apply them against fraudulent receivables that we have shown in our books.'

'Oh yes,' Aditya remembered. He felt a bit stupid that he had not figured that out when Shivinder had recommended opening the franchisees. Shivinder was smarter than what Aditya had initially imagined. The franchisee deal was a masterstroke: issuing new franchisee licences to the same set of franchisees against whose names they had booked the fraudulent sales—the very same franchisees who swore by Shivinder because he had built them up from scratch when he was in Step Up Shoes—and also making more money than what either of them would ever have made in their lives.

By December 2006, the entire receivables problem was taken care of and the Snuggles balance sheet was sorted out. Sixty-five crores had gone into the account and the overdue receivables had been settled. The financials that Snuggles India would present for the year in April 2007 would be squeaky clean. The thirty crore rupees in GB2 was safe. It did not have to be touched. Shivinder and Aditya were happy and relieved.

A parallel infrastructure had been set up. The opportunity it offered them for making money was limitless. But the thing about greed is that once it gets you in its clutches, it doesn't let go. The battle that day was won by greed. The war too had to go its way.

21

January 2007

Mumbai/Boston

Cardoza had just returned from his vacation. Like most other Americans, Cardoza too went on his annual jaunt in December. This time around, he had decided to camp in South Asia. On his way back, he had made a one-week stopover in India. A couple of lectures at the premier management institutes in Bangalore and Ahmedabad helped him pay for his trip. His prime motive though, was to spend a week with Cirisha and review the work she was doing in the field. He wanted to make sure that the grants were being spent in the right fashion. A fair bit of his time went into assessing the on-ground execution of his projects. The Bill & Melinda Gates Foundation had in principle agreed on a grant of thirty million dollars to MIT for research in the Asia-Pacific region and Cardoza wanted to make sure that they were geared up for it.

'Young man, why don't you too come to Boston? It's a fine place. Great campus. You will have a fabulous life there,' Cardoza said to Aditya, sipping on a hot cup of Americano. Aditya had driven Cardoza and Cirisha to the Barista Lavazza outlet in Bandra reclamation for a post-dinner coffee, a night before he was scheduled to fly out of India.

Aditya just smiled. 'I have a reasonably good career going, Michael. I can't just give it all up.'

'I am sure America wants some good people to come there. In

any case your bank is headquartered in Boston, right? Can't you pull some strings?'

'Sure. If things work out, why not? I would love to move. The family can be together more often.' He looked at Cirisha as he said this. She just smiled, a bit confused whether Aditya said this out of sarcasm or really meant it.

In the next two days, Cardoza was back in his office, in time for the kick-off meeting of the Office of Sponsored Programs (OSP) at MIT in the second week of January. The OSP normally met once a quarter. This meeting, the first of the calendar year, was critical, for it was in this session that the OSP took stock of the research grants available and those in the pipeline, to draw up a timetable for the entire year. Cardoza was keen not to miss it. He was also MIT's relationship manager for the Bill & Melinda Gates Foundation and was required to present a plan for the thirty million grant that they had at stake.

Presided over by the chairman of the grants committee, the OSP had six members, including Cardoza. Each of the six presented their respective research projects to be undertaken for the year and the grants they had managed to get commitments for, as also the deficit or the amount they would require from the overall grants made available to MIT by various governmental agencies.

The last presentation was Deahl's. He got up, went to the head of the table and began speaking. 'I have four research assignments lined up for the year.' And he outlined in detail every single research that he was undertaking.

'These three projects are backed by adequate grants from the industry. If everything goes well, I will not be digging into any of the federal grants that come our way.'

'That's good to hear, James.' The chairman of the grants committee could not hide his relief. In the year gone by Deahl was largely responsible for MIT spending twelve million more than the budgeted expenditure. The institute had been pulled up for that. 'But I thought you said four assignments. You have put up only three.'

'I am coming to my last project in a minute.' He pulled up the last two slides of his presentation on the screen.

When Cardoza saw what appeared on the screen, he suddenly straightened up. His body divorced itself from the back of the chair and moved forward. His elbows rested on the table in front and his palms pushed against his cheek. He continued to stare at the screen in shock.

Deahl had taken up the same research assignment that Cardoza had kicked out of the door. On the screen in front of the committee were the words: 'Correlation between poverty and gun-related violence. Does alleviation of poverty change group behaviour and result in reduced instances of gun crimes?'

And when the next slide came up, Cardoza nearly let out a muted scream.

Against the name of the organization sanctioning the grant was 'Department of Social Justice and Equality (DSJE)—Government of Arizona'. He knew the moment he saw it that the NRA had influenced Arizona, a state under the control of the Republicans. The DSJE fronting the project would lend credibility, something which an NRA-backed assignment could never have provided. The slide also had details of the sponsorship amount.

Twenty million dollars was a huge sum by any standards. Sounds of excitement resonated in the room.

Cardoza was agitated. He wanted to oppose the research citing professional impropriety, but then something held him back. It wasn't appropriate to interfere in each other's domains. The research had first come to him. He had turned it down. He had done his bit. If someone else took it up, it was not his problem. Also, he didn't want to play party pooper at a time when everyone was so excited about the twenty million dollars.

As he walked out of the meeting, part of him kept needling him into wondering if he had done the right thing by keeping quiet.

22

April–June 2007

Mumbai

It was a peaceful Saturday evening. Aditya was in the living room, watching the replay of the India vs Bangladesh World Cup cricket match held in March that year, when his phone rang. He answered and glanced quickly in the direction of the kitchen. Cirisha was stirring up some veggies for dinner.

'Hello?' he whispered into the phone and walked towards the bedroom.

'Adi. That bastard screwed us.'

'Who?'

'Deven. Deven Khatri.'

'Why? What happened?'

'He forged my signature on multiple cheques and transferred ten crore rupees into his account with Citibank.'

'What? Are you serious, Shivinder?'

'Why will I kid about this, Adi?'

'When did this happen?'

'It's been happening over the last fortnight. He has been withdrawing small sums to make sure that it remains below the radar. Today I casually logged into the account to see how much cash we have lying idle. That's when I noticed it. I was livid. I still am. I walked up to him and confronted him.'

'What did he say?'

'Nothing. He just picked up his bag and walked out. I have been trying to call him. His phone is switched off. He is not at home either. I don't know where he is.'

'What a jerk! I know the ACP. Should we call him and lodge a complaint?' Aditya was panicking now.

'Are you out of your mind? What will we say about how this account was created and how we came into so much money?'

'Hmm . . .' Aditya felt a bit foolish.

'Thank God I caught him before he could clean out the account.'

'Send someone to his house to pick him up and thrash him. He can't do this to us and get away.'

'I will kick him in his balls till they come out of his mouth. He can't run away with my cash.'

'Once you decide on what to do, let me know. Cirisha is around. Can't talk.' He hung up and turned around to get back to his cricket match. He froze when he saw Cirisha standing right behind him. He was not sure how much of the conversation she had heard.

'Was it Shivinder?'

'Yes.'

'What happened? Who were you guys planning to thrash?'

'Deven has apparently run away with ten crores of Shivinder's money. He is now trying to locate him and recover the money.'

'I always knew this Shivinder was a crazy guy. But how does this concern you, Adi?' she asked him once they had settled down in bed. 'Looks like the guys in his team are following his lead. They learnt fraud from him and are now cheating him. Do you have to be friends with him?'

'You are never here, and yet you have a view on who my friends are, who I spend my time with!' an irritated Aditya snapped back. Cirisha's timing was wrong. A piece of advice was the last thing Aditya wanted after hearing that he had just lost ten crores from the fortune which was supposed to be jointly owned by him and Shivinder.

'I'm only asking you to be careful, Aditya. He is like a scorpion inside your shoe. You will never know what bit you till you reach a point of no return.'

'I am not a child, Cirisha. I can handle it. I know what is good for me and what isn't.' His face had a ruthlessly cold look. It was as if he didn't really care. She was worried sick. In Shivinder, she saw a selfish, corrupt and immoral devil. She knew that if Aditya were to fall into his trap, he would never be able to extricate himself.

That night the simmering tension transformed into a full-blown war. There was a huge argument and, like every other argument of theirs, this one too led to a nasty conversation on the need for Cirisha to be in Massachusetts at the cost of family. There was no dearth of aspiration in the two of them, but for Aditya everything was measured in terms of money.

The fight that night was a clear indication of the fact that the distance was taking its toll. Aditya was fed up of the constant state of flux in their lives. 'When was the last time we took a vacation, Cirisha? Do you even remember? I am beginning to wonder if I matter to you, or is it only your MIT, Michael Cardoza and research projects that are paramount.' There was sadness in his eyes.

Pangs of guilt overcame Cirisha. She had not bargained for this when she advised Aditya on Shivinder. She backed away from the discussion. But one thing was clear. She needed to figure out a way to be in Mumbai more often. What started off as a one-week-Massachusetts–three-weeks-Mumbai arrangement, was now divided into two weeks each. Things had to change.

That night after making sure that Aditya was asleep, she called Cardoza. He had just got into work. 'Last night Hillary Clinton announced her intention to run for President in 2008. So now we have Edwards and Hillary who have confirmed. Let's see who else joins the fight. It's getting interesting, particularly for the Democrats.' Cardoza, like every other American, followed the presidential elections with a fair bit of enthusiasm.

'I like her. It will be interesting to see how she fares. Two exciting years ahead.'

'Absolutely,' Cardoza said and then after a pause added, 'Is there a problem, Cirisha? Why are you sounding low? Is everything OK?' Cardoza was extremely perceptive. He had an amazing knack of figuring out that things were not the way they needed to be.

Cirisha was quite candid. 'Michael, I'm having trouble at home. I have mentioned it to you in the past, briefly. I am beginning to feel that India needs me more. I don't know what to do. How do I manage? I don't want to give up research. I am so close to qualifying for my tenure too.'

'I understand, Cirisha. Living a nomadic life is not easy. And you have been doing it for so long.'

'I was wondering if I can get a break. Six months. I'll try and sort things out by then. A sabbatical, maybe.'

'Or maybe even get Aditya to come to the USA.'

'I wish.' Cirisha eyes were moist.

'But hey! Why do you want to take a break? I am sure we can work something out.'

'Six months is a long period, Michael. Moreover, I do not have any serious live project in India. There's not much to work on.'

'Wait.' There was some noise on the other end as if he was riffling through some papers. He was back in a minute. 'Cirisha, you there?'

'Yes, Michael.'

'Tell me, where is Dherevi?'

'Pardon me!'

'Dherevi . . . apparently it's a slum in Mumbai. The largest in Asia.'

'Oh . . . Dharavi.'

'Yes, yes . . . the same one. It is D.H.A.R.A.V.I,' Cardoza spelt out the name.

'What about it, Michael?'

'Last week the National Health Association came to us with a grant of two million dollars to study life in urban slums—Urban Curse or

Urban Boon. They want us to study two of the five biggest slums in the world and help them conclude whose residents are better off: the ones in the urban slums or those in the rural areas. Behavioural patterns need to be studied. What makes people leave the comfort of their villages and towns and migrate to slums in urban areas.'

'Wow! There comes Batman, saviour of my Gotham!' said an excited Cirisha. 'But Michael, two million seems like a small budget.'

'That's what I was going to tell them. But now after this conversation with you, maybe I will take it on. If there is any shortfall, I will ask MIT to bear it from their overall research allocations. They are in any case making shitloads of money on the NRA-sponsored research.'

'It's not NRA-sponsored, Michael.'

'Yes. Yes. We all know who is behind that, don't we?' Cardoza was sarcasm personified. For the first time that day, Cirisha smiled. She knew how much Cardoza hated Deahl's research project. More so after Cardoza had rejected it on the grounds of his principles and values.

'Anyway, Cirisha,' Cardoza continued, 'the National Health Association has given us a choice of five slums—Neza-Chalco-Itza in Mexico, Orangi in Karachi, Pakistan, Dharavi in India and there is one in Cape Town and one in Nairobi. I forget their names. These are the five largest slums in the world.'

'OK.'

'If we decide to take it on, we can do the study in Mumbai and in Mexico. Two Third World countries with significant economic diversity. What do you say?'

'Sounds interesting. Would it be possible for you to send me the research request? It'll help me structure my thoughts.'

'Right away.'

'When do we have to start?'

'Well, as far as I am concerned, you are already on it.' And he laughed. 'Jokes apart, when you get back here, we can fine-tune the research deliverables and get on with it.'

'I will be back in early March, Michael. Is that all right?'

'Suits me.'

'Thanks, Michael. I can't tell you how grateful I am to you for this.'

'Well, don't then!' he laughed. 'Isn't it late in the night there?'

'Yes. It's around 12.30 a.m.'

'Go to sleep now. Goodnight, Cirisha. And say hi to Aditya.'

The next morning, when she mentioned this to Aditya, he was quite ecstatic. Three to four months, maybe longer, at a stretch was quite a luxury by any standards.

~

In a couple of weeks, Cirisha was on a flight to Massachusetts for a briefing from the National Health Association on the research deliverables. Thankfully, by the time she was able to present her assessment and methodology to the board and to Cardoza, the budget for the research had been raised to a comfortable four million dollars. There was no need to dig into the university corpus for funds.

That evening Cirisha was in her room, taking stock of what she needed to carry back with her to India, when Richard walked in.

He looked quite harried. Dishevelled hair and tired eyes. It looked as if he hadn't slept for a few nights. Cirisha was worried when she saw him in that state.

'Richard! Are you OK? Where were you the whole of last week?'

'I was travelling on work, Cirisha. Just got back this morning. Heard that you were here and were leaving today. Just came around to say bye. We will all miss you.'

'Aww Richard! You are such a sweetheart.' Cirisha hugged him. 'You take care of yourself.'

'Yes. Thanks.'

'And go get some sleep. You look so sleep deprived.'

'I'm working too hard, Cirisha. This research on guns and crime is too stressful. James is paranoid about the results. They say that if you torture data hard enough, it sings. In James's case, he tortures—not the data but the data-gatherer—so much that even he starts to sing James's tune. He doesn't listen to anyone. He draws his own inferences and conclusions. Some of them highly debatable. But who is to tell? Eventually no one will question him given his stature.'

'You mean to say he is faking data?'

'No, no. That's not what I am saying. You can always look at the same coin in two different ways. What you interpret is a result of your discretion. James is interpreting data to suit his hypothesis.' Cirisha had a hunch that Richard was not telling her the entire truth. But it was not in her nature to probe unnecessarily.

'Won't it get stuck at the peer review stage?' Every academician knew that it is mandatory for research, before it got published in any journal, to be reviewed and cleared by a set of peers or individuals of repute. 'None of the peers will give him a positive review if James is not convincing in his report.'

'Haha!' Richard laughed. 'You really think so?' And with a generous hint of ridicule in his voice, he added, 'Peer review?'

'Hmm . . .'

'You have been around long enough to know that there is no bigger scam going around than peer reviews. It's all about "You scratch my back, I'll scratch yours". James will manage excellent peer reviews and will get the paper published just as he wants it. After all, the people who write his peer reviews will come to him when they publish their papers. If they screw around with his peer review, he will bludgeon the peer review when it's their turn. Which world are you in, Cirisha? I have seen James draft out his own peer review and send it along with his research report. No one ever dares to deviate from what James sends them. What he sends, comes back signed . . . Not a word changed.'

'I guess I'm a bit of a prude in these matters. I am hoping that if James does screw around with the research, the peer group will take a stand. Michael will, for one.'

Richard smiled. 'Michael will never get a chance to do the peer review. The researcher selects the peers who would review the findings. Why on earth would you send an important research report for peer review to a faculty who you know is antagonistic towards you?'

'But Richard, you should not keep quiet if you see something wrong. You should stand up and raise your voice. Otherwise you become as much party to it.'

'Not too sure if that's the approach for me. If I play along quietly, there is a lot for me to gain.' And he walked out of the room. 'Keep in touch. Remember, people will miss you here,' he said before the door shut on him.

That was the last Cirisha would see of him for a while. She was on to her next research assignment that would formally begin in a couple of months. It would take that much time for her to do the basic groundwork and get the research methodology approved by the sponsors. Slums were not the most exciting of places and the last thing she wanted to do was to complete her project and then figure out that her sponsors wanted her to do something completely different. Once it started, she would be in Mumbai for a long stretch—and that really excited her.

23

May–June 2007

MIT, Boston

Richard was Deahl's pointperson in the NRA research. They had also taken on three research assistants, students who were majoring in Social Psychology, to assist them in data gathering.

'The data for Chicago has come in,' Richard announced as he walked into Deahl's room.

'How does it look?'

'I need to drill deeper. On the face of it the data looks quite supportive of Lucier's hypothesis.'

'If it holds for Chicago, it is sure to hold everywhere. We will be able to prove the hypothesis in all the other regions. Chicago has one of the most restrictive gun ordinances in the United States of America. No civilian gun ranges. And gun shops are banned. No one can carry assault weapons or high-capacity magazines in public.'

'And despite such stringent gun-control laws, Chicago has the highest gun-related homicide rate,' Richard added.

'Yes, Richard. And that's why Chicago lends itself to such a wonderful analysis. By the way, what's the source of this data? Published data or is it classified?'

'Lucier and the Illinois State Rifle Association helped us get this data. While some of it is published, a lot of the core working data is not published by government departments. Nothing to suggest it is classified, though.'

'Lucier badly needs this to work for him.' When Deahl said this, Richard smiled.

'When will you be able to run your analysis on the data?'

'Give me a few days, James. There is too much of it.'

'This will form the basis of our next course of action. Let's get it out fast.'

24

July–September 2007

Mumbai

The suburban railway station at Bandra (West) was crowded. Gangu Tai got off the train on platform number ten and walked right towards the end. Two platforms to cross and she would be out of the station. She looked up. The asbestos sheet of the station roof was cracked. The sun filtered through a few tiny holes in the asbestos, exaggerating their size. The overhead walkway came in sight. She thought for a second and decided not to use the deserted walkway. Crossing the tracks would be dangerous, albeit easier. She jumped off the platform, dashed across two sets of railway lines and climbed on to the next platform. With swift steps, she walked across the platform, crossed two more tracks and in no time, she was next to the railing marking the boundary of the railway station. Manoeuvring herself through a gap in the railing, which had become a sort of a thoroughfare, she got out of the station and on to the road. A short walk from the station, across the Mithi river, was a civilization in itself. Dharavi. This was Gangu Tai's world. Her name was Gangu Bai, but because of her age everyone called her Tai, an affectionate term for grandmother.

Almost half of Mumbai lived in slums, of which Dharavi was the largest. Gangu Tai was returning after delivering a consignment of four hundred bags. Her steps were pacy, their span large. She was getting late for a meeting with Cirisha, who was waiting for her outside a small roadside temple below the flyover connecting Dharavi to Mahim, the nearest suburb.

It was an emotional reunion for the two of them. Cirisha was seeing her after four years. Gangu Tai had aged significantly from the time that she left her job as a domestic help at the Raisinghania household—a job that she diligently did for three years. A strange reaction to a problem at home had made her return to her village, promising never to come back to Mumbai. But return she did, after two years. The lure of money in this big city was too strong to resist. She needed money to take care of her drunk and chronically ill husband back home.

'Gangu Tai,' Cirisha called out affectionately as she hugged her, unconcerned that her Marks & Spencer top was getting messed up. 'How are you, Gangu Tai? How is my darling Kavita?'

'She is fine, Didi. Helping my brother in his fields.'

'After doing her BA?' Cirisha asked. She was both angry and troubled that such a bright talent was being wasted.

'What else could I have done? You are the only one who knows the state we were in.'

'Yes, I know. And if I remember, I advised you against it.'

'I didn't have a choice, Didi.'

'Hmm . . .' acknowledged Cirisha as the incidents which had occurred four years ago flashed before her eyes. Kavita was the eldest of Gangu Tai's three daughters. A smart and inquisitive girl, she was the darling of her teachers. Cirisha was fond of her. Kavita had just finished her graduation and was looking for a job. A few rowdy elements saw her one day while she was walking out for an interview and began harassing her. They began stalking her every day. The roads within Dharavi were narrow and congested. Taking advantage of that, the rowdies would collide with her while walking and often make snide, derogatory remarks. Kavita tolerated it for as long as she could and eventually, one day, she mentioned it to Cirisha in the presence of Gangu Tai. Aditya was also around at that time. He advised her to ignore it. 'The guys would stop it by themselves,' he said. Cirisha was appalled at such a suggestion and stormed out of the house with Kavita to the local police station to register a complaint. The cops, strangely, did not even bother to register a First Information Report, which they were obligated to in such instances, and instead, advised them to go back and talk to the rowdies and settle matters amicably. This only made the rowdies braver. When it became unbearable, Gangu Tai decided to leave Mumbai for good and headed back to her native place in Amravati. She returned to Mumbai within two years in search of a job.

Gangu Tai became Cirisha's guide through the bylanes of Dharavi, an unending stretch of narrow, dirty lanes, open sewers and cramped huts. It had its own laws; every basic necessity was run by the mafia like a parallel government. The teeming slum of Dharavi, home to a million people, had become the hotbed of political lobbying thanks to its location. Situated right next to the biggest commercial hub of Mumbai, the Bandra Kurla Complex, Dharavi was prime real estate, which interested every single construction lobby in the country, possibly even the world. Gangu Tai introduced Cirisha to everyone who mattered in the administration of Dharavi.

Cirisha spent entire days with families that had migrated from rural India. Though over 40 per cent of Dharavi comprised second- and third-generation residents of the slum, she spent most of her time with people who had migrated to Mumbai from remote parts of the country, and largely, for cost reasons, sought out the solace offered to them by the big heart of the largest slum. Most of them, as she figured out, had migrated to the city for a perceived better life for their children. At times, their commitment to their children, even at the cost of their own lives, brought tears to Cirisha's eyes.

Raghu was one such migrant from distant Amravati who had come to Mumbai at the behest of Gangu Tai. He had initially come to Mumbai alone, but three years back, his wife moved in with him. Now he had a two-year-old son who was born in the hustle and bustle of this urban jungle. Having sold off his land in Amravati before coming to Mumbai, Raghu was relatively better off than most of the other migrants. He had invested his savings prudently and started a small business. It had worked well for him, for he was now able to get more people from his village to come and work with him, for him. Working with familiar, loyal people was always better than unknown devils.

After spending a day with him, Cirisha went with Raghu to his factory, deep inside the guts of Dharavi. 'There is no way I can find my way out of this,' Cirisha thought as she made her way into the maze, led by Raghu. After a jumpy ride of fifteen minutes in a rickety autorickshaw, they reached a multi-storeyed building. The rotten smell of a tannery made her impulsively reach for her handbag to pull out a scented tissue. As she stepped out of the autorickshaw and walked towards the entrance of the building, she saw Raghu talking to someone.

'Gangu Tai? How come you are here?'

'Didi, I was the one who started this with Raghu.'

'Gangu Tai!' Cirisha exclaimed. A big smile lit up her face. 'Wow! You never told me that you run a business.' Cirisha was both surprised and amused. This was the same lady who used to mop the floor of her Pali Hill apartment.

Cirisha looked around. It was a large factory. 'How many people work here?'

'Around two hundred. And Didi, last evening you asked me what would make me go back?'

Cirisha nodded.

'You only tell me, how can I leave these two hundred people and go back to my village? With the money I have made for myself, I will live comfortably all my life. What will happen to the lives of these people and their families if I go? I will never be able to. My conscience will not allow me.' Cirisha was touched. Gangu Tai's victory felt like her own.

She walked through the leather goods manufacturing facility. The ground floor was where they manufactured bags. Handbags, slingbags and laptop bags. She could never have imagined that a facility like this would exist deep inside a slum. They walked up to the third floor. Being fit helped; Cirisha didn't puff and pant while climbing three floors. On the third floor was a dormitory where many of the workers lived.

Shoes were being manufactured on the second floor. Shoe tops, without the soles. 'We don't have moulding units. So we are not able to mould the upper of the shoe into the soles. That's why we just make the shoe uppers and supply them to the company. Someone else does the moulding,' Raghu volunteered. Cirisha picked a few of the uppers and looked at them. They looked absolutely top class. 'In the case of leather-soled shoes, we make the complete product too.' Raghu showed her some finished shoes. She picked one up and admired it. It looked like a branded product in a posh store. She brought the shoe to her eye level and looked inside.

She was handing it back to him when she saw it. Hastily she pulled it back and looked inside the shoe. This time, she carefully lifted the tongue of the shoe—the flap beneath the laces—and there it was.

'Snuggles!' she exclaimed. 'You make shoes for Snuggles.' The tongue of the shoe had a label of Snuggles stitched on it.

'Yes, Didi. Even handbags. We work exclusively for them.' Cirisha was surprised that an MNC like Snuggles got their shoes manufactured in Dharavi. Cirisha turned towards Gangu Tai, a look of anger swelling in her eyes. 'So you run a fake shoe racket, Gangu Tai?'

'No, no, Didi,' Gangu Tai responded hurriedly. 'These are genuine shoes. I can show you the order copies too.' Gangu Tai, feeling a little insulted, went out of her way to convince Cirisha that their business was genuine. She walked to the office and pulled out a file. By the time she came back, Cirisha had clicked images of a few shoes on her iPhone, making sure that the Snuggles tag was captured. She wanted to show it to Aditya.

As she walked through the facility, the sight of young girls, barely in their teens, working there irritated her. Even Gangu Tai's youngest daughter was there, packing shoes into boxes.

What got her worked up was that if Snuggles was getting contract work done in that factory, it should have made sure that the work environment was up to the mark and more importantly, that it adhered to the 'no child labour' policy which most good companies have. She despised Shivinder, and this only made it worse.

Aditya was already home by the time she reached. 'Hi Cirisha!' he said as he opened the door, making a feeble attempt at giving her a hug. Cirisha pushed him away. 'Sorry, Aditya. I'm feeling very dirty after a day inside Dharavi. Let me take a quick shower and then you can give me a big, big hug.' She smiled and rushed towards the bathroom. Aditya could hear the splashing of water on the floor. He sat down on the bed. 'Adi, you there?' Cirisha screamed from inside the bathroom.

'I am right here waiting for you.'

'You know Gangu Tai has her own business now. She employs close to two hundred people.'

'Yeah? What does she do?'

'She works for your friend.'

'Who?'

'Shivinder. Who else?' she screamed above the noise of gushing water.

'What rubbish!' Aditya exclaimed. The bathroom door opened and Cirisha was standing there, a towel wrapped around her, arms akimbo. 'What did you say? Rubbish? Eh?' And she walked briskly to her bag and pulled out her mobile phone. She quickly flicked through a few screens of her new iPhone and held it out towards Aditya. 'See.'

Aditya took the phone from her hand and browsed through the pictures.

'Look at the last few pictures.' Cirisha referred to the labels. She wanted Aditya to see the images that she had clicked.

Aditya reached the image of the label and stopped. 'You took these pictures at Gangu Tai's factory?'

'Yes. Gangu Tai and her partner, a guy called Raghu. Both are from the same village.'

'And you said the factory is in Dharavi?'

'Right.'

'Are you serious?'

'Yes.'

'Must be fakes then.'

'No, Adi. I thought of the same thing. But only until I saw the order from Snuggles. It was an original letter signed by Deven Khatri.'

'Deven Khatri?'

'Yes. He is the same guy who ran away with Shivinder's money, right? I took a picture of the order copy too. And you know what, Adi, when I saw what was going on there, I was pissed off as hell. They don't even bother about working conditions in these sweatshops. Children work there, Aditya. Children. It's shameful for an MNC like Snuggles. You must tell your friend.' Aditya just nodded. He hadn't heard a word of what she said. He scrolled through the images and reached the last picture—of the order copy. It was on what looked like an original letterhead of Snuggles. And it was indeed signed by Deven Khatri. Dated March 2007, it was an order for shoes and bags to be supplied over the next six months.

Two questions clouded Aditya's mind. First, why would a CFO sign a manufacturing order? And second, Snuggles did not have a manufacturing unit in Mumbai, leave alone Dharavi. Then what was this unit of Gangu Tai doing?

His newly acquired iPhone was lying next to him. He tried calling Shivinder whose phone was not reachable. That's when he remembered that Shivinder was away on a vacation, an exquisite Alaskan cruise. 'Such discussions can't happen over the phone,' he said to himself and decided to wait for Shivinder's return.

Cirisha was hit by a bout of insomnia that night. She was in an extremely agitated frame of mind when she remembered that Richard had done some work with the American Apparel and

Footwear Association, and sought him out. She wrote to him in detail about what had transpired at the footwear factory and requested him to raise it with Snuggles if he had any contact with them through the footwear association. She obviously didn't want to route the request through Shivinder.

25

Early October 2007

MIT, Boston

Deahl was in his room, engrossed in a serious discussion with Richard, when there was a knock on the door.

'Later, please,' Deahl thundered without even looking up.

'Dr Deahl.' The visitor was unfazed and stood there adamantly.

Deahl had heard the voice earlier. 'Aah. Lucier. Why is it that you insist on giving us the pleasure of your company at the most inappropriate of times? Especially when you should not be seen here.'

'Good evening, Dr Deahl. Mr Avendon.' Lucier looked at Richard and just nodded his head, completely ignoring the sarcastic comment. Richard acknowledged him. He had seen him a couple of times in the past. He was not at all fond of Lucier, particularly his near-perfect sense of dressing—expensive Zegna suits, handcut black shoes, a briefcase in hand, which Richard always suspected held more than a few sheets of paper. 'It is urgent, Dr Deahl.'

'Please take a seat.' Deahl shut the file he was looking at. Turning towards Richard, he said, 'We will discuss this later.' He looked at Lucier with eyebrows raised. 'Would you mind if Mr Avendon stays? He is . . .' Lucier interrupted him. 'Yes I know. He is driving the research for you. Please be my guest.'

Deahl reached out to the telephone to call his secretary. 'Don't worry, Dr Deahl. I have told her not to disturb us for the next twenty minutes,' Lucier said.

111

'OK. That's kind of you. What brings you here? Your presence here gets me nervous. I can't be seen conferring with you on anything, least of all my research. It's the institute's reputation at stake.'

'Have you seen this?' Lucier didn't even bother to listen to Deahl. He threw something on the table. Seeing the blank look on Deahl's face, he added, 'You might want to read it.'

Deahl picked it up. It was a copy of the *New York Times*. Right on top was a big picture of Senator Barrack Obama with a headline, 'Obama: The Most Anti-Gun President in the History of America'. And in fine print, it carried the line, 'If He Becomes One'. The article went on to suggest how Obama the senator supported the blanket ban on buying and carrying guns in the state of Illinois.

'If this man comes to power, we will be in a serious spot.' Lucier had a concerned look which made wrinkles appear on his forehead. 'We can't let him come to power. The only way we can counter him is if your research comes out favourable to us and we are able to drive public opinion based on that.'

'I am aware.'

'Then why is it taking so much time? The Democrats will announce their candidates for the elections in another four months. It's likely to be an Obama vs Hillary game. In all likelihood Obama will win the nominations by the time the March primaries are done with. A Republican win seems unlikely given the public mood. Our hopes for a favourable report for the NRA are receding really quickly. Obama cannot become the President, we have to do everything possible to counter his anti-gun stance.'

'Thanks, Lucier. We do understand the urgency.'

'No, you don't.' Lucier's fists came thumping down on the table. 'The NRA needs the research done and dusted by December. Not later than that. The NRA can't go down. We haven't paid twenty million dollars for nothing.'

Deahl nodded his head as Lucier got up from his seat and swaggered out of the door.

A nervous Richard looked at Deahl. 'Weird guy.'

'The NRA does function in a strange manner. Look, Richard. No one in his or her right senses will oppose some form of gun control in this country. But the NRA guys know their business, which is why they have bought out our research even before commissioning it. The twenty million dollars that they have pumped into this research puts the onus on us to prove why gun control is not required. By linking gun-related crime and poverty, they would have done enough to deflect all the pressure from gun-control laws to the broader issue of economic development. Twenty million dollars is a lot of money. And our research will give them lots of credibility. I won't be surprised if they have related research being conducted by different universities across the country.'

'True.'

'And Richard, don't bother about the politics of gun rights. A good report here can propel you into your tenured position. Just remember that.'

Richard smiled and walked towards the door. Wasn't he willing to do anything for a tenured position? In any case he was extremely confident that this time around he would make it. He had enough going his way.

'And Richard!' Richard stopped and turned around. 'Where are we on the prison data?'

'Data gathering in three prisons is done, James. It is being tabulated and analysed now. I'll send it to you tomorrow. Will that do?'

'Yes. That will be fine.'

The door banged shut behind Richard and Deahl got busy with his papers. He had a class to prepare for the next day.

26

3rd October 2007

Mumbai

Cirisha had got up early that day. Gangu Tai had promised to take her to the other end of Dharavi, which housed the glass and metal-forging facilities. A morning cup of coffee for her was always accompanied by a quick checking of emails.

Richard had responded to her email sent a few days ago.

Cirisha,

Hope all is well. I checked with the Snuggles office in Boston. I did apprise them about the issues you had mentioned. I even told them that in case the media picked that up, it would lead to significant erosion of their brand value. But I got a very strange response from them. It's self-explanatory. Forwarding it to you. I'm off to Chicago for a conference tomorrow morning. James was to go. But he got busy and asked me to go. In case you want something from the Magnificent Mile, drop me an email. I'll get it. Pay me later. ☺

When she read the response from Snuggles, it irritated her no end. How could that be? How could an MNC lie and that too so blatantly? She wrote back to Richard.

*Can you give me the email ID of their compliance/HR or whoever
looks into it? It's a bit unclear from this email. I will write to them.
What they are saying is not true. I have seen it with my own eyes.
And thanks for the offer on Magnificent Mile. I don't need anything
from there. My needs aren't so sophisticated.*

She looked at her watch. It was past seven. If Gangu Tai had to be
met at eight, she had to leave in fifteen minutes. The cup of coffee
touched her lips for one last gulp. She dumped the glass into the sink
and ran into the bathroom. She was late for the meeting.

27

Mid-October 2007

Mumbai

Shivinder returned to India in the first week of October. Aditya met him the same evening. Skipping the niceties, he got to the point.

'What's with this new contract manufacturing in Dharavi? I didn't know you had one.'

'Dharavi?'

'Yes. Cirisha visited a facility which was manufacturing shoes for you.'

'Are you sure it was for Snuggles?'

'She showed me the order copy.'

'It must be manufacturing fakes.'

'It was signed by Deven Khatri. Dated prior to him running away with our money.'

'Is it? Let me find out.'

'Are you sure you are not doing something behind my back? We are in this together. Don't try to play games with me, Shivinder.' Aditya was livid.

'You must be kidding, Adi.' Shivinder was unfazed. 'You have helped me when things were difficult. Do you think I will shortchange you?'

'You better not.' Aditya walked out of Shivinder's office, got back in his car and drove to his office. Back home that evening, he wanted to tell Cirisha about his conversation with Shivinder. But he held back. What would he have told her in any case? She knew nothing about his deals with Shivinder.

~

As they were sitting down for dinner that night, Cirisha's phone rang. She ran to pick it up.

'Hello?'

'Can I speak to Ms Narayanan?'

'Speaking. May I know who is on the line?'

'Ms Narayanan, I would like to meet with you sometime tomorrow. Will that be possible?'

'Well, would you care to introduce yourself?'

'My name is Nick Rand and I am from Boston.'

'Do I know you? What is this regarding?'

The moment he told her who he was, she looked up at Aditya. He was busy reading the newspaper while enjoying his rotis. She walked into the bedroom, whispering into her phone.

And when she walked back into the dining room, she was clearly excited.

28

Mid-October 2007

MIT, Boston

'So it's clear, James. Very clear,' Richard said while shutting his laptop. They were in the conference room, debating the data.

'Hold it! Hold it!' Deahl exclaimed. 'Can you pull up that table on the screen again? Let's go through it once more.'

Richard fiddled with his laptop and in a jiffy the chart was up on the screen. He looked at Deahl, whose eyeballs were fixated on the table on the screen ahead of him. (See facing page)

'This is only Chicago, right?'

'Yes,' Richard replied. 'And James . . .' Richard began to explain, only to be cut short by Deahl, who was holding up his palm to silence him. He wanted to draw his own inferences. 'So the data indicates that the homicide rate is highest in areas which are high on the poverty scale.'

'Yes, James. And . . .' Richard hesitated.

'And what?'

'An even more damning correlation is the combined effect on gun-related crime, of poverty, lack of education, unemployment and concentration of African American people in the neighbourhood.'

'Yes. That is obvious in this summary. Poor locations with a high African American concentration have a very high homicide rate.'

'I can understand, James, if the homicide rates in the poor black areas were twice as much as the rates in the white upmarket areas.

Poorest Locations in Chicago

	% of Population below Poverty Line	No High School Diploma (% of people aged 25 years and above)	Unemploy-ment (% of people not in labour force aged 16 years and above)	Assault Rate (homicide-related) per 100,000	Firearm-Related Crimes (per 100,000)	% of African American Population
Riverdale	61.4	24.65	26.41	36.31	37.33	97.28
Fuller Park	55.5	33.72	40.54	62.94	36.31	96.22
Englewood	42.2	29.40	21.37	47.52	44.15	98.43
West Garfield Park	40.3	26.23	25.22	36.48	32.74	95.18
East Garfield Park	39.7	26.29	16.49	42.31	39.29	91.45
Average of five poorest areas		28.02	25.86	45.08	37.92	95.63

Richest Locations in Chicago

	% of Population below Poverty Line	No High School Diploma (% of people aged 25 years and above)	Unemploy-ment (% of people not in labour force aged 16 years and above)	Assault Rate (homicide-related) per 100,000	Firearm-Related Crimes (per 100000)	% of African American Population
Mount Greenwood	3.1	4.59	6.96	2.26	9.31	2.04
Edison Park	5.1	8.53	7.49	0.00	7.04	0.31
Beverly	5.2	5.16	7.84	4.63	6.45	3.74
Norwood Park	5.9	13.52	7.37	4.18	8.89	6.89
Clearing	5.9	18.57	9.62	7.39	11.63	1.92
Average of five richest areas		10.02	7.85	3.64	8.62	2.94

But here it is roughly fifteen times higher. That is a ridiculously high number.'

'Our story will be simple. Places high on the poverty scale, low on education and high on unemployment will be high on drug abuse, alcoholism, violence and resultant gun-related homicide. Children born in these areas are less likely to have a normal childhood and hence are more likely to grow up into violent teens.'

'Yes. Children reared in such environments have a high propensity to turn to crime.'

'And if you want to pull them away from crime, taking away guns is not an option. Focusing on their economic development is probably the only way out.' And he looked at Richard. 'So we have a story.'

Richard smiled. 'We have a very good story, if the Chicago example were to be looked at. It screams from every nook and corner of the city that gun control hasn't worked. Economic development and social initiatives to get the African American community into the mainstream will bear more results than any change to the Second Amendment.'

'Wonderful, Richard! Let's also look at gun ownership patterns over the year across the United States and see if there is anything for us to report. A few more examples like Chicago will add meat to the study.'

'Sir,' said Richard and shut down his laptop. He had made his point. He then opened his notepad where he had jotted down some notes. 'James, just a couple of points that I wanted to discuss with you, if you have the time.'

'Tell me.'

'The prison data for three locations has been compiled.'

'Of felons convicted of gun crime?'

'Yes. The results there are a bit warped.'

Deahl just raised his eyebrows.

'We interviewed felons across a few prisons. The purpose was to figure out if they would have committed the crimes for which they had been convicted had they not had easy access to guns. Our hypothesis going in was that the non-availability of guns would not have prevented these crimes. That these felons would have committed the crime irrespective. If not guns, they would have made use of some other weapon of destruction.'

'That would prove beyond doubt that gun control would not have stopped the crimes that did take place.'

'Absolutely. That's why we interviewed these convicts in detail, asked them relevant questions and compiled this data. However, James, when I look at the data which has come in from inmates in Vermont, it presents an entirely different picture.'

James hastily turned towards him. 'What do you mean?' There was a touch of concern in his voice.

'Data from Vermont suggests that without guns the convicts would not have committed those crimes.' Deahl's look turned to that of anxiety. He closed his eyes and let out a deep sigh. Shoulders drooping, he looked at Richard and asked him, 'Are you sure, Richard?'

'Yes, James. That's how it looks as of now.'

'Have we got data from any other prison?'

'Florida. We interviewed seventeen inmates. Same result. Sixteen said that without guns they would not have had the courage to commit the crimes for which they got arrested. Phoenix. Same result. Eighteen out of twenty-two inmates said they wouldn't have done it. Surprisingly, it points to the fact that had guns not been so freely available, over 80 per cent of gun-related crimes, many of them leading to homicide, would not have been committed.'

'This is bad news.' Deahl went into deep thought. His palms moved up to cover his face and he rubbed his eyes with his fingers.

'We will dig deeper into this. Maybe there is more to this.'

'The Chicago example proves that gun control has not yielded results. The convict interview shows that gun control could have prevented crime. We are back to square one.' He looked at Richard. 'Who is helping you in data gathering?'

'Caroline and Philip. It's just the two of them and me on this prison assignment. I did the Vermont, Florida and Phoenix interviews myself.'

'Great. You focus on the Chicago analysis. Ask Caroline and Philip to see me. I will oversee this directly. It is of critical importance to our research.'

Richard was surprised, but didn't show any emotion. After all, Deahl had committed to his tenure this time around. He would rather play along. 'James, I'm off to the Boston prison tomorrow. They have given us permission to meet their inmates. This meeting has come about after numerous rounds of discussions with them. They needed a fair bit of convincing.'

'It's OK. Don't bother. I will coordinate that. Just ask Caroline and Philip to see me. As I said, I need you to focus on the Chicago data. That's the most critical piece for me.'

Richard got up from his chair. He had a confused look on his face. He was wondering why Deahl didn't want him involved in the prison interviews. 'OK. I'll let them know,' he said and walked out of the room.

The research report was due in a month. They could at best stretch it to two. Any later than that and Lucier would flip.

29

November 2007

Coimbatore

Narayanan's phenomenal success had attracted a number of people to the emu trade. The most prosperous emu farmer of Tamil Nadu launched a new scheme in November 2007. The paper emu scheme.

It was a big hit. The scheme was simple. Invest two lakh rupees and have six emu chicks allocated to you. Unlike earlier schemes where the customer would take the chicks and rear them at a farm set up on his own land, this time around, Narayanan set up his own mammoth emu farm and simply allocated a specific number of emus to the customer. These chicks would then be reared on Narayanan's own farms.

For the investment made, the investor would get a fixed return of ten thousand rupees per month for the first two years. After two years, the money realized from the emu meat, skin, toenails and any other by-product would be passed on to the investor after retaining a certain service fee.

A full-grown emu was expected to fetch thirty thousand rupees. For six emus, the amount would be a lakh and eighty thousand. The monthly payment of ten thousand rupees meant a realization of two lakh and forty thousand rupees for the customer over two years. After deducting Narayanan's share in this, the investor would get roughly three and a half lakh rupees for an investment of two lakhs. All this, with no effort from the customer. This scheme was particularly designed to appeal to people living in apartments and small houses, people who did not have the space to set up their own farms to rear emus. The middle class loved it and demand skyrocketed.

In the span of just a month after the launch of the scheme, Narayanan was able to sign on five thousand customers. An amount of over hundred crores was collected in a month. If all went well, through the sale of emu oil, meat, toenails and skin, Narayanan expected to make a profit of fifty crores in this business. Perhaps even more.

The corpus in GB2 Geneva was growing by the day.

30

December 2007

MIT, Boston

It was a chilly December morning when Deahl walked into his office. There was a spring in his step that day. The lounge chair was to his right. He flung his bag on it and walked to his desk. The black chair was where he had left it the night before. He pulled it back, sat down and looked at the table in front of him. The tiny red light on the bottom right corner of the telephone instrument was blinking. Nonchalantly, he stretched out his right hand and flicked the button next to the light. He was in a great mood.

'Morning, James. Can you please call me once you get in? I need to speak with you,' the voice on the telephone crackled. A smile lit up his face. So the feathers had been ruffled. He had expected that. He got up, pushed his chair back and walked out of his room. In a few minutes, he reached his destination. He pushed open the door and walked in.

'Yes, Gordon. You wanted me to call you. I thought I might as well come over and grab a coffee with you.' Gordon Meier, the provost of MIT, looked up from the pile of papers on his table as Deahl strode into his cabin.

'Hey, James. Good to see you.' He got up to welcome Deahl into his room. His secretary walked in at the same time. 'Should I get you another cup of coffee, Gordon?' Gordon nodded and she left, shutting the door behind her.

'Is this necessary, James?' he asked the moment they were alone.

'What are you referring to?'

'You know very well what I am referring to, James. Over the weekend I read the research report, which you plan to send out for peer reviews.'

'I didn't send it to you. How did you get it?'

'The OSP did. They were concerned about the impact of the research.'

'Impact! Have I said anything wrong in my report, Gordon?'

'Technically . . .' he said, thinking for a moment before continuing, '. . . no. Technically nothing is wrong. It's an extensive research. But given the public mood and the general drift against gun activism, do we really need to muddy the waters by releasing something as controversial as your report? There is already a fair bit of shit going around, given that the ten-year ban on assault rifles was allowed to just lapse into obscurity.'

'That was two years ago, Gordon.' Deahl remembered that in 1994 the Bill Clinton administration had banned nineteen types of assault weapons. The ban was in force for a period of ten years and, unless explicitly authorized by the Congress, was to lapse in 2004. Congress did not act on the ban, causing it to lapse.

'In its hundred and fifty years of existence, James, MIT has steered clear of political affiliations. This breaks the tradition. Your report is too volatile.'

'My research is the reality, Gordon. Everything else is fantasy. Political or non-political, I don't know. My report calls a spade a spade.'

'James, I understand where you are coming from. You have been a part of this university for a long time. Don't you think this could eventually lead to erosion of credibility for our university? We will be branded as siding with the Republicans. The only university in the entire United States of America to get such a reputation. I can't let this happen, James.'

'On the contrary, the public at large will respect the honesty of this university. Our credibility will only improve.'

The argument went on for another fifteen minutes. Finding it inconclusive, the provost finally took a tough stance. 'I will disallow this university from putting its official sanction on this research.'

'Must I remind you, Gordon, that the very basis of giving academicians a tenure is to make sure that they don't succumb to bullying of the sort that I am being subjected to right now, and to make sure that they speak their mind.'

'James, you have the right to speak out against gun control if your research states so. But you are wrong in doing so at the behest of the NRA. It kills any objectivity that the research was expected to have in the first place. It is a case of moral drudgery. How can you accept and complete a research which has been sponsored by the NRA and present a result favourable to them in exactly the same manner that they wanted?'

'Firstly, if the research findings are data backed, I really don't care what the findings are. And secondly, it is not an NRA-sponsored research.'

'It is.'

'Says who?' demanded Deahl.

'Me.' It was Cardoza. He had just walked into the room and was standing at the door listening to the two of them. The dean of the Social Psychology department was with him.

'When you walk into a discussion, courtesy demands that you knock,' an irritated Deahl snapped at him. Cardoza and the dean ignored his snub.

'Lucier had met me with the research request. I had turned him down. In you he found an ally. The funds for research were funnelled in through the Department of Social Justice and Equality, Government of Arizona, so that no one could connect the dots. I can say with complete confidence that the research has been compromised.'

'Ridiculous. This accusation is nonsensical.'

'Not as ridiculous as the genesis of this research, James.'

'What if I disagree with the two of you?'

'As I said, you will not be able to publish this research as an MIT-sponsored research.'

'And how could you deny me that right?'

'You need three peer reviews to get this research published,' the dean said. His body language was aggressive. Meier had been balanced in his approach and communication, but the dean was arrogant and aggressive. This did not go down well with Deahl.

'Oh. So you will make sure that no one from the faculty at MIT reviews my research. This kind of arm-twisting is appalling. I guess I will need to talk to my lawyer, gentlemen, before I do anything further about this.' Deahl got up and walked out of the room in a huff. As he was exiting the room, he turned, looked at the dean and thundered, 'My three peer reviewers don't necessarily have to be this university's faculty. The peer review can be from any individual of repute and standing. I hope you realize that! You can't stop the world from reviewing my research. Can you?' He turned and walked out of the room. Deahl had no fear. After all, he was a long-term tenured professor.

Meier smiled. He looked at the dean and said, 'You ticked him off. He will not put it up for peer review now.'

Cardoza didn't share his confidence. 'Don't underestimate James. We don't even know what he is capable of.'

'It doesn't matter.' Meier stepped in. 'Even if he puts it up for a peer review, he has to keep the OSP informed. Once he does that, I will bring in sanctions on the project citing misconduct. The university rules give me adequate authority to do so, as long as the investigation gets completed in a hundred and twenty days. So we have time to figure out what to do.' He turned to Cardoza and said, 'Michael, can you please inform the OSP to keep me posted if and when James puts it up for peer review.'

'Sir,' Cardoza acknowledged as he got up to go. There was a knock on the door.

'Coffee!'

The hundred and twenty days that the university rules gave him to investigate any wrongdoing would be enough to figure out a way to scuttle the issue. At least that's what the provost thought.

31

End-February 2008

MIT, Boston

A furious Meier stormed into Cardoza's room. The latter was in a discussion with the dean on some academic and student-related issues. Meier was clearly agitated as he walked up to Cardoza's table and, in one swift action, he lifted his right hand and banged what he was carrying down on the table. A loud thud echoed.

'Were you aware of this?'

Cardoza rose from his chair. It was impolite of him to have continued sitting when the provost was standing. The door opened. His secretary walked in hurriedly. Cirisha was standing behind her. Her India project was over and she was back to her Boston–Mumbai grind. Both of them had rushed in hearing the loud noise. It had sounded as if something had collapsed.

'It's OK. Nothing to worry about.' Cardoza faked a smile and hastened to add, 'Cirisha, don't go away. I need to talk to you after this meeting. Hang around.'

'Yes, Michael.' The door shut behind them.

Cardoza flipped through what Meier had flung on his table. He didn't like the look of it. 'When did this happen?'

'No clue. I will get him. We had specifically told him not to do it. And what does he do? Just the opposite.' The provost was fuming.

'It's a free country, provost. You will not be able to stop him. At least legally you cannot.'

'Now I know why the OSP did not get any intimation of a peer review request being sent out. It's simple. He didn't send one out. That arrogant son of a bitch.' Everyone in the room was shocked. They had never heard the provost mouth profanities before.

'Let's talk to him. Maybe he can explain his actions.' It was a poor attempt at calming him down.

'Talk to him? You must be kidding. This calls for action. Send out a message to the disciplinary committee. Call a meeting in an hour. If the members are in the classrooms, send someone and ask them to assemble in my room.' And he walked out.

Cardoza heard the door slam shut. But he didn't look in that direction. His eyes and his mind were focused on the book Meier had slammed on his table.

On the cover, in bold letters, were the words *Staring Down the Barrel*. Authored by James Deahl. Instinctively, his hands reached out for it and he flipped open the cover. On the first page was a message. 'Dear Gordon, with best wishes . . . Hope you enjoy reading this. James Deahl.' Along with it was a bookmark prominently displaying the Barnes & Noble logo. 'In all Barnes & Noble Stores, March onwards.'

There was a feeble knock on his door.

'Michael?' It was Cirisha.

'Come on in.' He was still flipping through the book.

'What's this, Michael?'

'James decided to give the peer reviews a skip. Instead of getting it published as a research paper in one of our research journals, he has gone ahead and published it as a book. A hardback which will be available in all bookstores. Accessible to anyone who wants to buy and read.'

'What?' she exclaimed. 'Isn't that inappropriate?'

'Yes, morally speaking. Though legally, he is well within his rights. As long as it is a sponsored project and the university does not pump in its grants, he can do it. Article 4.3.12, para seventeen of the research guidelines gives him that right.' And he went back to flipping through the pages. 'Though I have never seen anyone exercise this right ever. James is a smart cookie.'

32

March 2008

India

In early 2008, GB2 was hit by unprecedented losses worldwide. The subprime mortgage crisis of 2007–08 had taken its toll. GB2 had bought Mortgage-Backed Security (MBS) from the market, which were subprime in nature. In late 2007, a number of Americans stopped making payments on their home loans; to make matters worse, the real estate market tanked on account of massive foreclosures and the MBSs were not even worth the paper they were written on. With billions of dollars in open position on the MBSs, GB2 was faced with a crisis. And as most organizations in that situation, GB2 too had a knee-jerk reaction. The businesses were realigned. Investment banking was downsized and severe restrictions were imposed on how the investment banking business was conducted across the globe. It was like killing the goose that laid the golden egg, but desperate situations called for desperate measures. GB2 was forced to show the market that it was in control of the situation. India too was impacted.

Against this backdrop, Aditya's nervousness when Kevin Moore, the CEO, called him for an unplanned meeting, was only natural. The CEO had also requested the HR head to be present. Only the previous afternoon, a Sunday, Aditya and Moore were playing a game of golf together. Moore had not mentioned anything to him then.

Aditya walked into the CEO's cabin and found him seated at the far end of the room. Seated next to him was the HR head, Piyush Shrivastava. Aditya was flummoxed. Why was HR in the meeting? 'You wanted to see me, Kevin?' he whispered.

'Yes, Aditya. Please take a seat.'

'What happened? Hope all is well.'

'Not really, Aditya. We would like you to read this, before we begin.' And he handed him a letter.

~

Cirisha took a flight out of Boston the same night. Whatever be the reason for his sacking, she couldn't have left him on his own. She had made up her mind to give him a chance to explain. If he was not able to, she would then decide on the next course of action.

33

March–April 2008

Boston

The disciplinary committee meeting chaired by Meier ended in a stalemate. A strong pro-faculty lobby shot down Meier's demand for action, including possible termination for Deahl. Conflicting perspectives emerged. And when the meeting ended, all that Meier could do was to push a resolution curtailing Deahl's teaching duties, the rationale being that if he was allowed to freely mingle with the student community, he was likely to dump his ideology on unsuspecting students.

Staring Down the Barrel released on the designated day to a fabulous response. In no time, the book flew off the shelves. Scandalous excerpts from the book had been leaked to select sections of the press. Deahl was all over the papers and on television. The *New York Times* reviewed the book on the day of its release and gave it a thumbs up. As a result, in the first week of release, the book became a non-fiction bestseller on all the three major lists: *New York Times*, *Wall Street Journal* and *USA-Today*. This was just the beginning.

On the electoral front things were heating up. The North Carolina and Indiana Democratic primaries were to be held on 6th May. Hillary Clinton and Barack Obama campaigned extensively before that. The contest thus far was too close for the NRA's comfort.

They had a single-point agenda: keep the Democrats out of power and even if they did manage to win, make sure it wasn't Obama who would be President. For the NRA, Deahl's book couldn't have come at a better time. They bought space in leading newspapers to campaign against Obama's perceived anti-gun ideology and the book was their tool, their bible, which proved that crime was not related to proliferation of guns amongst the masses. Tighter gun-control laws were not required nor were they good enough to build a robust, progressive country of peace-loving people.

In all this chaos, one man gained. Deahl had become an overnight star. There was a swagger in his walk. An arrogance in his approach. He had publicly defied the higher-ups in the university and they couldn't do anything about it.

One evening in the last week of March, Richard went to meet Cirisha. Her cabin was locked. He looked around. The entire floor was dark, save the far end where Cardoza's room was located. He walked towards it, only to see Louisa typing away furiously. She looked up and saw Richard.

'Hey Richard, what brings you here? You are on the wrong floor.' She raised her finger and pointed upstairs. That was the floor where Deahl and his team had their workspace.

Richard smiled. 'How are you? I came to meet Cirisha.' It was more of a question.

'She is in India, sweetheart.'

'Isn't she back yet? She had told me that she would be back in office today.'

'Change of plans. Should be back on the 30th.' She smiled back at him and noticed that he was sweating profusely. 'Is everything OK, Richard? You are sweating badly!' It was not particularly hot in there.

'A fencing tournament is on. I'm coming straight from there. Try getting into that gear and jump around a few times. It really gets your body temperature racing.'

That night he called Cirisha in India. It was early morning and she was awake and working, responding to a few emails . . .

'So 2nd April it is. Wow! I'm so happy for you. You will rock it, Richard! Have faith.'

'I know. I qualify on all parameters. That I did even last time around, but things didn't work out. This time I am worried that this *Staring Down the Barrel* controversy will turn the entire faculty against me. After all, I was assisting James in this.'

'Look, Richard. Can you wish it away? You can't. A few in the faculty will be jealous of James's success and fame. Some of them will be genuinely irritated because of what James did. But you shouldn't worry about what everyone thinks. There are four people who will make your tenure decision. The dean, Michael and two others on the committee. The dean will vote against. Michael will play straight. That's the way I have known him. Others, I don't know.' And then she paused, hoping for a reaction. 'Richard, you can't go into this discussion assuming that they are all against you. It's a matter of life and death for you.'

'Yes,' said Richard, 'life and death,' and hung up. It was quite abrupt. She went into the kitchen, got herself a cup of hot water, picked up a sachet of green tea and walked back to her laptop. On the way, she heard a chime, indicating that she had received a new email. By the time she reached her laptop there was another chime. She settled down at her desk and opened her inbox. There were two emails from Richard. She opened the first one. It was a response to the email that she had sent Richard long ago, giving him details of Snuggles's Dharavi factory. She could see the entire text of her previous mail below Richard's response. But it was Richard's reply that surprised her. It had three cryptic-sounding words. She couldn't make head or tail of it.

She was confused. What could it be? A strange mail, that too on top of and in reply to her earlier mail on Snuggles. Very unlike Richard. In this confused state, she clicked open the next mail.

And she smiled.

The second mail just had one additional line and was sent as a response to the first mail: 'Sent by mistake.'

'Mad fellow,' she said to herself and smiled again. She knew his mind was stressed.

Cirisha looked at her phone. It was only six-thirty in the morning. She walked back into the bedroom. Aditya was still sleeping. She remembered the day she had landed in India. Aditya had come to pick her up as usual. He had hugged her and sobbed like a child. Aditya had always been an achiever. An ambitious corporate executive for whom winning was everything. That ambition was also probably the reason why he was sacked. Terminated for having invested GB2's money in a local start-up for personal gratification. From what she could gather, GB2 had invested two million dollars in a Mumbai-based start-up at Aditya's behest. In return, the company had given a 5 per cent stake at no cost to Aditya. Everything had been hunky-dory till the time that another private equity honcho had squealed to Kevin Moore at a dinner the previous evening. Moore had then called up the head of HR, who in turn contacted the promoters of the company in question and confronted them with the information, which they couldn't deny. Why would they, especially after they had got their money?

Armed with this confession, they had cornered Aditya, who could not say anything in his defence. He was summarily dismissed. The CEO's parting words had been, 'Integrity is a very potent skill. Try to build it in your repertoire.'

When Cirisha had heard this, she was filled with disgust. How could Aditya do something like that? Was money all-important? What about dignity? Self-esteem? How could she have gone so wrong in assessing an individual? For a moment, she had even considered leaving him. But she was not one to give up on things easily. She had to make it work. That night Aditya begged for forgiveness. She relented. He promised never to tread down that path again.

'Come with me to Boston. We will figure out what to do. In any case we have enough to live comfortably. Let's get away from this place and from people who don't matter.'

Left with no choice, a guilt-filled Aditya agreed.

Thankfully for Aditya, he had managed to hide from her the fact that Narayanan had been the frontman for the deal and that the entire stake had been routed through him. Had she even got a whiff of it, she would surely have walked out on him and Narayanan.

34

April 2008

Boston

Aditya and Cirisha landed in Boston on 30th March to chart a new beginning. Cirisha resumed work on the 2nd of April, the day Richard was scheduled to have his tenure interview. Cirisha had called him the previous evening. They had chatted for a long time. She even wished him luck. His big day was stressing him out. 'You must relax, Richard. Behave like a forty-year-old man!' she tried to cheer him up. He had turned forty in January that year. Despite her best efforts at calming him down, he was very edgy. He even apologized a few times for having sent her the emails erroneously. Cirisha had completely forgotten about them.

On the morning of 2nd April, dressed smartly in a freshly laundered suit, Richard walked into the war zone—a carefully chosen room, normally used as a classroom. It was quite early in the day. Session had not yet started so no one was around.

Cardoza saw him first and ushered him into the chair meant for him. It faced the panel that was seated on a slightly elevated podium in front of him. Richard quietly walked up to the chair, nodded in acknowledgement at the panel and sat down. The reaction thus far had been cold.

Quietly, Richard surveyed the room. The door was to his right, the seats normally occupied by the students were behind him and the classroom writing board was right in front. Between the board and him were the men who would play God that day—Cardoza was the first in the panel, closest to the door. Seated to his right was the dean, Henry Liddell, further away from the main door, to the right of the dean were a Brazilian, Sandy Gustavo, the head of the research and grants team, and Frederick Lobo, the head of the FEC.

The discussion began. It centred on Richard's academic credentials. Lobo put on record the feedback that the FEC had received from the students. Richard was quite a popular faculty. So no problems there. Teaching record was a 4/5. The peer evaluation report was put up for discussion. In all, four peers had submitted their reports. So far so good.

That's when Liddell began to question Richard on the research. 'Richard, the last time around there were accusations of your having solicited your peers for co-authoring research papers to which you hadn't contributed at all.'

'Those allegations were unproven.'

'Seriously suspicious. But not proven. That's what the report of the previous FEC states because no one came forward. Even those who had initially complained backed off. Probably someone coerced them into doing so.' He looked at Lobo, who was nodding his head. 'Who are we to say? In any case, we cannot go by that report.'

'OK. So we ignore that.' The dean was surprisingly magnanimous.

'Richard, the committee has unanimously taken a view to ignore your contribution to the book, *Staring Down the Barrel*, despite the author giving you due credit. The university has decided not to recognize it as a valid research paper,' Cardoza said. He looked at the others in the team and added, 'What does the committee feel about the other research papers submitted by Mr Avendon? Even if we ignore this latest work of research, he still has enough published papers to be considered, right?'

Without waiting for anyone from the panel to answer, Richard went on to elaborate on all the research that he had done and the impact that each of those had had on the university, academia and society at large. 'I have received fabulous peer reviews for each of these. All of them have been rated very highly.' He had come prepared.

'Richard,' the dean began. 'We have seen the quality of research work done by you. We have also analysed the grants that you have been able to mobilize for research purposes and looked at the various committees that you serve on. On purely the classroom academic front, you are amongst the best non-tenured assistant professors that we have. But we cannot approve a tenure position for you. The main reasons being your unproven grant-raising capabilities and your inclination to let your political leanings impact your research work. Since this is your second and consequently last attempt, you will not be granted tenure at MIT.'

'What?' Richard was shocked

'Isn't it obvious? Do you have anything to say to this committee before we call it a day, Mr Avendon?' The dean's tone bordered on ridicule. It was clear. He was being punished for having been a part of the *Staring Down the Barrel* saga. Richard looked at Cardoza from the corner of his eye. He seemed to be disagreeing with the group.

'We need to discuss this, dean,' Cardoza started off, only to be interrupted harshly. 'Well, on a pure committee vote, it is three to one, Michael,' the dean thundered.

'So much for anonymity of votes,' Cardoza responded sarcastically. 'This discussion is not supposed to happen in front of the candidate. And the decision, after due consultation among the members, has to be communicated to the candidate at a later stage. And in the case of Mr Avendon, there are enough positives to call for a debate.'

'Thank you, Michael.' The dean was in no mood to listen. He turned and looked at Richard. 'Do you have anything to say, Mr Avendon?'

'Yes, I have lots to say. For years you have ignored my achievements. Looks like tenure is all about conformity to your stupid process as opposed to achievement. My research can at worst be called original, and not playing to the gallery of old, obese professors on the verge of retirement. Unfortunately, you value collegiality over originality. I have done few research projects but the ones I have done are pure quality. Ones that make a difference to society. To the United States of America. I should have learned my lesson earlier that there is no place for useful and profound research unless it is fashionable.'

'You are getting worked up, Mr Avendon.' The dean had a smirk on his face. He was enjoying every bit of this flare-up. It was a proxy war that he was fighting with Deahl through Avendon.

'Oh yeah? Worked up? I should have got worked up a few years back. You fat sloppy son of a bitch.' Richard was getting really hostile now. He had no fear. In any case, it was the end of the road for him at MIT.

Cardoza sensed it and got up from his seat. He tried to pacify Richard, who was now beginning to sweat profusely as though he was on some sort of drug. 'Richard. Calm down. Easy. Easy.' But it was of no avail. This was not going the way he wanted it to. Realizing that this could get out of hand, Cardoza hurriedly walked outside.

He dialled Cirisha's number, the first number on his speed dial. 'Cirisha, are you on campus?' he asked the moment she answered.

'Yes, Michael.'

'Can you please ask the chief of MIT Police to rush some backup to the admin block? I think Richard Avendon is getting out of hand.'

'Right away. I hope it's not serious.'

'I don't think so. But he is screaming his guts out, calling people names, swearing at everyone in the room. I just stepped out to call for help. Please do this right away. I'll talk to you later.' And he walked back towards the room.

Within moments, the sound of gunfire reverberated through the admin block. By the time the MIT Police reached the spot, Richard had shot everyone in the room dead, before shooting himself in the head with the last bullet. Cardoza was hit on his shoulder by the penultimate bullet in Richard's 0.22 calibre revolver and was wheeled away to the campus hospital.

35

First quarter of 2008

Coimbatore

The first three months of 2008 were defining ones for the emu farming business.

While the second half of 2007 was marked by rapid growth, it was not without its impact. The paper emu scheme launched by Narayanan was easy to replicate. This led to the mushrooming of small-time players and, consequently, to a phenomenal increase in the number of emus around Coimbatore. The supply of emu eggs increased, as did the supply of emu meat.

The demand didn't keep pace with the supply. Soon there was excess supply. And that meant a fall in prices. Initially, the drop was negligible, but soon enough, the prices crashed. Revenue realization on the birds dropped. Smaller emu farmers were suddenly finding it difficult to feed the birds, or even pay the initial lot of customers who were now coming back with full-grown emus, demanding payment in return. Monthly payouts to the customers who had subscribed to the paper emu schemes began to suffer. Initially, it was a one-off issue with a few small-timers. But within a matter of months it grew into an epidemic.

In April 2008, for the first time, cheques issued by Narayanan to the participants in his emu farming scheme bounced. Ten thousand customer cheques were returned because the bank refused to honour them.

The monthly payout that he had to make to his paper emu customers was in excess of ten crore rupees. Narayanan had a working capital limit, and many times in the past he had been allowed to exceed it because of the credibility he enjoyed with the bank. But April was the beginning of a new financial year. New rules, new policies. Emu farming had suddenly, over the last three or four months, become a bad word in banking circles. A number of small farms had gone bust, leaving banks to hold the baby. This did not go down well with the management and there was a clampdown on banking facilities for emu farms.

In the first week of April, over four hundred people gathered outside his corporate office and started shouting slogans and demanding payments. Thankfully, he had a better reputation than most others in the trade and hence the number of people was relatively low. Faced with no other choice, he called his RM managing the Geneva account. Two million dollars were pulled out from GB2 in Geneva and used to pay off the investors for April. It didn't take much for him to realize that with the emu meat price collapsing, no takers for emu eggs and a sluggish investor interest, he was staring at a long dark period. The crisis had been managed for one month. He had to figure out a long-term solution. This could not go on for long.

36

April 2008

Boston

'It is with utmost grief that we condole the death of our favourite dean, Henry Liddell. As someone who has led MIT to a number of significant achievements, the dean was one of the greatest academicians and finest human beings that I have ever met. I feel sad for his family,' Lucier said with tears welling up in his eyes. The world knew that it was an act. Addressing a press conference was not easy in modern-day America.

'But sir,' a reporter butted in, 'don't you think that the life of three honoured academicians and one promising faculty member has been cut short by the Second Amendment? The same amendment that the NRA has been opposing for years now.'

'No. This assessment is incorrect,' responded Lucier. 'If Mr Richard Avendon wanted to harm the committee members, he would have come prepared even if guns were not available. If not guns, it would have been something else.'

'But guns make it easy to kill from a distance. You don't need to be close to the person being harmed. Had he carried something else, maybe, just maybe, the members could have overpowered him.'

'The suggestion is ridiculous. Have you considered the fact that narcotic drugs like heroin are banned in the United States? Where do druggies get them from? Even if you ban guns, there will be criminal elements who will make a business out of supplying illegal weapons.

Had Mr Avendon been denied access to a legal weapon, he would have been able to acquire it in the same manner that criminals do today. From the mafia. The end result would have been the same.'

The shooting of the dean and the three academicians had become the talk of the nation. It brought the Liberals and the Democrats together.

The chief of MIT Police, who had initially been called in when the gunshots had been fired, did the preliminary investigation. It was an open-and-shut case. Richard had a history of emotional outbursts. His desperation to get the tenure was not a secret. He had worked himself up into believing that he wouldn't get past the committee this time and had come prepared. He had brought his own handgun. And had shot everyone from close quarters, before killing himself.

The day after the incident, Cardoza was a devastated man. Cirisha and Aditya were at the hospital to meet him. 'Thank God that Richard was not carrying an assault rifle. Else you would not have been in our midst today,' Cirisha said with tears in her eyes.

'This is what the Second Amendment does to us, Cirisha. It's sad. Really tragic. Does James realize that he has a responsibility to society? Does he even care?' Cardoza was getting worked up.

'Richard was obsessed with getting his tenure, Michael. He called me in Mumbai last week. He was worried that you would obstruct his path to a promotion.'

'You know, Cirisha, my last words to the dean were that we should have another discussion on Richard's tenure and then decide. I even wrote to the dean a few days ago that the time is not conducive for this committee meeting and that we should put it off by a few weeks. He didn't agree. And when he didn't, I wrote to him that we must make sure that we do not let the James issue cloud our mind and that we must promote him. Unfortunately, once the dean made up his mind, he never listened to anyone.'

Cirisha noticed that Aditya, who was by her side, was getting bored. She got up to leave. A copy of *Staring Down the Barrel* was lying on Cardoza's table. 'If you don't mind, can I borrow it from you?'

'Sure. Be my guest.'

'When will you be back at work, Michael?'

'Thankfully, the bullet just scraped my shoulder. It's just a superficial injury. My arm will need to rest for two weeks, but I should be out of here and at work in two days.' He looked at Aditya and said, 'How are you liking it here, my friend? I am sure with you around Cirisha will be happier and less worried.' And he smiled. Aditya just patted his arm and smiled in return. His mind was somewhere else. He had to meet Shivinder, who was also in Boston on a Snuggles Global CEO meet.

37

April 2008

Boston

The Snuggles Global CEO conference was in full flow. The India presentation had just got over and Shivinder had received a standing ovation. After all, India was the number one country in terms of growth for Snuggles across the globe. Next was the presentation by the Latin American team, the last for the day. While their presentation was in progress, a short and hefty African American discreetly walked into the large ballroom of the Hilton Plaza, went straight up to the global CEO and whispered something into his ear. The CEO got up with a pained look on his face, looked at the congregation and said loudly, 'You guys carry on. I will be back soon.' He then followed the man out of the room.

In the next twenty minutes, Shivinder was called out. He was ushered into a room where four people were already present: the Asia-Pacific head of Snuggles, the legal head, the global CEO and a fourth man he had never met.

'Hello, Mr Singh. I am Nick Rand.' The fourth man seemed to have read his mind.

'Have we met before, Mr Rand?'

'No. We haven't.' Nick was curt. The expressions on the faces of the others were quite cold, making Shivinder wonder what was going on.

'You actually thought no one would find out, Mr Singh?' Nick began to speak.

'Find what out, Mr Rand?'

'Fraudulent sales figures, padded up receivables, increased profitability and valuations. I don't know where to begin.' And he paused before getting up from his chair. 'It all started last year, Mr Singh, with a lady complaining to Snuggles Inc. through her American associate about child labour at a factory manufacturing Snuggles shoes and leather accessories.'

'So, did you find children working at any Snuggles manufacturing unit? I don't think we have underage labour anywhere, Mr Rand. We follow strict procedures at all our manufacturing sites.'

'Hold on! Hold on!' Nick hurried to put all speculation to rest. 'I have just begun.' And he started pacing up and down the room, as if he were narrating a film script to a group of producers. 'The complaint came to us through a professor at MIT who wrote to us on behalf of the complainant. The professor had done a fair bit of research for us in the past.'

'So? What is this all about?'

'The address where child labour was being used, as indicated by the complainant, did not match with any of our manufacturing facilities.'

'It could be a unit manufacturing fakes. We have them all over the world, don't we?'

Nick nodded his head. He raised his eyebrows and tilted his head to the left. 'Possible. We would have assumed the same and intimated you had the images accompanying the complaint not been shocking.'

'What image?'

'Of the label stitched on to the tongue of the shoe. A label which indicates the size, place of manufacture, price, etc. But most importantly, a label which has a code.' Shivinder knew that at Snuggles, every label had a unique code to indicate the model, serial number and the place and month of manufacture. 'Strangely, the label in the image which was sent to us had that code too.'

'Why would that be strange?' Shivinder was being difficult. Aggression, he thought, would get him out of a difficult situation. 'These days fakes look identical to the real shoes.'

'Because, Mr Singh, I am yet to come across a fake which has a genuine code on the label. The worst we have seen thus far is that all the fakes manufactured at a given facility have the same code. They just pick up a label and replicate it across shoes and models. But in this case, the four images sent to us had different numbers—that too codes which matched the shoe models. Which meant there was a high probability of the labels being genuine. They had been generated using the same algorithm that we use in our factories.'

Shivinder raised his eyebrows and ridiculed Nick. 'What are you trying to say, Mr Rand?'

Nick was not intimidated by Shivinder's approach. He was used to such reactions. 'Just out of curiosity we ran the codes through our database. And guess what? Shoes with these codes had already been sold through a certain franchisee in Mumbai.'

'Maybe someone got hold of the numbers and generated the labels. If you want I can check it out and come back to you. This breach is easy to plug. Wish you had told me earlier.'

'That won't be required once you have heard us out, Mr Singh.'

'Nick was in India for a few months, Mr Singh.' The regional manager Asia-Pacific spoke for the first time. Unknown to Shivinder, or for that matter anyone else from his insider team, Nick had spent six months in India in an undercover operation, trying to dig deep into the Snuggles scandal.

Nick continued, 'I went to the factory located deep inside a slum. A four-storeyed building. Big facility. Over two hundred and fifty workers. Forty-five of them children. As in forty-five I could count as being visibly underage.'

'You just said that it was not listed amongst our manufacturing sites. So I don't know. I'll have to check.'

'Thanks, Mr Singh. But you know about the facility.'

'The presupposition is ridiculous.' Shivinder was losing his cool now.

'You might want to see this.' Nick handed over the order copy, signed by Deven Khatri, to Shivinder. 'I picked up a copy when I was there.' Shivinder didn't have an answer and was beginning to look defeated. Taking a deep breath, he looked up. In a voice filled with sorrow, he said, 'I hope you are aware, Deven Khatri disappeared a year ago. A missing person complaint has been registered with the Mumbai Police, who have been unable to trace him.'

'Yes, we are aware. We are really sorry about that. He has signed this purchase order.'

'I just wish what you are saying is not true. Deven seemed like such a nice guy. Committed to the organization and to me.'

'We are sure about the latter. A bit doubtful about the former, though. Moving on,' Nick continued, 'we went to the store from where shoes with these numbers had already been sold. This is the one on Linking Road, in Bandra, Mumbai.'

'Yes, we have a showroom there.'

'We visited that store. The retailer proudly told us that he had another store—half a mile from where we were. He took us there and showed off his store. A new one, opened in the last twelve months. And guess what?' He paused and added, 'There is no record of the new store in our central systems.'

'Oh, is that so? I am sure it's a mistake which can be corrected.'

'It's not a mistake, Mr Singh. The code on the tongue of each shoe at the second franchisee we went to matches a shoe which has already been sold elsewhere. This store is not connected to our global system. No one at Snuggles knows of this except your confidants in India. And this is not the only such store.'

'Are you insinuating that we run a fraudulent set-up?'

'Your game is up, Mr Singh. You took advantage of your knowledge of our internal systems. You knew that the only time the code is used after a product is sold is if it comes back for warranty. And in case it did come back, you managed it at your end, so that it never blew up into a service issue.'

Shivinder knew he was exposed but fought on. 'I am appalled at this accusation.'

'Well, you would have had reason to be if this was just a mistake. But it seems to be a conscious effort at defrauding the company. I have visited most of your franchisees in western and southern India and personally compiled a list of outlets which appear to be fraudulent. My list has two hundred and sixty-eight stores. God knows how many such stores there are in the country. And each one of them claimed to have paid twenty thousand dollars as a non-refundable deposit.'

'Never in my wildest dreams would I have imagined that Deven could do something like this.' In a last-ditch effort, Shivinder tried to shift the blame onto Deven.

Nick looked at the head of Asia-Pacific. There was a look of disgust in their eyes. 'Greater Boston Global Bank.'

'What about it?'

'The account in the name of Snuggles India Private Limited. Opened and operated by you and your CFO, Deven Khatri. Can you explain why the amounts in that account never made it to any of the financial statements?'

'No clue. Why are you asking me questions which you should ideally be asking the CFO?'

'Because, Mr Shivinder, there is no way that you didn't know about the account. You have made the payout to this manufacturer of fake shoes in Dharavi from the GB2 account. You signed the cheques, Mr Singh. You.'

'I sign most of the cheques which have been validated by the CFO.'

'Maybe then you could explain how and why you continued issuing those cheques even after Mr Khatri disappeared. Mr Khatri was not authorized to sign the account on his own, whereas you were. The slumdog millionaire shoe manufacturer that we visited had been paid through cheques from GB2 signed by you as recently as two months back. It can only mean you knew about the account, the fake shoe manufacturers and the mysterious franchisees.'

'And Mr Singh,' the Asia-Pacific head spoke up again, 'this only points to the fact that you knew about this entire operation and ran this clandestinely. You opened over two hundred and sixty-eight franchisees, unauthorized by Snuggles, despite being explicitly prohibited from doing so; flooded them with fake shoes manufactured at a dirt-cheap cost, siphoning off the money in the process. Not to mention the enormous risk of brand dilution.'

'Would you care to tell us where the money is, Mr Singh?'

'I don't know what you are talking about. I need to talk to my lawyer before I comment.'

'You will have an opportunity for the same. But just as a professional courtesy to the CEO, I would like to let you know that we debated if we should let you resign. But the consensus was that you should be terminated with immediate effect and legal action be initiated.' The Asia-Pacific head was angry but firm.

Shivinder got up from his seat. 'I will consult my lawyer and let you know what needs to be done. Thank you, gentlemen.' And he walked out. He knew that his game was up.

The Asia-Pacific head and Nick continued smiling as he opened the door. 'Before you leave, you might want to see the charges filed against you this morning in India,' said Nick as he got up to follow Shivinder outside the room. Shivinder stopped in his tracks. A police complaint had been filed against him? Was his game really up? He turned and took the papers from Nick's hands. It was a six-page document which he read till the last word and then looked up. 'You can't do this.'

'Just fifteen minutes ago, Mr Singh. Fifteen minutes. We did just that. Charges against you for siphoning off money and causing losses of over fifty million dollars to Snuggles Inc.' The global CEO was categorical.

Shivinder turned and headed for the exit. The moment he stepped out of the door, three uniformed officers surrounded him. They had badges on their shirts which Shivinder recognized as the Boston Police Department's logo. Below the logo were three words which made him shiver—Economic Crime Department. He quietly walked with them, even as they read him his rights. As his steps slowly dropped in sync with those of the police officers, a strange look appeared on his face. It was pure unbridled rage. It was all because of Cirisha Narayanan that he had got into trouble. Everything was going smoothly until she visited his factory in Dharavi. He would make her pay for it.

38

March–May 2008

India

As Shivinder was fighting a battle with the team at Boston, an entirely different saga was unfolding halfway across the globe. In Delhi, an anti-corruption crusader had cornered the government on its inaction with regard to bringing back the thousands of crores of black money stashed by Indian politicians and entrepreneurs in tax-friendly and privacy-intensive banks overseas. Issuing a clear threat to make public the names of Indians with accounts in overseas tax havens like Switzerland, he had sent a chill down the spines of everyone involved. GB2 was specifically named by him as one of the banks involved. He claimed to be in possession of a list of over three hundred Indians who had clandestine accounts overseas and that too with GB2.

Narayanan was worried that his name would be on that list. His withdrawal of over ten crore rupees from the GB2 Geneva account to pay creditors and investors their dues had caught the fancy of the media. In larger cities like Delhi or Mumbai, this amount would not have raised eyebrows. But in Coimbatore, a few hawks from the media watched his every move. A hungry, hyperactive media, busy speculating on who those three hundred people could be, egged on by a few jealous small-time competitors of Narayanan, suddenly took note of the fact that the latter had produced ten crores out of thin air and paid back the investors in cash. The issue blew up into a scandal. And when the local media took note, could the national media have been far behind? The source of the funds started being questioned. This intense trial by media had its impact.

The day Narayanan realized that he might be exposed in the GB2 Geneva account scam, he applied for an American visa. The reason given to the visa authorities at the American consulate was that he was going to visit his daughter in Massachusetts. And the day the media included his name in the possible list of Indians with black money overseas, he decided to bail out. Leaving his emu business in the hands of a few caretakers, he took the first flight to Boston from Chennai. Cirisha was at the airport to receive him. She was very excited. Her father was coming to visit her for the first time after her marriage.

After Narayanan went to bed to sleep off his jet lag, Cirisha retired for the day with a book in hand. Keeping her company in bed was Deahl's *Staring Down the Barrel*. She was in a good frame of mind. Narayanan's arrival had cleared the gloom surrounding the death of Richard. And she found Deahl's book interesting enough to divert her mind.

As she read the acknowledgements in the beginning of the book, she became emotional. A few drops of tears sneaked out from the corners of her eyes and dribbled down along the edge of her nose. Their superiors were at loggerheads, but she was quite affectionate towards him. Richard had been one of her favourite faculty members.

39

May 2008

MIT, Boston

On the morning of the first Saturday of May, MIT was hit by another shocking bit of news. Meier had resigned. The president of the governing body, Juan Antonio, announced the resignation of the provost to the faculty, students and the media.

'The provost has been severely emotionally impacted by the events that have transpired in the last few days, leading to the death of four of his colleagues. He has expressed his inability to continue in the post.' Till the morning of that Saturday, Meier was thought of as a person who had the credentials to succeed the president.

Intense speculation began on who the chosen one would be to succeed Meier. An earnest search began. The president constituted a search committee, which looked at the list of eligible candidates.

A shortlist was to be arrived at after a rigorous procedure, which entailed feedback from the faculty, the sponsors and even the students. A specific email ID was created for this and everyone directly or indirectly involved was requested to send in their inputs.

The process lasted a week. It was down to a shortlist of four candidates who would finally be scored by the faculty search committee and their candidature put to vote by the institute's executive committee, also called the governing body, which comprised five members, Meier and the president.

40

May 2008

Boston

Staring Down the Barrel was ruffling feathers everywhere. Its contents made it a topic for intense debate. Parents of victims of gun crime condemned the book and lobbied against it, calling it a shameful blot on the highly respected literary scene in America. Some called it opportunistic.

The NRA milked it dry. They used the research to prove to the government and the public that gun crime was not in any way linked to the Second Amendment. It was more than that. And that logic helped them demonstrate that the choice of President should not depend on who holds a strong opinion on gun control, rather it must be based on who promises economic growth for the weaker sections of society. The choice must be the one who not only promises jobs to the blacks but also works towards reducing the wide chasm in the economic status of the haves and have-nots.

The Democrats rubbished the research. Obama ignored it. But try as hard as they did, in each and every remaining debate between Hillary Clinton and Barrack Obama, *Staring Down the Barrel* continued to figure prominently. Someone from the audience was sure to ask them a question on this subject. Such was the impact.

Deahl had done a thorough analysis. His research was based on multiple lines of argument. One was the fact that gun deaths were unnecessarily hyped and often turned into front-page news.

His contention was that over the past quarter of a century, gun massacres killed close to six hundred people, while over three and a half thousand people had died in lightning strikes alone. Gun violence was not as serious an issue as it was made out to be. There were more serious issues to be dealt with. Whenever there was gun-related violence, everyone was quick to jump to the conclusion that the incident happened because of the gun, without getting to the bottom of why the psychopath used the gun in the first place. He had extensively quoted examples like that of a nanny in Colorado who had knifed two infants to death. In that case everyone was concerned about the mental state of the nanny, her racial profiling and her family background, and there were multiple discussions on what could have prompted her into killing the two children, but no one really spoke about the fact that the weapon used in the crime was a knife. Should knives be banned? he asked. Were guns responsible or was it the mental state of the murderers that needed to be considered? If gun violence was on account of the latter, then would the gun-related crime have taken place had guns not been made available to them? This was the thinking which led him to do a detailed analysis of the thought process of these murderers. For this, his team interviewed various people who had been convicted on charges of gun crime and were serving their sentence in prisons across the country.

His second line of argument was that guns were great equalizers. It helped old men, women and other vulnerable individuals to protect themselves against attacks of any kind. In the absence of guns, such individuals would be rendered helpless and unable to defend themselves.

The third was the propensity of the economically weaker sections for crime. This was demonstrated through an in-depth analysis of segmentation of crime rates in places like Chicago, Texas, Massachusetts and so on, split by geography. Apart from these, there were quite a few other research elements which relied on data regarding ownership of guns, how areas with higher ownership of guns had lower crime rates primarily because the possibility of the prospective victim being armed prevented a number of assaulters from committing a crime, and most importantly, the correlation between gun crime and drug abuse.

'How the hell can he say that gun control will not have the desired impact?' Cardoza got excited when Cirisha brought up the book in a conversation with him. His left hand was still in a sling, but that didn't sober him down. 'I read it. Found it repulsive. When young kids pick up their parents' guns and shoot unsuspecting victims, when an adolescent youth walks into a movie theatre with an assault rifle and fires indiscriminately, who is to blame? Not the guns for sure, if James is to be believed. His logic is ridiculous.'

'I don't think he is completely wrong, Michael. He claims that gun control will only take rifles and other weapons out of the hands of law-abiding citizens, whereas criminals will continue to get them through other means. Places like Chicago, and even Massachusetts, where gun control has been in force for some time, haven't really been able to control crime. Right?'

'That's because half the guns in Chicago are sold on its outskirts, in Riverdale. Gun-control laws don't apply in Riverdale.'

'Precisely. That's what he says. If you ban guns, criminals will find a way to get their guns, the same way as they procure narcotic drugs. And law-abiding citizens will become easy prey.'

'Hold on, Cirisha!' Cardoza's voice dropped to a whisper. 'Do I sense a convert here?' He looked worried and irritated. The last thing he wanted was an ideological defection from his camp.

Cirisha laughed. She found Cardoza's reaction quite funny. 'No, Michael. In fact, everything about the book is so fresh in my mind. Maybe that's why I was trying to debate it.'

'Merci.'

Cirisha smiled. She realized that she should not have argued in favour of Deahl. Cardoza would never like it. 'It is time for Richard's memorial service. Let's leave.' She changed the subject quickly.

'Where is it being held? I thought the university had declined to give an official sanction.'

'Yes. But a small group is still going ahead with it. It's in the same lecture hall that Richard was interviewed in by you, the dean and the others. Apparently there was a request to hold it on Richard's floor, or at least outside our block. But Gordon refused to give permission. That's why it's taken so long.'

'How many people are expected?'

'Not many. Just a small peaceful gathering.'

'You think I should come?'

'Your call, Michael. I am going. I heard that James is coming too.'

'OK. Let's go.' Cardoza acted as if something had shaken him out of his slumber. He got up and walked with her.

They walked to the venue of the memorial service. It was a very moving moment for all of them. Cardoza put his right hand around Cirisha and hugged her by the shoulder when he saw her weeping silently.

The speeches began. Cirisha was also slated to speak. There were two speakers ahead of her. In her mind, she went over the points and pulled out her phone to read through the notes that she had prepared. While she was looking at it, her phone rang: Aditya was trying to reach her. Thankfully, the phone was in silent mode. She looked up, the speaker was a student who was completely in awe of Richard. And why not? After all, Richard was indeed one of the best teachers on campus. She didn't pick up the call.

Within ten seconds, Cirisha's phone rang again. She picked it up this time and tried whispering into it. The call got disconnected. Aditya never bothered her with multiple calls. Thanking her stars that she was sitting next to the rear exit, she walked out, shutting the door carefully behind her.

'Yeah, Aditya,' she said in a whisper. She didn't want to disturb the others. 'I am at Richard's memorial service. Remember, I told you.'

'Yes, I know. But this was urgent. Shivinder has been picked up by the cops.'

'Who?' She did not hear the name clearly as she was focusing partly on the person giving the memorial speech. He was still going strong.

'Why is there so much of disturbance in the background? And who is that guy speaking to you? Why can't you focus on me when you are talking to me?'

'Aditya, the memorial speeches are going on. Anyway, let me get away from here.' She started walking away from the room and turned back. Something didn't seem right, but she couldn't figure out what it was.

'Tell me,' she said, walking ahead. The student could still be heard. 'Can you hear me now?'

'Yes, it's better. Tell that idiot to speak softly.'

'Shut up, Aditya. The door is closed. I am up next. So tell me quickly. Who is arrested?'

'Not yet formally arrested but has been taken into custody. Shivinder.'

'Shivinder? Why?'

'Some confusion with the Snuggles HQ folks. They called in the cops.'

'What charges?'

'Apparently on some fraud that he committed in India. Possibly related to the Dharavi factory that you complained against.'

'Oh, so Shivinder is involved. Hope he rots in jail.'

'Come on, Cirisha. He is not that bad a guy.'

'That's what you think. What do you want me to do?'

'Help him get out. You know people here. I don't.'

'Impossible. You know what my views about him are.' Cirisha was very strong-minded. There was no point in trying to get her to change her mind about Shivinder.

'Then I am going to at least see what can be done. I'll be back in the evening or late tonight.'

'I won't stop you. And now if you will let me, I need to go. I am the next one to speak.'

'OK. I expected that when I heard that idiot in the background stop.'

'OK.' She did not know what else to say. As she walked back to the room, she couldn't help but feel again that something was wrong. But she just couldn't put her finger on it. She pushed open the door and walked in. Her name was being called out. She walked up straight to the front of the room and began speaking. As she spoke, she could see Cardoza and Deahl in opposite corners of the room, exchanging dirty glances. Even though Deahl had been suspended, till such time that any firm action was taken on his tenure, he was within his rights to carry on with work as usual except for his teaching assignments, which had been put on hold.

41

26th May 2008

Boston

The shortlist for the Bancroft Prize was announced. Awarded annually by the trustees of Columbia University, the Bancroft Prize was given to authors of books of exceptional merit in the fields of American history, biography and diplomacy. That year, *Staring Down the Barrel* was one of the books shortlisted.

The entire faculty of MIT was up in arms. How could something which had been dismissed as mischievous and evil by the late dean of MIT even be considered for the award, leave alone make it to the shortlist? It was even suggested that the NRA was behind the nomination.

Cardoza was upset. The notoriety of *Staring Down the Barrel* was making him angry. Deahl seemed to be winning all the rounds in this battle of egos despite the university trying to pull him down.

The *Boston Globe* had carried a detailed interview of Deahl and even excerpted his book. It was a part of its feature on books shortlisted for the Bancroft Prize. Cardoza was reading it when Cirisha walked in. Hurriedly he shoved the newspaper away. Cirisha couldn't resist a smile.

'You know, Michael, everyone says you are a far better boss to work for than James.' She knew that the comparison would cheer him up. 'You never take credit away from your team. And look at James. The only thing he can say about a guy who spent his entire life at MIT working with him is that Richard helped him gather and analyse the data. As if Richard was a clerk.'

'Everyone is not the same, Cirisha.' And he finally smiled. 'How does your day look?'

'Two classroom sessions today. One research discussion. And balance I have to catch up on a couple of things which are bothering me. In the afternoon I have to meet someone from the Boston Police. Crime investigation team.'

'Why? What are you up to now?'

'Nothing serious, Michael. Last year, I had complained to Snuggles against instances of child labour at their manufacturing facility in India. Apparently their CEO has been arrested while on a visit to Boston. The Boston Police wants to meet me for some first-hand information.'

'Great. How is Aditya coping up with life here?'

'Oh, he is doing fine. He is learning fencing at the MIT Fencing Institute. Keeps him busy for a few hours. He has company at home in the form of my father. So no complaints.'

Cardoza smiled. 'God bless the great Indian family,' he said and went back to his computer screen. Cirisha walked away.

In her chamber, she logged in to her computer and manoeuvred to the *Boston Globe* website. The interview with Deahl was on their home page. There was still an hour to go for her classroom session, and she was already prepared for it. There was adequate time for her to go through the interview. Even though she had seen it that morning, she hadn't had the time to read it. She began reading the article—her training in speed-reading was helpful.

Deahl had managed the Q&A very well. He had presented the research in its true form, without giving it any political overtones. 'I am not a politician. Though I support the Democrats, I don't support all their policies, particularly the one on gun control. This book is an honest attempt at presenting facts, which resoundingly confirm that gun control is not the way out for all our problems. We have researched over a thousand cases of gun-related crime, individually met the felons, tried to understand the criminal psychology and what goes through their minds, and then analysed if he or she would have committed the crime even if access to guns had been denied.'

Cirisha found this very interesting. She had done loads of research, but the idea of doing research with convicts enthused her. And when she read in the interview that Richard had spearheaded the research, her respect for him went up a few notches. Not that it really mattered.

She shut the browser on her laptop, picked up a few papers and walked to her class. The students section was a few minutes' walk away.

Lieutenant David Windle was waiting for her when she returned. It was not too difficult for Cirisha to make out from the uniform and overall demeanour that he was the person from the Boston Police crime investigation team who had come to meet her. David was about six foot two. Cirisha seemed diminutive in front of him.

After the initial formalities, Cirisha told him about her visit to the slum in Dharavi, the factory where Snuggles shoes were manufactured, the children working there and the Snuggles labels. When the officer told her that Shivinder had been taken into custody on account of the company filing charges against him—charges of defrauding the company to the tune of fifty million dollars—she was surprised.

'But officer . . .' She was hurriedly interrupted. 'Lieutenant Windle. Please.'

'Oh, I am so sorry. Lieutenant Windle, isn't that something the Indian Police would be worried about?'

'Yes, you are right. That's why I am here. There isn't enough clarity with regard to the jurisdiction. But that's for the courts to resolve. If the crime is committed in India, even if it is against an American citizen or entity, the law prevents us from keeping anyone under detention for more than twenty-four hours. The extradition process would kick in if the Indians were to make a request. The legal team at Snuggles had said in their complaint that the issue was precipitated by your email to them.'

Windle was quite friendly and chatted with her for over an hour. 'Some guys got killed here a few days back. You knew them?'

'Yes, there were four of them.'

'There was quite a buzz around the incident in the Boston Police headquarters. MIT is not directly under our control. We don't get in unless it's too serious an issue or the MIT Police requests help from us.' Cirisha just nodded. 'That Avendon fella . . . apparently he did it. I can't imagine him shooting down everyone. Even the coroner was shocked. He was to come and visit us a few days back.'

'Visit you? What for?'

'Said he wanted to interview a few felons who were convicted for homicide. We have quite a few of them up there in the Greater Boston area. Apparently for some research project.' Cirisha could tell that Windle was not aware of the research and the huge controversy that Deahl's book had stirred up. He was a cop whose life revolved around criminals and their arrests.

'Oh. OK. He was doing some work which revolved around people who were propagators of gun-related crime.'

'Wonderful. All these guys who use guns should be bundled up and sent to Guantanamo. There is no place for them in mainland America.'

'That would be a nice idea. By the way, what did Richard Avendon do in Greater Boston then?'

'What did he do? Now that, you tell me. I wish he had done something because he never came.'

42

26th May 2008

Boston

Around the time Windle was with Cirisha in Cambridge, Aditya had travelled down to Greater Boston to meet Shivinder.

'Until the preliminary investigation is over, he will remain in custody,' the officer-in-charge announced. 'In any case, Lieutenant Windle is handling this case. We will have to wait till he returns.'

'Lieutenant Windle?'

'Yes, he is the in-charge of the precinct. He is visiting MIT in connection with this case. You could either wait in the visitors' room or you may choose to come back later.'

'Thanks, sergeant. But when I had called yesterday, I was asked to come in today. And that's the reason I have driven all the way from Cambridge to meet him. Do you think it will be possible?'

'Let me see what I can do.' And he disappeared. In three minutes he was back. He had probably conferred with Windle in the interim. 'Please follow me.'

'What happened? How did you land up in this mess?' Aditya asked Shivinder the moment he saw him.

'It's all because of your wife.'

'Come on, Shivinder. You did all this because you were blinded by money. You should have stopped after we got rid of the shoes in the warehouses. Instead you went a step ahead and started manufacturing low-cost fakes and stuffing them into the fraudulently opened stores, and pocketed the money for yourself.'

Shivinder laughed. 'What about you? You were the one who got me into all of this.'

'Come on. Don't pull me into this. It's your problem. You deal with it,' Aditya whispered. 'I came here because you called me. Only because you said you needed help. For old times' sake.'

'Adi, I am stuck here with my reputation in tatters because of you and your wife. Without your manipulation, I would not have got into this. I am not an idiot, dude. There is enough on record to prove your involvement. If I go down, I take you with me. And as far as that wife of yours is concerned, let her know that I am going to come after her. Just watch out.' The look in Shivinder's eyes scared Aditya. He was worried. More than anything else, he was worried that Cirisha would find out about his involvement in the Snuggles scam.

'What do you need from me? Why did you call me here?'

'I need to make sure that my money is safe. These guys here can't do anything to me. I haven't committed a crime on US soil. Sooner or later I will be out. Even if they file against me in Indian courts, it will take some time before the courts there charge sheet me and ask for my extradition. Till the time all this settles down, I need to make sure that the money we have accumulated in GB2 is safe. Not only the floats in India, but also in Geneva. You have to make sure of that.'

'But how?'

'You are the banker. You know how to move money. Figure it out.'

Aditya gave him a long hard look. There was no way he was going back into GB2 India to pull the money out. In any case Snuggles would have flagged it off as a suspected fraudulent account. Surveillance by the bank authorities would be high now. If he tried to do something, he would be in trouble. He decided to take it as it came.

As he turned and made his way out of the room, he looked at its dark walls. His future seemed as dark. 'And Aditya,' Shivinder said,

'I am sure you don't want your wife to know what happened on the night of your promotion.' Aditya turned, looked back at Shivinder in disgust and left. The sergeant quietly shut the door behind him.

'Why did I let myself be lured by the wily Shivinder?' Aditya thought to himself as he recollected the evening after the party when he, along with Shivinder and a few others, had gone to the infamous Mumbai dance bars. One thing led to another and even before he knew it, they were back in Shivinder's car with two women. All that happened was on impulse, fuelled by alcohol and anger at Cirisha for not being able to make it to his promotion party. He had regretted it the morning after, but he couldn't have turned back the clock. He left the prison and drove back home, a disturbed man.

'You met Shivinder?' Cirisha asked him the moment he parked his car and walked in.

'Yes, I did.'

'Hope they lock him up for good.'

'Come on, Cirisha. What has he done to you?'

'It's not always about what he has done to me. Isn't it also about the conscience-less animal that he is? About what a man like him does to society?' And she walked away.

Narayanan, who was quietly standing in the corner of the large living room, came up to Aditya, put an arm around his shoulder and quietly said, 'Let it be. She is different.' Aditya was fuming. He hadn't even had a chance to calm down after the meeting with Shivinder. And here he was, at home, hearing all this nonsense. The elephantine ego of an unemployed investment banker was beginning to get hurt.

That night Cirisha started rereading the book. *Staring Down the Barrel.* Something in the book amazed her. Intrigued her. Scared her.

As she rested her head on the pillow, her body on the mattress, eyes firmly riveted on the concentric rings in the false ceiling above, her mind wandered to a thought that had been bothering her for quite some time. Was she responsible for Richard's death? One of her closest associates, her confidant at work and the only one she connected with. Yet she was not there for him when he needed her most. The time they spent together had helped him keep his impulsive behaviour in check. Unfortunately, for the better part of last year, her presence in India meant that her calming influence was missing from Richard's life, exposing him to the upheavals of his own aspirations. Becoming a tenured professor was the single most important thing in his life. More important than life itself. He was willing to do whatever it took. Make any compromise required. Academia should have been the last place for such tribulations, but sadly, the politics and aggression of the corporate world had permeated through the world of academics. 'When paranoia hits academia, it's time to hang up your boots,' Cardoza had once told her.

Staring at the ceiling, she wondered. First it was Ahmed Siddiqui who died in strange circumstances, and now, four faculty members had been killed in a conflict over tenure promotions. Was it worth it? Should she just call it quits and go back to India? In any case, Aditya was not too happy with her move here. And her father too lived all alone in Coimbatore.

It was a restless night. Her mind wandered all over the place. At one point, Aditya, who had come in by then, shook her and asked her if she needed something. 'Do you think we should see a doctor?' he asked her out of concern.

The Dharavi slum, the factory, Gangu Tai, the children in the factory, she remembered all of it. And then today's conversation with Lieutenant Windle. It had raised more questions in her mind. She had promised to give him a copy of the email she had initially sent to Richard, seeking his help with the Footwear Association of America and Snuggles HQ. In that email she had detailed everything that she had seen at the Dharavi factory.

Worried that she might forget it, and driven by a restless, insomniac spirit, she got up. 'You sleep. I am going to the study,' she told Aditya. He opened his eyes for an instant and shut them immediately. In any case, he was tired after the drive to Greater Boston and back. The stress of the various discussions had only added to the fatigue.

Cirisha turned on her laptop and opened her inbox. The Dharavi email that she was looking for was over a year old. She couldn't find it. It struck her that since it was over six months old, it would have been archived. Retrieving it from the archives was a painful process. That's when she remembered. A few days ago, Richard had sent her an email erroneously. Wasn't that on top of the mail she had sent Richard detailing the Dharavi findings? The entire sequence would be there in chronological order in that email. Thankfully, that email was easy to find.

Windle had specifically requested for a printout. She fired one. The printer took some time to warm up. She waited for the four pages to print. While she was waiting, she went back to her computer and read her initial email to him. She was reminded of Richard. His bubbly energetic self. She thought for a minute. Had she not been married to Aditya, she would have seriously considered Richard as someone she would want to spend her life with. His childlike, mad passion for academia was endearing. She would have loved to see the look on Cardoza's and Deahl's faces on being told that the two of them were getting married.

She went back to reading the emails. Two emails had come in from Richard that day, just about a week before his death. The first seemed to be a normal email, which had the word 'Details' in its subject line. Richard had erroneously forwarded the Dharavi slum email back to her. It was a cryptic message. The body of the email contained three meaningless words. She read it three times. And then a fourth time. She couldn't figure out what it meant. In any case it was not meant for her. That's what Richard's next email had said. 'Sent by mistake.'

The printout was ready. She picked up the papers from the printer and put them in her bag, even as she realized that she could have printed it out in college. She needn't have done that at three in the morning.

The next morning, Windle produced Shivinder in front of the Massachusetts district court judge, who refused to grant him custody. Much to Windle's despair, Shivinder was allowed to go free. However, he was ordered not to leave Boston till the police in India filed their charges. He was asked to appear in court in sixty days' time to decide on the future course of action, in case Mumbai Police did not file charges till then.

43

27th May 2008, morning

MIT, Boston

For the first time, Cirisha was late for work that day. Cardoza and the research team were waiting for her to begin their discussion on her project.

'I am sorry, Michael, I overslept. I'm really sorry for wasting the team's time.'

'It's OK, Cirisha. Since you were not here, we started discussing Erica's research. We will be done in fifteen minutes. Come and grab a seat. You too can listen in.'

Cardoza knew, as did everyone on the team, that Cirisha was not a habitual latecomer. Cirisha joined in. It was an interesting study on the reasons for rising suicide rates across various universities in America. Erica had done a detailed research on the causes and commonly used methods of committing suicide, and even presented some ideas to predict occurrence. Cirisha was left wondering if Richard too would eventually become a statistic for the study.

Erica was done in fifteen minutes and Cirisha got down to presenting her findings. Within ten minutes of Cirisha beginning to speak, Cardoza got up. 'Folks, my apologies. I completely missed it. I just saw on my BlackBerry that I need to be in another meeting. Seriously sorry, guys. Let's continue the discussion tomorrow.' He looked at Cirisha and said, 'Can you walk with me to the coffee shop? I need to get a dose of caffeine before I head to my sleepy meeting.'

On the way to the coffee shop, a quarter of a mile away from the Academic Block in the direction of the duPont Center, Cardoza spoke. He looked concerned. 'Cirisha, take a break if you need to.'

'Sorry, Michael.'

'Richard was a good friend of yours. I am aware that you are extremely disturbed. But Cirisha, we need to move on. As long as we are at work, we need to make sure that we are not distracted. It's been close to two months since that unfortunate incident.'

Cirisha looked up. This was the first time ever that Cardoza had told her to pull herself together. 'I am sorry, Michael. I am not able to focus. I was awake for most of last night. And that's the reason I got late today.'

'It's not about being late, Cirisha. For the last forty-five minutes or so, I have been noticing that there is something else going on in your mind.'

Cirisha turned her face away from Cardoza. She could not lie to him, he would see right through her. 'Would you want to take off for a couple of weeks? Come back refreshed and charged up. I am fine with it. We are slightly behind schedule on this project but we will pull back.'

'No, Michael. I will manage.' Cirisha was firm. 'I won't give you reason to complain.'

'That's like a champion,' said Cardoza and gave her a hug. It made Cirisha feel good. And when the coffee came in, she felt even better. 'When will you be back from the meeting, Michael? We can finish this discussion today itself.'

'What meeting? This is the meeting I wanted to have. There is no other meeting. I made it up because I found you so distracted that it was futile going on like that.' Cirisha smiled.

Cardoza swiped his card and they walked back.

'Yesterday I met a lieutenant from the Boston Police Department,' Cirisha mentioned to him as they walked back.

'What for?'

'In connection with the Snuggles case. Remember I had told you about the Indian arm of Snuggles?'

'Oh yes. Now that you say it, I do.'

'The CEO has been arrested.'

'Yes, yes. I recollect. You did mention it. Why do people take advantage of their seniority and do stupid things? The incremental benefits of doing such acts are negligible. Remind me. This could be a good subject for us to research. Behavioural impact of authority and hierarchy in a global organization. Getting sponsorship won't be difficult. Some MNC will be happy to shell out the money for this.'

'Not a bad idea.' And then after a pause, she added. 'So, are we doing the rest of the discussion now?'

'No, Cirisha. I've lost the flow now. And in any case, most of the team would have disappeared. Let's continue the session tomorrow.'

'Sorry, Michael,' Cirisha looked extremely apologetic. Cardoza smiled. 'I will be in my room then. Please call me if you need anything.' Cardoza nodded and they went their respective ways.

Cirisha got busy with the closing analysis of the Dharavi slum research. She was alone in her room, collating the data and arranging it in a presentable format, when her phone rang.

'Cirisha Narayanan?' A heavy voice. It was familiar, but Cirisha couldn't make out whose it was.

'Yes.'

'Lieutenant Windle. I came by the day before.'

'Oh yes. How can I help you, lieutenant?'

'I called to inform you that Mr Singh has been released from custody, as per a court order.'

'Oh, is that so? Thank you very much for letting me know.' She didn't seem too bothered.

'Do you see any threat from this individual? I have also spoken with the chief of MIT Police. We would be happy to provide you with cover for the next few days in case you feel the need.'

'That won't be necessary, lieutenant.'

'Do let me know should a need for that arise.'

'Sure. I appreciate the help, lieutenant. And by the way, I have printed out the emails that you asked for. I'll send them out today.'

'I will have them picked up from your office either tomorrow morning or latest by the day after, miss. We are in any case waiting for a response from the Indian side.'

'Sure. Thank you, lieutenant.'

Cirisha looked at the far right corner of her table. A folder with the printouts was kept ready for Windle. She prided herself on being so organized. She turned her attention to the iMac. In the time that she was talking to Windle, the computer screen had got locked. She had to key in her ID and password again to log in. She did that. Her mind was somewhere else. Her fingers moved on her iMac as if they knew the topography by heart. The moment she pressed 'enter', her eyes opened wide. Her hands, which were on the keyboard, started shivering. The right hand lifted itself and came to rest on her forehead. 'What the hell was that?' She hurriedly pulled out her laptop from her bag and brought it up. Despite having an iMac at work, she always carried her laptop. It was necessary given her travel schedule. After logging in, she searched in her laptop for something she had seen not so long ago. In a few seconds, it was up there. She looked into her screen and copied something to her phone. It would be safe and accessible there.

That's when it dawned on her that what she was looking for was right there on her table. In one of the folders on the top right corner.

44

27th May, night

Boston

'I will be late, Adi.' When Cirisha told him this, Aditya was not too happy. But of late he had reconciled himself to the fact that Cirisha and he were progressively being torn apart from each other. The fact that Cirisha did not tell him why she would be late made it worse. The loneliness too was killing. Sitting at home doing nothing was not something he was too kicked about. And life in the United States can get pretty boring for someone who is used to the hustle and bustle of an Indian metropolis.

By seven in the evening, the campus was pretty deserted. Cirisha looked out of the window. The road to the parking lot was empty. Not a soul in sight. Three cars were still parked there. One was hers. The headlights were on in the other, which meant that someone was about to leave. The third looked like Deahl's. Ever since he got suspended from academic activity, James had come in to work every single day, without fail. He would come in at 8.45 a.m. and leave around 5.30 p.m. Today, for some strange reason, he was still at work.

She was pacing up and down her room. Nervous. Was she doing the right thing? She couldn't say. Maybe she shouldn't do it after all. What if she got caught? A thousand and one questions went through her mind as she settled into her chair. She looked out of the window. Deahl's car lights came on. She let out a muted scream.

So Deahl was leaving. There would be no one on the second floor. Just thinking about what she was about to do made her legs start to shake. She forcibly held them still with her right hand. The clock on the wall in front said 7.43 p.m.

Convinced that the wait was enough and that there would be nobody on the upper floor, she got up and strode towards her cabin door. Turning right, she walked with measured steps towards the main door, which connected her floor to the elevator lobby. The fire escape was to the right. She walked straight ahead and pressed the elevator button, only to realize that she had only a floor to climb. Opening the door to the fire escape, she took the short flight of steps and reached the second floor. She looked at her watch. Ten minutes to eight.

She breezed through the glass doors into the corridor, which had faculty rooms on both sides. All the rooms were closed. She knew that Deahl's room was the last one on the left—the closest that any academician could get to a corner office. She walked half the length of the corridor and stopped.

The door to the right had two names on it.

She pulled out a card from her jacket. With shivering hands she brought it up and held it against the swipe recorder on the door. The door didn't open. She swiped it twice, thrice. Nothing happened.

'Damn!' she exclaimed. Holding the knob, she tried to force it open. She couldn't. Her access card was programmed to open all rooms on the first floor, but not on this one. She had assumed it would work, but it didn't. This was Deahl's territory.

She stood there for ten seconds, rooted to the ground. And then as if she remembered something, she dashed out of the corridor, down the fire exit to the first floor, straight into her room. She rummaged through her drawers and pulled out something. Holding it in front of her, she blew a kiss at it and ran back again to the second floor. The entire sequence had taken three and a half minutes. This time when she swiped the card on the door, it opened with a click. She looked around to see if the noise had alerted anyone. No one was around. The only sound heard on the floor was her breathing. She entered, taking care to shut the door behind her softly. It was a large room, bigger than hers. She glanced around. The workstation on the right was where she wanted to go to. She walked around the table and reached down below, powering on the iMac. It came up in a jiffy. The screen prompted for the password. What was it?

With nervous hands, she reached into her trouser pocket and pulled out her phone. She kept it on the table and with both hands she started typing. Her eyes alternated between the phone and the iMac screen. First came a capital letter, followed by three letters, two numbers and an alphanumeric. She was praying that it was the right password. Just to be sure, she deleted the password and keyed it in again. Her mouth curled into a prayer. Her eyes shut for an instant. And she pressed the enter key. Her face betrayed thrill, joy, worry, fear and anxiety all at once. Just before she pressed 'enter', she had seen the fine print below the password prompt, which said, '27 days to password change'. It meant that the password was changed sixty-three days ago. At MIT, passwords are required to be changed every ninety days.

The blur started clearing a bit. The email which Richard had sent her was not a mistake. It was part of a carefully thought-through plan. But plan for what? She had no idea. He had anticipated something and written to her giving her his login password. It had to be for a reason. Had he planned to kill everyone well in advance? A week before the tenure interview? Did he kill the panel members only because they declined his tenure or was there more to it? What was Richard trying to tell her? Rather, what had Richard hidden from the world that he wanted her to know?

She wanted to check the files in Richard's iMac to see if there was anything he would have wanted her to see. She had even brought a portable data drive to transfer data from Richard's computer. The moment she opened the finder window, she went pale. Beads of sweat appeared on her forehead. Richard's computer had been wiped clean. There was not a single file. It was as if someone had run a sanitizing program on it, which had wiped out the entire contents of the iMac. A click on the hard disk icon told her that over 90 per cent of the data storage was free. Did the MIT technology team format his disk to allocate the computer to someone else? But had they done that, Richard's login ID would not have shown up when she switched on the iMac. Someone had intentionally deleted all the files.

Confused and worried, she got up and dragged herself to the door. Quietly, she opened it and stepped out. Lost in her thoughts, she walked to the main door, opened it and made her way to the lobby. The moment the glass elevator came up to the second floor, she rued her decision. Why didn't she take the fire exit?

'Aaah. Look who's here!' Her heart jumped out of her mouth when the elevator door opened. Inside, was Deahl. 'What are you doing here, sweetheart? Can I help you?' Her hands went cold with fear. How did she get so engrossed in thinking about Richard that she ignored the basics?

'I came up to meet you. I wanted some pictures of Richard for my blog post. I had a few, but they are all of Richard with someone else. I was hoping you would have a solo one.'

'I am afraid I don't have any. You can check with my assistant tomorrow.'

'Or else we can even check his iMac. I'm sure he would have some.' She felt stupid the moment she said that.

'The investigating agency was working on this a long time back. Maybe they sanitized it. We will have to wait for the forensic report, sweetheart.' Cirisha nodded. 'I will try and check with them if they found anything in the computer,' Deahl said.

'Thanks, James,' Cirisha said as she took the elevator down to her floor. She couldn't help but wonder how and why an investigative agency would sweep all the data away and wipe it off the hard disk. For forensics, they would either carry away the entire computer, or take a mirror image of the hard disk. Why would they erase it completely? Someone had wilfully cleared off the data. Why was Deahl lying? Was he? She didn't have the answers. The only positive thing to arise from that evening's adventure was that now she had very strong reason to believe that Richard had not sent her the email by mistake. The elevator stopped on the first floor and Cirisha got off.

~

The caretaker from Coimbatore called Narayanan again. Things had got worse. One of the emu farm owners, unable to repay his consumers, had committed suicide. That was not all—the anti-corruption crusader had made public an alleged list of people who had their money stacked away in Geneva.

At Narayanan's insistence, Aditya hunted down the list on the internet that evening. Two names got him worried. At No. 239 was Narayanan and on No. 286 was Shivinder Singh. Both were accounts facilitated by Aditya Raisinghania. Somehow, the crusader had got access to a list of Indians having clandestine accounts with GB2 Geneva.

Aditya looked at Narayanan. Only one thing came to mind. 'Let's figure out a way of moving the money out of Geneva to somewhere safer.' He walked to the phone kept in the living room, picked it up and dialled a number. 'Good evening, Greater Boston Global Bank, investment banking, how may I help you?'

~

'How did you get into Richard's room?' Aditya asked her that night when she told him how she had run into Deahl.

'On the day of his tenure interview, he was running late. I was entering the Academic Block when I saw him running towards me. He threw his ID card at me and yelled, "I don't want to give them a chance to screw around with me for even the smallest of reasons.

Can you please swipe me in?" I shouted "best of luck" to him and he ran for the interview. Never came back.'

'Thank God for IT inefficiencies. But I still think what he did was an innocent mistake.'

'He is not the kind of guy who does unplanned things. He is very organized, extremely disciplined. Someone who is very particular even about the way his teacup is kept on the table. Walk into his room, all his pens would be kept straight on his writing pad, perpendicular to the table corner,' Cirisha argued.

'How does that prove anything?'

'You are forgetting that he sent me his password. Something you don't just share with anyone. It can't be by chance. Would you ever, by mistake, send your password to anyone? Damn! I don't know your password, leave alone anyone else's. And Aditya, if by mistake you do send it to anyone, then the next thing you would do is change it. Despite sending it to me in end-March, his password is still the same. He didn't change it. Isn't that a good enough reason to believe that he sent it to me deliberately?'

'Ciri, you must relax. If Richard wanted to tell you something, he would have. He had enough opportunities to. And more importantly, Cirisha, it is a bit dangerous to be caught by your seniors stealthily creeping into other people's rooms.'

'Let it be. It's my headache. I will manage.'

Sensing that this could lead to an argument, Aditya changed the topic of discussion. 'I'm meeting Cambridge Partners Hedge Fund on the 30th. Nalin has helped set it up.'

'This Friday? Are you still in touch with him?'

'Yes. Spoke to him a few times. He called me today. He knows some people there. Asked me to go down and meet them. He has also lined up a meeting for me with a boutique investment banking firm in New York tomorrow.'

'Despite the fact that you cheated GB2.' Aditya didn't know what to say. He just hung his head and walked away.

'In any case, if you are going to New York tomorrow, take Dad with you. He is getting bored here. Maybe both of you can do some sightseeing after the interview.' Aditya smiled when Cirisha said this. It was as if she had spoken his mind.

Cirisha turned back and walked towards the window. It was still not dark. She could see the road in front of their house. A black pick-up truck was parked on the road, albeit a bit ahead, in front of the neighbour's house. She had never seen that truck there. It seemed to be out of place. She stood there for a minute, staring blankly at it. And then she drew the curtains and walked back. She hunted for *Staring Down the Barrel*. But she couldn't find it. That's when she remembered that she had taken it with her to work, but hadn't got it back. She made a mental note that she had to bring it back the next day.

45

28th May 2008

Boston/Mexico

The inability to get to the bottom of what Richard was trying to communicate to her, if at all he was, was beginning to affect her. It was making her edgy, irritable and short-tempered. She was careful not to run into Deahl lest he ask her some uncomfortable questions about the previous night.

Meanwhile, Aditya and Narayanan took an early morning flight to Mexico. It was an eight-hour flight, and by the time they checked into Camino Real hotel in Mexico City, it was three in the afternoon. Built by Luis Barragan and Ricardo Legorreta, two of Mexico's finest architects, Camino Real was a riot of colours. Narayanan and Aditya did not venture out of their rooms for the next three hours. They made no attempt to explore the city that they were visiting for the first time.

At six in the evening, there was a call from the reception. Someone was waiting for them in the lobby. Narayanan was a bit apprehensive. He had never been to Mexico or dealt with Mexicans. Aditya calmed his nerves and led him to the lobby.

Standing there below a towering Tamayo mural were two gentlemen in suits. Short even by Mexican standards, one of them was clean-shaven. A rectangular badge hooked to his belt hung slightly below his waist. The other individual was wearing dark glasses, which made him look a bit sinister. The duo led Aditya and Narayanan to a quaint little bar in the lobby, opposite the La Huerta restaurant. Narayanan was stunned when he saw the décor. The bar was built over water. He could see exotic fish swimming right below his chair. Aditya had to tap him to get him to focus on the task on hand.

'I was told that there would be only one person,' Aditya began the conversation. He looked at the clean-shaven man, who had introduced himself as Gurria Trevino.

'Yes. Only one. But what you want to do, you need him for that,' he spoke in broken English. 'He Enrique Nieto,' Trevino introduced the other Mexican.

'OK.' Aditya didn't know what to say.

'He got account in San Diego.'

'Do you know what we need?' Aditya asked him.

'Yes. We get call. Our bank in Boston call yesterday.' Aditya heaved a sigh of relief. So GB2 Boston had called their Mexico City branch and got Trevino to meet him. Nalin's contacts had worked. 'You want to transfer forty million dollar to America.'

Aditya nodded.

'Bank fee one million. Me fee one million. Enrique fee half million. OK?'

Aditya was shocked. He didn't know if this was usual, but he didn't have a choice. Narayanan wanted to move his money out of Geneva. Neither of them wanted to be caught bringing in forty million dollars of unexplained money into the United States of America.

Narayanan started to say something. Aditya kept his hand on his leg and stopped him. 'I am fine with this deal.' He stared at Enrique, wondering who he was. Trevino understood what was running through Aditya's mind.

'Enrique have account in San Diego. Account in Mexico too. You transfer money to Enrique account in Mexico. He give you access to forty million in San Diego account. You get chequebook, online password and ATM card. You change password. Use account. Enrique forget his account in San Diego.'

'How do I trust you?' Aditya asked him.

'You come all the way to not trust?' And Trevino opened his bag and pulled out his credentials. In any case, his GB2 Mexico identity card was hanging at his waist. Aditya excused himself and stepped out of the bar. He called Nalin in Boston. He had made this trip on Nalin's recommendation. Putting Aditya on hold, Nalin called his counterpart in Mexico. Within three minutes, he was back on the line. 'Trevino is one of the best they have. You can blindly do as he says.'

Aditya returned to the bar visibly relaxed. The hostile look that had appeared on Trevino's face when Aditya had spoken about trust had gone. Enrique opened his laptop. The deal was about to go through.

'Can we do this on my laptop?' Aditya recommended.

'Sure.' Enrique shrugged his shoulders. That was the first time he spoke.

'First transfer full fee.' Trevino demanded. 'Only bank fee.' Aditya electronically transferred a million dollars into the fee account of GB2 Mexico. An account whose number was provided to him by Trevino.

After that, Enrique logged in to his account with a local bank in San Diego. When Aditya looked at the account his heart skipped a beat. It was in a completely different name. Enrique gave all the details to Aditya. Aditya changed the password required to access the account, to make sure that Enrique could never access the account again. Narayanan kept all the related documents in the bag he was carrying with him.

The next transfer was of thirty-nine million dollars to the account of Enrique Nieto with GB2 Mexico. Enrique took over and transferred thirty-seven and a half million dollars from another American account to the account in San Diego.

In exchange for forty million dollars which were lying in an account in Geneva, Aditya and Narayanan had got control of thirty-seven and a half million dollars, accessible in the United

States of America. Something which no one in India would even get a whiff of. He had derived comfort from Nalin's words that this was the standard operating procedure for laundering money into the United States. GB2 Mexico, Nalin said, had full accountability and if something did go wrong, they always recovered the money.

Early next morning, the two of them took a flight back home, and by late afternoon, they were back in Boston.

'How was the interview?' Cirisha asked him the moment she saw him enter the house.

'Not worth it. No point pursuing further. Let's see what Cambridge Partners has to offer,' said Aditya as he walked into the bathroom for a long warm shower.

46

29th May

Boston

In a glittering press event on the evening of 29th May, the final shortlist of three books for the Bancroft Prize was announced. As expected, Deahl's book had made it. He was tipped by most people in the know to be the frontrunner. The NRA had put its muscle behind this book. The organizers of the Bancroft Prize were known for their Republican leanings, making them favourably disposed towards *Staring Down the Barrel*. But in the final analysis, all that mattered was that Deahl was a step closer to the award.

News channels that night were sharply divided. Appearing on Fox News, Deahl spoke in depth about how he and his team went about their research. Cirisha was at home, watching it on TV with Aditya. Narayanan was asleep, he was tired after the stressful trip to Mexico.

'It took the team over nine months of intensive data gathering and analysis to get down to this level of detailing.'

'Oh yes,' the anchor agreed. 'You even went down to state prisons and interviewed felons and convicts who were involved in gun crime, didn't you? Tell us about that.'

'Yes, Stella. It was an absolutely fascinating experience. My team went to various state prisons and interviewed over a thousand convicts. From Vermont to Miami and from Seattle to Los Angeles, the team visited over four hundred prisons and interviewed inmates. Ninety-five per cent of those convicts had committed the crime using illegally obtained weapons. Something which gun control can't fix. And over 70 per cent of them had said that even if guns had not been available, given their state of mind at the time that they committed the crime, they would still have done what they did. That's not it, Stella. A significant number of inmates in various prisons across the country—California, New York, Boston and many others—said that the possibility of the victim being armed had prevented them from committing more crimes. Guns have, in fact, kept our crime rate low.'

Cirisha was appalled when she heard this. 'What a liar!' Aditya looked at her, wondering what was getting her so excited.

'David Windle told me that Richard was to visit the Boston state prison, but never did. Windle had sought the required permissions and got them for Richard, who never got in touch with him. So what Boston prison inmate analysis is James talking about? Ridiculous.'

'Are you sure?' Aditya tried to calm her nerves.

'Absolutely. Unless of course they didn't do the analysis in Windle's prison, but went to some other prison in Boston. There are three prisons that I know of. Something doesn't seem to be right here. I need to talk it out with Michael tomorrow. He needs to know.'

'Just make sure you have your facts right before you accuse anyone, Cirisha. Richard could have been the culprit here. He could have fudged the data without telling James. We can't be sure James did it. We Indians are genetically wired to be suspicious about everything.'

'Hmm . . .' Her gut told her that something was wrong. She knew that Richard couldn't have committed what she thought was a basic mistake. She chose to keep quiet.

47

30th May

Boston

Cirisha called Windle five times that morning before he called back.

'Only lawyers call me a dozen times. You are the first civilian to do so. I am sure it was important enough.' Cirisha knew that Windle meant no offence.

'Lieutenant,' she began, 'you mentioned to me that Richard had called you sometime last year to fix up a meeting.'

'Oh, Mr Avendon, the guy who did target practice in the classroom. Well, yes. Mr Richard Avendon had called up. He wanted to interview some prisoners. He even came and met me. Procedurally we need the state police department head's nod to let anyone treat inmates like research subjects. We had gone through the entire rigour. Got all the approvals. But he never came after that.'

'In his place, did anyone else come and meet the inmates?'

'No, no one came. My office might still have the approval copy. No one even bothered to collect the approval from the state police HQ.' And after a pause, he added, 'But why this sudden interest in the research, Ms Narayanan?'

'I heard the author of the book, *Staring Down the Barrel*, speak on Fox News yesterday. He spoke of the research conducted by his team in the Boston state prison. I remembered our conversation and that's why I was surprised. So I thought I would check with you.'

'I'm not sure if that was an accurate representation by the author.

But now that you ask, let me check.' There was a moment's silence followed by some chatter. Windle walked over to his assistant's desk and asked her to check on the approval for the research given to Richard. Cirisha held on. Within a couple of minutes, Windle came back on the line. 'I just found the copy of the approval. It's right here. No one even collected it, let alone meet the inmates.'

'Then how?' Cirisha wondered.

'There is no chance that anyone came and interviewed the inmates. I can confirm that.'

'Is there a possibility that they went to some other prison under the state jurisdiction?'

'Miss, there are three county prisons in Boston. When such approvals are granted, they are prison specific. And until and unless the approval granted for one prison is either utilized or revoked, no other approvals are given. Hence the chances of them having interviewed inmates of some other prison in Boston are as remote as Bin Laden walking into the White House on Christmas day, all wrapped up in red, and claiming that Santa dropped him there.'

'Thanks, lieutenant.' The moment she hung up, she reached for the book lying in front of her. She had specifically checked this last night after she heard Deahl's interview. Page 228. The table clearly showed the number of inmates interviewed and their location. Against the Boston state prison, was a number: 23. 'God only knows how many of these are fabricated in the name of research,' she said, picking up her cup of espresso and taking a sip. The book had conveniently hidden behind the façade of confidentiality and steered clear of divulging the names of inmates who had been interviewed. She kicked herself for having ignored the data when she read it the first time.

As she was glancing through the book to discover possible anomalies, Aditya called. 'I'm leaving, Cirisha. Let's hope things work out.'

'Best of luck, Aditya.'

'Thanks. What did the cop say?'

'Nothing different from what he had said in the past. James is lying, Aditya. No clue why he would do that. It's wrong and revolting. Such a senior person fabricating his research. He could lose his tenure if this is proven. THE professor James Deahl has fallen from grace.'

'Hmm. I need to leave now, let's talk later at night.' And he hung up.

Cirisha checked if Cardoza was in office, picked up the book from the table and walked straight into his cabin.

'Michael, I need to talk.'

'You look harried. What happened?'

'I have evidence that James fudged his research. The research that half the country is going ballistic about is based on data which is a figment of James's imagination.' And she told him about her conversation with Windle. James was a liar. He had committed one of the three cardinal sins of academia.

'James is a seasoned player. I seriously doubt that he would have fudged his data.'

'Maybe he did that in bits and pieces. Not the entire data. The part about the Boston state prison surely is fudged, Michael. Why he did that I have no clue. But I spoke with the lieutenant from the Boston Police Department. He has confirmed whatever I have mentioned to you.'

'What do you want me to do? Take it up with the institute?'

'Yes, Michael. Don't you think that will be the right thing to do?'

'I do, but I am trying to pre-empt what the institute will say. For all you know, they can just turn around and say that it was not an officially sanctioned research report. He published it outside the university, without waiting for the university's blessings.'

'Does that mean we will not take it head on?'

'No, no, Cirisha. That's not what I am saying. We have to do something about it. If after this revelation the book wins the Bancroft Prize, it will be tragic. But how and what is something we have to think through carefully. We cannot fail once we take it up. Let's make it a watertight case before we take it up with the institute.'

'True.' Cirisha thought for a moment. What Michael was saying made sense. They only had evidence that the Boston prison information was incorrect. What about the rest? One mistake could be put down to human error. She had to dig deeper. And if the Boston prison was the only mistake in the research, Deahl was sure to dump it on Richard's head.

She turned to leave.

'And Cirisha,' Michael called out, 'we are meeting at three today to finalize the analysis for both your project and Erica's. I hope you are feeling up to it?' She just nodded.

~

Aditya walked into the forty-eight-storeyed building in downtown Boston. The imposing building was home to Cambridge Partners, one of the largest hedge fund firms in America. He was led on to a superfast elevator which took him straight to the chairman's office on the forty-seventh floor. There he was ushered into a large room appointed with exquisite furniture. Tables of pure teak and seats upholstered with pure leather straight from the tanneries of South Asia and designed by fashion designers from Italy added a dash of arrogance to the room. A chairman of a hedge fund had to have such luxuries.

'Good afternoon, young man.' Aditya turned, only to be confronted by a short pot-bellied man. He would have at best been in his mid-forties. He looked like a man used to living well. They hit it off. The interview was a breeze. After about forty-five minutes, the chairman got up, excused himself and walked out. He requested Aditya to wait.

It was not a long wait. In a couple of minutes, three other men joined Aditya. Dressed in pinstripes, they all looked like accomplished bankers.

'Good afternoon.' Aditya stood up out of courtesy. The three of them just nodded. The one in the centre, a well-built tall gentleman—would have been six foot four at least—seemed to be more senior than the rest. The body language of the other two confirmed that hypothesis. The lack of introductions peeved Aditya.

'Mr Raisinghania,' the one in the centre began, 'Mr Chairman was lavish in showering his praise on your candidature to join this fund.'

'Thank you. He is being kind.'

'We know that.' The reply was curt and unexpected. It wiped the smile from Aditya's face. 'We believe your wife works at MIT?'

'Yes, she is an assistant professor there.'

'Social Psychology. We have also heard that she is showing undue interest in investigating the incongruities or rather the alleged inconsistencies in the research conducted by a colleague. Quite unnecessary, I must confess, Mr Raisinghania.'

'How is that relevant to this conversation? The chairman never mentioned anything about his interest in my wife's career.'

'Let me explain. As you might be aware, a hedge fund invests its patrons' money in various industries and papers that give high returns. Most of these investments are not made public.'

The look on Aditya's face showed that he didn't understand the context. 'So?'

'We have investments in various gun-manufacturing units. To be precise, 22 per cent of our investments are in such firms. So we wouldn't want any of our employees' families to sabotage our investments. If your wife does not give up the tirade against *Staring Down the Barrel*, which is such a wonderful piece of research, the controversy it is going to stir up will hurt us. And we can't have someone like you in the team, especially at a time when your wife is hell-bent on harming us.'

'I have no control over that. It's her life. She does what she pleases.'

'Maybe then you should try talking to her. Else she might end up harming herself.'

'What the hell? Are you threatening me?'

'Mr Raisinghania, you seem to be an intelligent man. It would be tragic if we were to lose you on account of something so frivolous. And mind you, Mr Raisinghania, the gun manufacturers are known to be extremely ruthless.' They turned and walked out, leaving him alone in the room shell-shocked. Aditya picked up his bag a worried man. This was becoming bigger and scarier than what he had imagined it to be. He walked out of the room, with none of the fanfare with which he had been ushered in.

'Thank you,' he heard someone say. He turned just in time to see the chairman shake the burly man's hand. 'You are welcome, Lucier. Anything for you.'

When he mentioned this conversation to Nalin, the latter had no idea of how and why the conversation had taken the turn that it had. 'But Aditya, it's better to be careful and not get into a conflict with these people,' Nalin told him. Aditya didn't say anything, he just hung up. He was worried because Cirisha would not listen to him. She always acted on instinct. However, this time, he was worried it had gone too far.

'You are making too many enemies, Cirisha. I am getting worried. Your safety was the first thing that crossed my mind when these guys at Cambridge Partners spoke to me. They are rich guys with connections. And rich guys don't like to get hurt. This is the first time someone has threatened me. I was too shocked to even respond.' When Aditya said this, much to his annoyance, Cirisha smiled.

'You know, Aditya. This only strengthens my resolve. It proves that there is something there which they don't want me to go digging for. Don't you think so?'

'I don't know about that. All I know is that these Americans will do anything to protect their turf.'

48

31st May 2008

MIT, Boston

The search committee had come up with four names as possible replacements for Meier. Of the four, two were from the Social Psychology department: Deahl and Cardoza. The two others were renowned professors who had served MIT for over a decade and a half. Deahl's name, however, came with a rider. The executive committee had to first clear him of his partial suspension.

Meier was furious when he saw Deahl's name on the list. However, he let the process take its course.

The university executive committee met that Saturday to discuss Deahl's suspension from faculty and research duties. In a strange turn of events, the suspension was overruled. The executive committee was of the view that Deahl was well within his rights to publish his work outside the university, as long as he did not claim academic credit for the published piece of work and the sponsor didn't have an issue with it. The university rules did not prohibit such an act. And once published outside, the OSP or the dean did not have any jurisdiction over it.

It was also agreed that the appointment of the provost would be taken up at the next meeting. The committee also requested Meier to continue in his position as the provost till such time that it decided on his successor.

49

2nd June 2008

Boston

'What time will you be back?' Aditya asked Cirisha as she was about to get into her car.

'What happened?' Cirisha glanced at her watch. She had a couple of minutes to indulge Aditya. He had been really stressed over the weekend, particularly on account of the Cambridge Partners discussion.

'Can you pick me up on the way back? I will be at the Fencing Centre. I don't feel like taking out the new car.'

'Why? It's not a new car that you are getting so protective about it!' Cirisha chided him. She was referring to the used car they had bought for Aditya about a month back.

'Protective? Rubbish. I don't feel like going alone. Gavin will pick me up while going. He has to go somewhere after the session. So he can't drop me back. If you can't come, I will take my car.'

'No problem, Adi. I will pick you up. Second floor, duPont Center?'

'Yes, yes. Same place.'

'You seem to be enjoying it.'

'It's an awesome place. You must come and see.' Fencing had become a new passion for Aditya. When he had joined fencing, it was more to keep himself occupied and learn a new sport in the bargain, but now he had begun to enjoy it. It helped to take his mind off his frustrations.

'I've been there in the past. Richard was the faculty support for fencing.'

'Yes, I know. Some people were talking about him yesterday.'

Cirisha smiled. 'By the way, who is the academic support these days? Have they nominated anyone to replace Richard?'

'Jung Hoon Chun.'

'Who? The one in the physics department?'

'No clue. Why do they even have faculty as academic support? This fellow is an ass. Fat guy, must be over 250 pounds. Just comes and sits there doing nothing. I doubt if his hand would even get into the sabre guard,' Aditya said.

'Sabre?'

'The sword. The handle of the fencing blade is called sabre.'

'Oh, OK. Don't know about Chun, but Richard was an absolutely fabulous sport. He could take on champion student fencers and beat them. I hadn't seen him miss fencing even for a day.'

'You haven't seen me. Once you see me, you will forget Richard.'

'In such a short time? Hahaha,' she laughed. 'Give me a break, Aditya. In any case I have no interest in these gory games. You have fun. Just make sure you don't injure yourself.' She glanced at her watch again.

'The equipment they have is fabulous. Very unlikely that anyone will get injured. Anyway, are you sure you will be able to pick me from there this evening?'

'Yes, yes. Absolutely no problem,' said Cirisha as she got into her car and drove out of the garage. The black pick-up van was still there. It hadn't moved for two days. She lowered her window and slowed down as she approached the van. As she passed the parked vehicle, she heard a faint hum. Which meant that the engine was on. It worried her. Was there someone inside the van? Was someone keeping a watch on them? The moment she passed the van, she pressed her foot on the pedal and accelerated. She did not want to get into trouble.

As she was crossing her block, she dialled 911. 'I believe there is an unmarked black van parked in the exit carriageway of Glen Evelyn Drive. It's been there intermittently for the last few days and there is someone in the car. I don't think the car belongs to the place.'

Within minutes, three cars with blaring sirens drove into Glen Evelyn Drive. And in five minutes, Cirisha got a call.

'Madam, there is no black pick-up van in Glen Evelyn Drive. You sure you saw it there?'

'Yes. I was worried because the car had been parked there for the last two days and had been in idling state.'

'It's not there, madam.'

'OK. I'll call again if I see it. Thank you for taking care of it promptly.'

'Not a problem, madam.'

That evening, Cirisha picked up Aditya from the duPont Center. After a quick stopover at the International House of Pancakes, from where they picked up a takeaway dinner for Narayanan, they drove back home.

50

3rd June 2008, morning

MIT, Boston

Cirisha's class got over at eleven. She was walking back to her room, when a few men in uniform crossed her and moved towards the exit. They seemed to be coming out of Cardoza's room. Dumping her papers on the table, she walked down the corridor, straight into Cardoza's room.

'Hi Cirisha.'

'Morning, Michael. Were these guys here in connection with Richard's death?'

'Yes, Cirisha. The coroner and the chief of Boston Police were here. They had a meeting with Juan. Juan requested me and Gordon to join in.'

'Here?'

'Hmm,' Michael nodded. 'Juan wanted to be discreet and didn't want the meeting in his office. He asked me to host it. The chief left some time back. The coroner too just left.'

'Oh. What did they say?'

'Nothing that we did not know of. It's been sixty days since Richard and the others died. They wanted closure on the case. The coroner has certified the reason for the deaths of the dean, Henry Liddell and Frederick Lobo as homicide. As death caused by firing from a close range. Richard's death has been put down as suicide using his own gun. They have concluded the investigation and have named Richard Avendon as the first and only accused.' He handed her a piece of paper. Cirisha read through it. The coroner had waived the need for an inquest given the open-and-shut nature of the case. The weapon used in the homicide was owned by Richard. They had done a preliminary investigation, which included things like a sweep of his workstation, talking to a number of faculty members about Richard's mental health and so on. Cirisha was surprised that they hadn't spoken to her.

Amongst the other papers left with Cardoza was the forensic report of Richard's iMac. Cirisha started reading through it. 'For your eyes only. I have to bundle all this up and dump them in Juan's office.' Cirisha nodded without moving her eyes from the papers.

'According to this, the data on Richard's iMac had been wiped clean on the morning of his death. There is one school of thought which believes that Richard destroyed all the data before he came for the tenure discussion,' Cardoza summarized for Cirisha.

'That's not correct, Michael. I saw him coming in that morning. He was late for the interview. He was rushing in. Seeing me, he threw his card at me and asked me to swipe him in. He was to collect the card from me later in the day, after the interview. But that never happened. He didn't even go to his room that morning.'

'According to this report, Richard's death happened around the same time that his iMac was wiped clean. Hence the presumption that he cleared it or timed the wipe on his iMac.' And then she paused and said, 'Unless someone who was aware of what Richard was planning to do quickly cleared it out. Who could it be?' She answered the question herself, 'Could it be James?'

'Rubbish! You are hallucinating. Do you mean to say that James knew that Richard was going to die?'

'Probably.'

'Unlikely.'

51

3rd June 2008, evening

Boston

Cirisha reached the duPont Center well in time. Like the previous evening, she was there to pick up Aditya. One look at the clock on the dashboard told her that she was half an hour ahead of time. Thirty minutes was too long a time to wait in the car. She locked the car, entered the building and walked up to the second floor. Maybe it was time to test Aditya's claim of being nimble-footed. When Cirisha saw him practise, she was quite surprised by his agility and the speed at which he moved. When Aditya turned and looked at her, she gave him a thumbs up. 'You look handsome in this gear, Mr Raisinghania.'

'Thank you.'

'Well, you shouldn't have become an investment banker. You should have become a fencer. Maybe India would have won a few medals at the Olympics.'

'Thanks for the compliment. Give me a couple of minutes. I will change and come,' he said and disappeared into the washroom.

Five minutes later, he emerged in his regular jeans and T-shirt. 'What's for dinner?' The workout had made him hungry.

'Let's stop at the International House of Pancakes again. I am in no mood to cook. For Dad I will make some parathas. There are two frozen ones left in the freezer. What do you say?'

Aditya made a face. 'Again?' But then realizing that Cirisha was also getting back home after a long day at work, he agreed. 'Come, let's go,' he said and smiled at her.

They reached the parking lot, got into the Honda and drove to the closest International House of Pancakes. 'You wait here. I will get it.' Aditya got off the car and ran inside. He ordered banana caramel pancakes for Cirisha and a plate of crunchy battered shrimps for himself. It was their standard order.

'Twenty-four dollars, please.' The girl at the counter had keyed in the order.

'Sure.' Aditya felt the back pocket of his jeans. His wallet was missing. 'Oh shit! I think I dropped my wallet. Can you wait for a minute? I will check in my car and be back. I am so sorry.' And he turned and ran.

'Next, please,' the girl called out to the next person in the queue as Aditya ran out of the door. He ran straight to the parking lot. The car was missing. He looked around. Cirisha was nowhere to be seen. He panicked. He ran to the other end of the parking lot. He still couldn't see the car. He felt his pockets. He had left the phone in the car. Sweat broke out on his forehead. Morbid thoughts crossed his mind. He did not know what to do. He decided to call the cops and turned when a car drove into the parking lot.

'Where the hell did you go?'

'Chill, Aditya. What happened? I needed some stuff for the house, so I picked it up from 7-Eleven there.' She pointed in the direction of a 7-Eleven departmental store. Aditya turned and saw the logo glowing brightly. 'Couldn't you have waited for me? I was worried sick.'

'I am fine, Adi. I am fine. Nothing can happen to me.' And she smiled. He bent down and hugged her through the window. 'Come, let's go,' she said, but noticed that the food was missing. 'Where is the food?'

'Oh, yes. I need cash to pay. Hand me my wallet.'

'Where is it?'

'It would have slipped from my back pocket and fallen on my seat.'

Cirisha switched on the light inside the car and looked around. In ten seconds she turned back towards Aditya. 'Not here.'

'Oh shit!' After a moment's pause he added, 'I think I didn't pull it out from my locker. Completely forgot.'

'Locker?'

'At duPont. I left in a hurry because you were waiting. So I might have left it there. It's OK. Give me some cash and I'll get the food. I'll collect the wallet tomorrow.'

'Hold on. You left the wallet in the locker?'

'Yes. Not to worry, though. It's my other wallet. Would at best have about a hundred dollars in it. I don't take the one with my credit cards when I go fencing. I play it safe.' He said it with a great deal of pride, as if his decision of not taking his regular wallet had been vindicated.

'How many lockers are there?'

'Quite a few, in fact. Almost everyone has one.'

'Really?' And then her eyebrows shot up. She looked up at the sky as if she was thinking about something. Almost instantly, she looked back at him and whispered, 'Get in. Quick.'

'What happened?' He looked at her and pointed towards the pancake outlet just a few metres away. 'Food?'

'Just get in. Now!' she whispered a scream.

Aditya got in. 'I am hungry.' But Cirisha was not listening. She reversed the car like a maniac. It made a screeching noise as she left the parking lot. A few passers-by were stunned at the way she drove. Aditya hurriedly put on the seat belt trying his best not to slam into the windscreen. 'Cirisha!' he screamed. 'Are you OK?' No response.

Cirisha was driving at over 100 mph on a road with a speed limit of 65 mph. 'Cirisha, will you please tell me what the hell is wrong with you? Why are you driving like this?' He could barely hear himself over the noise of the revving car. Cirisha did not speak a word. She was completely focused on the road ahead. The traffic on the Cambridge Turnpike was thin. She took the 94th exit and turned towards MIT. About half an hour ago they had driven on the same stretch, albeit in the reverse direction. In another five minutes, she was back in the parking lot of the duPont Center.

'Why are we back here?'

'Your wallet. Where is it?'

'It could have waited till tomorrow. I was not in any hurry. And it's safe there. It's my personal locker.'

'I know, I know. Come, let's go.' Aditya just followed her as she rushed into the building. It was late in the evening and the place was deserted. Aditya's practice session was the last one for the day, and that had ended over an hour ago.

'Where is the locker room?' she asked him as they got off the lift on the second floor. 'There,' Aditya said, pointing to the right-hand corner. She made a dash for the locker room and entered. 'It's a men's room, Cirisha.'

'I know. But there will be no one here at this time.' It was a room full of lockers. 'Richard had a locker here. Which one is that?'

'What? How would I know? And for God's sake, why do we need to look for Richard's locker?'

'Help me look for it. It has to be here somewhere!' Cirisha was in a world of her own.

'There are hundreds of them here. How will we know which one is Richard's?'

'Do you guys tag your names on lockers?'

'No. There is no place for that.'

'Shit! How do we find his locker?' She looked around. There were hundreds of them. All tiny 1-foot by 2-foot lockers. There were a few big ones towards the bottom. Aditya counted them. He was good with mental math. Six blocks of lockers, each having seven rows of eight lockers each. Close to three hundred and fifty of them.

'Three hundred and thirty-six, to be precise.'

Cirisha completely ignored Aditya's calculation. 'Adi, if you were to choose your locker, how would you? Which one would you prefer?'

'It would depend on which ones were available. One may not always get the locker one wants.'

'Yes. But Richard is the faculty support.'

'Was.'

'OK, OK. Richard was the faculty support. He had been here since the time this facility opened. He would have had the first go at selecting the locker he wanted. So availability would not have been a problem.'

'Good point.'

'So tell me, which lockers would you have preferred?'

'Either the big ones at the bottom . . .' Cirisha looked at them. Unlike the others which were a foot high, the ones at the bottom were two feet each. 'Or this row.' He touched the fifth row from the bottom. 'This is at eye level. Easy to operate.'

'Great. Richard was about six inches shorter than you. He would probably have taken the fourth row. Worst case, the fifth row. That brings our search down to the fourth or fifth row in six blocks, or ninety-six lockers to be precise. Down from three hundred and fifty.'

'If you ignore the bigger ones at the bottom,' Aditya confirmed her calculation.

'Correct. We will look at the big ones if the fourth and fifth rows don't work. And normally no one prefers the ones in front. You would rather choose the ones at the back. It gives you privacy.'

'Absolutely right,' Aditya agreed.

Cirisha walked to the last block of lockers. 'Let's see if his locker was one of these.' She pointed to the fourth and fifth rows in the last block. 'Sixteen lockers. It has to be one of these.'

'How will you open them? Unless of course . . .'

'Yes.' And she took out her mobile phone and flipped through a few screens. She memorized the code on her phone and keyed it in to open the locker.

'Incorrect code.' The message flashed with a beep. She tried again. Same result. She moved on to the second locker. Same result. She keyed in the number on the keypad of the third locker.

'Are you sure we are in the right place?' Aditya asked.

'We will find out,' she said. 'Why don't you begin from the other end? That will be faster.'

'Code?'

'Messaging it to you right now,' and she sent the image of Richard's email to Aditya's phone. Aditya was a bit worried that they were breaking trespassing laws. He started from the opposite end with the fourth row from the bottom.

By that time Cirisha was already keying in the code in the fifth locker. Nothing happened. She moved on to the sixth one. Silence. She waited for a beep that just wasn't coming. Aditya held back whatever he was planning to say and looked at the locker. For a second there was pin-drop silence. And then there was a sound of something moving. As if some levers were shifting into place.

The word 'OPEN' appeared on the locker screen.

'Yes!' she shouted jubilantly.

She reached up to the locker and opened the door. It was dark inside. Her hand holding the mobile phone automatically came up. Faint light from the phone screen filled up the dark abyss.

'There is something here,' she whispered.

'Careful. Let me pull it out for you.' Aditya reached into the locker. He had to stretch to his fullest to reach something which was safely tucked away right at the back. It was heavy and bulky. Cirisha looked on in wonder as he dragged out a pile of papers in a yellow envelope.

Cirisha opened it and was about to take the papers out, when Aditya advised, 'Let's get out of here. It might not be safe.'

Cirisha turned to walk out of the room, envelope in hand. 'Wait!' cried Aditya. He came up to her, hugged her tightly and began kissing her on the lips. 'Are you out of your mind, Aditya? You just said that we must get out of here.'

'Shut up, you idiot.' And he kissed her again. Holding her close to him, his arms around her, his lips seeking hers, he turned and walked out of the locker room towards the lift. It was a distance of about fifty feet. Throughout the stretch, he held her firmly in his grasp. Even for a moment he did not let go of her. Once they were in the lift, he released her from his clasp and pressed the button for the ground floor. Cirisha was wondering what was going on. He repeated the same thing the moment they got out of the lift on the ground floor and held her close to himself till they reached the car.

'What has got into you?' she yelled. Aditya smiled. 'Now drive. I did this because there are many security cameras in the lobby and on the ground floor. I didn't want any of them to capture images of the envelope that we were carrying outside. We should have brought a bag and dumped the envelope into it. But we didn't know that we would be carrying back something like this. So I didn't have any option but to hide the envelope between you and me. And for that I had to kiss you and hug you.'

Cirisha didn't know what to say. 'And by the way,' continued Aditya, 'that's the longest you have kissed me in a long time.'

'Shut up.' Cirisha smiled as she shifted the Honda into drive mode and drove out of the parking lot towards home. She couldn't wait to get home. In the car, Aditya opened the envelope. There were several papers on which something had been scribbled. He could not make head or tail of it. Cirisha was driving. The papers had to wait till they got home.

'Is this what Richard wanted us to find?'

'You are assuming he wanted us to. Maybe he left this the night before he killed himself. Or maybe earlier. And forgot about it. We just happened to stumble on it.'

'Unlikely. How many times do I have to tell you about Richard? I have known him for seven years now. If he left it there, it ought to have a meaning.'

'And that's for us to figure out.'

'That's correct, sweetheart,' said Cirisha with such a confident undertone that Aditya couldn't say anything. He was getting increasingly worried about the repercussions.

52

3rd June 2008, night

Boston

It was a long night for the Raisinghanias. The documents in Richard's locker were nothing short of dynamite. Safe inside the envelope was the entire raw data of Deahl's research. The complete set of questionnaires of the interviews arranged by the prisons, it contained the names of people interviewed, along with the date, time and contact details. The interviewers' names and signatures were there on every questionnaire. The material was good enough to recreate a chunk of the qualitative part of Deahl's research. Data pertaining to another leg of the research conducted in Chicago and a few other cities was there too.

Cirisha was curious about the interviews conducted at the Boston prison. She hurriedly sifted through the papers till she found them: twenty-three of them, in a separate set labelled 'Boston state prison'. When Aditya saw the way the documents had been arranged and labelled, he knew what Cirisha meant when she said that Richard was one of the most organized souls she had ever met.

'See.' When Aditya looked up, Cirisha waved a set of papers at him. 'This says that twenty-three inmates of the Boston state prison were interviewed. It also has their names and the dates of the interviews. According to these questionnaires, Aditya, Boston prison inmates were interviewed in August last year. It's the prison in Windle's precinct. He is clueless!' Cirisha passed on the papers to Aditya, who looked at them and agreed with her.

'I will talk to him tomorrow morning. Let's see what he has to say,' she said. After a moment's thought, she added, 'I'll go and meet him tomorrow.'

'Why don't you call? It will be easier,' Aditya reasoned.

'It is better to meet him in person. His body language speaks more than him.'

'Don't go alone, then. I will come with you.'

'It's OK, Aditya. He may not open up if you are there.' Looking at the concern in his eyes, she added, 'I will be careful, Aditya. I am not going into a war zone. Don't worry.'

Cirisha got down to tabulating the interviews done at the prisons. Once done, she intended to compare them against what was mentioned in *Staring Down the Barrel*.

She did not have the time or the tools to validate the complex regressions and detailed analyses. Consequently her focus was entirely on the basic data and tables. That too only the ones pertaining to the main question—whether the felons would have committed the crimes if the guns had not been available. A quick analysis would do, at least for the time being. Any error identified here would call for a more detailed investigation.

She started tabulating the data from the prisons into a simple table.

Prison location	Number of felons interviewed	Dates of interview	# Felons who said yes	# Felons who said no	Interviewed by

Prison by prison, the two of them started comparing what they found with the data in *Staring Down the Barrel*. The data from the questionnaires tallied with what was there in the book. 'I told you this is a red herring,' Aditya commented three hours into the exercise, inviting a deadly stare from Cirisha.

'I will get some coffee,' said Cirisha and got up to go to the kitchen. 'We have eight locations still to go.'

'Yes. I wouldn't mind a strong dose of filter coffee,' Aditya agreed. 'If we find that the remaining eight are in order, we will go to sleep. OK?'

Cirisha smiled and walked to the kitchen. She took a short detour to wash her face and freshen up. It was going to be a long night. She took some clothes out from the drier and put in another set waiting to be washed. Then she headed to the kitchen. Hardly had she poured water into the coffee percolator when she heard Aditya call out. 'Ciri! Come here fast! Quick!'

She put the glass down and rushed to the living room. 'What happened?'

'Look at this.' Aditya gave her a piece of paper. 'Vermont.'

Cirisha looked at it. Aditya had quickly tabulated the information collected from the prison in Vermont. 'Shit!' she whispered. Her hand instinctively came up to her mouth. She was very particular about her language. 'We have the first one.'

Aditya nodded. 'Vermont. According to the data in the questionnaires, 80 per cent of the inmates said that they would have hesitated and probably not committed the crimes they did had the guns not been easily available.'

'And James's book says just the opposite. Eighty per cent of inmates say that they would have committed the crime they did even if guns were not available. This is clearly a misrepresentation.'

'It could be an honest mistake,' Aditya tried to reason. 'Somebody could just have messed up the columns while capturing the data. Human error.'

'Unlikely. But before we start jumping to conclusions let's see the remaining seven locations too.'

By the time they were done with all the prisons, it was clear. There was a problem. Intentional or not, they couldn't say. The data tallied for every single prison except three: Vermont, Florida and

Phoenix. In all the three cities, the original data was contravening Deahl's thesis in *Staring Down the Barrel*. Why didn't the data for these three prisons tally with the book, especially when it tallied for every other prison?

She looked at the questionnaires for these three cities carefully. She recognized the handwriting. It was Richard's. 'There's no way he could have made a mistake,' she said to herself. That's when it struck her. She hurriedly picked up the paper on which they had formulated the table. One didn't have to be a rocket scientist to figure out a weird correlation.

'Aditya!' she called out. 'There is a strange coincidence.' Aditya, who was getting up to dump the coffee mugs into the kitchen sink, stopped. He came close and looked at the papers she held in her hands. 'The data-gathering interviews for these three locations have been done by Richard. Someone else has done all the others. What surprises me is that these three locations are the first locations to have been researched. Look at the dates of the interviews. All the other prison interactions were done later by someone else.'

'Does it mean that Richard was deliberately kept out of the subsequent ones?'

'Why? Why would anyone do that? Richard was the seniormost and the most capable guy on James's team.'

Aditya shrugged his shoulders.

'I think I know.' Cirisha recalled Richard's conversation. His statement that Deahl tortured the data gatherer till he sung Deahl's tune, resonated in her ears. 'Richard carried out the research at Vermont, Florida and Phoenix. The results were not in line with what James wanted. He moved Richard out and got someone else to give him the data he wanted—Philip and Caroline seem to have done all the rest. And Aditya, this is only the most basic analysis we have looked at. The book has a lot more detail and more scientific analysis. It will take us days to recreate it. But if the base data is flawed, the output would be junk too.'

'This has to be the biggest sham in the history of research not only in MIT, but probably in the entire United States of America,' Aditya said.

'And to think of it, the guy has almost pulled it off.'

It was about 4 a.m. by the time Aditya and Cirisha went to bed. She cuddled up to him and whispered. 'Do you think these papers have anything to do with Richard's death?'

'Maybe. He was so stressed by all this that he lost his mental balance.'

'Maybe. But then, Adi, we need to make sure these papers are safe. Do you think they are safe here? At home?'

'Ciri, these papers are not a national secret. Just plain data. They are perfectly safe here, and so are we.'

'I don't know. I am worried,' she whispered and buried her face into his chest. By that time Narayanan was in the next room snoring his way into his fourth dream sequence.

53

4th June 2008

Boston state prison

'You've come all the way to meet me regarding this?' Lieutenant Windle was surprised when Cirisha showed him the set of documents. 'It's always good to see you, though.'

Cirisha nodded her head and faked a smile. 'Lieutenant Windle, this is the data the research conducted by Richard Avendon has been based on. I wanted to double check with you before I look at it with any degree of seriousness.'

Windle took the questionnaires from her and looked at them carefully. 'Strange.'

'I remember you saying that no one had come from MIT for this research. But now these . . .' and she left the sentence hanging.

'Put it down to my old age, young lady,' he said with a smile. He was never perturbed by anything. Cirisha admired this trait in him. 'Do you mind if I check on this and call you back in a while?' he added.

'Sure, lieutenant. Thanks for all your help. I appreciate you going out of your way to help me.' She handed him a list of Boston prison inmates who were supposed to have been interviewed, and took back the questionnaires. She needed them. They were evidence.

'Anything for a pretty young lady.' Windle smiled. She liked him. Not quite like the cops back home in India.

After thanking him, she walked back to her car. This was just the first of the many checks she would have to do. She still hadn't been able to figure out why Richard had got her involved in this entire game. If Richard had really wanted to, he could have become a bigger hero by walking out on Deahl and exposing him. Why he chose not to do that was a surprise.

She was lost in these thoughts when her phone rang. She hurriedly picked it up.

'Ms Narayanan, I have checked all twenty-three names.'

'Oh wow! That was quick, lieutenant.'

'I didn't need to do much, you see.'

'As in?'

'Four of them are dead. The last of them died two years ago. Seven of them were released from jail on account of good behaviour quite some time back. Their prison terms were commuted. In fact, none of the seven has been in this jail for over eighteen months. Twelve of the twenty-three are still in prison. They don't remember having spoken to anyone regarding the research that you are mentioning. There is something fishy going on here.'

Cirisha slammed the brakes hard when she heard this. She thanked her stars that there was no vehicle close to her, else she would have been a part of a mangled lump of steel. Pulling herself together, she released the brakes slowly, moved the car to the shoulder lane and parked.

'Are you sure, lieutenant?'

'As sure as I can be.'

'Can you give me the names of the people who are dead and those who have been released?' She took down the names of the eleven convicts for her records and got back on the road. She remembered what Cardoza had once told her. There are three cardinal sins in academia: stealing from research grants, sleeping with a student and plagiarizing or fudging research results. From the looks of it, Deahl had broken the third cardinal rule. And to think that a book based on such research had been shortlisted for the Bancroft Prize! It was criminal. She would have to ask Cardoza to intervene.

54

4th June 2008

Boston

'We will have to take it to the provost. With the dean no more, it falls under Gordon's remit to take a decision on what he wants to do with this. So what if he is only a caretaker provost? If he doesn't do anything, I will go up to Juan. At least, as the president of the institute, he will do something about it. This is ridiculous!' Cardoza thundered. 'How can someone who is dead be part of the research? He can't fabricate data in such a brazen manner. Not at the level he is. This clearly demonstrates that he drastically changed the research just to make sure that the result he got was in line with what the NRA wanted.'

'Slow, slow, Michael. I brought this to you not for you to jump at it. Remember you had said the last time around that if we take this up, we cannot fail. Didn't you say that James has not submitted his data to the university? He technically doesn't need to unless there is an investigation and he is specifically asked for it.' Cardoza nodded. 'I still stand by it.'

'And Michael, even if James is asked for it, he can get away by not producing it, citing privacy, confidentiality and tens of other reasons.'

'If so, then why go through the process of creating the data? Just create the end results. Period. Write a fictional research and call it science.'

'There could be a background to this. Richard did the interviews at the first three sites. The results went against the NRA. Richard was the one who was slated to go to Boston state prison. He had arranged for everything. But he didn't go. Windle says no one went. But if one were to believe the questionnaires that I have with me, Philip did the interviews there, the results of which are overwhelmingly in favour of gun rights. There is a serious disconnect here. What also surprises me is that after Vermont, Phoenix and Florida, Richard had not participated in data gathering in any other place. Obviously, he was kept out.'

'What does it show?'

'If I were Richard, I would be mighty peeved at being kept out. Richard too would have been. I believe that the data was created first to keep Richard happy, so that he felt that he was in control. Second, to keep people within the team happy and make sure they didn't squeal to the outside world that the data was completely cooked, which normally happens when you have a dissatisfied soul on your team. And lastly, to anyone on the outside too, it would seem as if something serious was on. I checked this morning before coming to you. Both Caroline and Philip are no longer with the institute. They have left for greener pastures. Significantly richer too, I guess. So, I am reasonably confident my assessment is correct.'

'Very possible. There could have been one more possibility, though.' Cardoza was in a very agitated frame of mind and he was looking angry.

'And that is . . . ?' Cirisha left the question hanging.

'Maybe they did the prison interviews in most places. Remember, it's almost impossible to get away by stating that they did the interviews all over the country, without actually doing any research interview whatsoever. Some jailor somewhere will stand up and scream that what's stated in the research is false and that the interview in his prison, as mentioned in the book, never took place.

My take, Cirisha, is that they would have done the interviews in most, if not all the prisons that they have mentioned in the book. After the interviews, they would have cooked up the data and falsified the questionnaire responses to suit their objective. In such an instance the chances of getting caught are minimal.'

'Possible. In fact, what you are saying is more likely. These cooked-up questionnaires would then have been given to Richard for his assessment. But as far as Boston is concerned, we are sure the interviews never took place. We have to find out what actually happened.'

'The only way out is to confront him. We can't just keep it to ourselves. Let's get the others involved in this.'

'Don't you think we must wait till we have multiple points of conflict? As of now, we are sure that the data reported out of Boston prison has been tampered with. Let's do a sanity check on some more data points. I am sure even those will turn out to be false. We can confront him after that.'

'I agree. But what's the harm in talking to the provost? He can at least be sounded off.' Cardoza reached for his telephone and asked Louisa to put him through to the provost's office. Within thirty seconds, Louisa called back. 'Gordon Meier is travelling. He is on vacation somewhere in Canada. He'll be back only tonight. You want me to connect to his hand phone?'

Cardoza thought about it. 'No, it's all right.' He looked at Cirisha and told her what Louisa had just said. 'Gives us a little more time to think this through, I guess.'

'Let's build an airtight case, Michael.'

'Hmm,' Cardoza agreed.

'I need your approval to travel to Phoenix for the next level of my verification.'

At that very instant, Cardoza's phone rang. 'Hi,' he said into the receiver. There was a long pause. 'Do you want me to come now? We can take him right away. Or do you think we can wait till later in the evening? I checked with the pharmacy, they have the medicines. I will get them on my way back.' Again a long pause. 'OK. I'll try and come early.'

He kept the phone down and looked at Cirisha. 'No problems about travel to Phoenix. Send me the bill.'

'Thanks, Michael. I will leave tomorrow evening.' Before she turned to leave, she couldn't resist asking, 'What happened, Michael? Who is unwell?'

'Champ's not been keeping too well. The vet saw him yesterday. He may not survive. I will leave early today. I need to pick up some medicines and injections on my way. It's been upsetting me. Apologies if I sounded distracted.'

Cirisha knew how fond Cardoza was of Champ, his Dobermann. But Champ was over nine years old. At best he would live for another couple of years. Outside of work, Cardoza's life revolved around Champ.

'Let me know if I can do something for you.'

In the evening, out of courtesy, she checked with Cardoza. By the time he had got home with the medicines and injections, his wife had taken Champ to the hospital. Doctors were not hopeful of Champ living for more than a couple of weeks, at best. Cardoza had sounded quite distraught.

That night Shivinder called Aditya. It was a long call. After he put the phone down, Cirisha asked Aditya what the call was about.

'Apparently the Economic Offences Wing of Mumbai Police reached him. He had been avoiding calls on his phone, but somehow they got his hotel address and called him on the hotel line. They wanted to know when he was coming back to India. They even briefed him on the charges mentioned in the FIR filed against him. He is in deep shit.'

'So?'

'He has spoken to Kali Fariman, one of the biggest lawyers in Mumbai, to represent him. Kali will go through the papers and advise him in the next couple of days. Shivinder has bought time. He has asked us not to talk to the police. They apparently told him that the additional commissioner of police from the Economic Offences Wing of Mumbai Police will be calling you tomorrow.'

'Let them.'

'Shivinder wants you to deny any knowledge of anything that he has done.'

'And why does he think I will listen to him?'

'He is not requesting.'

'As in?'

'He says he will make sure you don't talk to them.' Aditya was worried.

'What the hell!'

'He is a dangerous guy, Cirisha. I was mistaken. I should not have engaged with him. But now it's becoming messy. If he goes down, he will take me down with him.'

'Meaning?' Cirisha was unsure if she had heard him right. Where did this come from? She anyway had enough on her plate.

'I had advised him on some of the things that he did. We manipulated the balance sheets of Step Up Shoes in order to make it attractive for Snuggles to buy. We set up a fraudulent franchisee network, inflated sales, collected payments from dealers which were routed out of the country through GB2. If he goes to jail, he will make sure that I too go with him.'

Cirisha was flabbergasted. She just shook her head and threw her hands up in disdain. 'Aditya! Please tell me you are kidding.'

'No, Cirisha. I should have told you earlier.' Aditya was ashamed of himself. For the first time, he genuinely regretted what he had done. But Cirisha was not willing to listen.

'No, no, no . . . this is not possible. I can't go wrong for the second time in a row. I always thought you were a good man. When GB2 sacked you, I thought it was a one-off mistake, but now it's evident. You are a criminal. A habitual fraudster. All you men are. All of you. Oh my God . . .' and she held her head in both her hands, elbows on her thighs, and started crying.

'Cirisha. Please. It was a mistake. I will never do it again. I promise you.' Aditya walked up to her and hugged her. She shook him off, stood up and slapped him across the face. It sent Aditya stumbling back a few steps.

'You said the same thing before. How do I believe you? God only knows how many times you have lied to me.' She continued sobbing. Aditya held her tight, but Cirisha didn't care any more. And then, in one inspired moment, she looked up. 'Go. Tell that friend of yours that I don't care even if you are involved. I will tell the Mumbai Police everything that I know. I will not lie to them. Even if he exposes you as a result. My self-esteem and integrity are important to me. Probably more than they are for any man that I know.' And she got up, walked straight to her room and slammed the door shut. It was the first night that the two of them were together under the same roof and Aditya slept on the couch.

The next morning, by the time he woke up, Cirisha had left. He tried calling her on her mobile a few times. She didn't answer the call. He checked the garage, her car was not there.

'She left very early and she looked upset. Did you guys have a fight?' When Aditya turned back, Narayanan was standing right behind him.

'No. Nothing serious. Just regular husband–wife stuff.'

55

5th June 2008, 10.45 a.m.

Boston

Cirisha had not returned. Calls to her phone had gone unanswered. It was very unlike Cirisha not to answer calls irrespective of how peeved she was.

A remorseful Aditya was standing in the lawn outside his house when two police cars came to a stop on the opposite side of the road. Three officers of the Boston Police Department got off, crossed the road with swift steps and walked towards him. Aditya was wondering why they were there when one of them called out to him, 'Mr Raisinghania?'

'Yes.' Aditya's heart skipped a beat. There was a tremor in his voice. 'Is there a problem, officer?' Was this the end of the road for him? Had Shivinder confessed to his involvement in the Snuggles scam?

'We need you to come with us.' When the officer said this, Aditya turned towards one of the cars parked on the other side of the road. Another deep-blue SUV had just driven in and come to a halt behind the police car. The doors opened and two people stepped out.

When Aditya saw Antonio and Cardoza come out of the car, he knew something had gone horrifically wrong. And when they told him what had happened, he knew his worst fears had come true.

Earlier that morning, the cries of a few women returning from their early-morning jog at the Boston Public Garden drew the attention of a few people, who hurried towards them. In no time, a crowd gathered around. Thankfully, one of the passers-by was a medic. He felt the pulse, looked at the dilation of the pupils, tried to listen to the heartbeat. But the body bore no signs of life. The person lying on the ground was dead. There were no physical injuries on the body to suggest murder. Probably a tired jogger who had suffered a cardiac arrest while jogging.

911 was called. The cops arrived with the paramedics in the next fifteen minutes and the body was wheeled away to a nearby hospital. The victim was declared 'brought dead'. A few credit cards found in the waist-pouch of the victim had helped identify her.

The name on all the cards was: Cirisha Narayanan.

56

7th June 2008, morning

Boston

MIT was in mourning once again, for the second time in two months. Cirisha was as popular an individual as Richard, if not more. But more than Cirisha, the incidents that had plagued the university over the last few months worried Antonio.

'It is unfortunate that we have lost a fabulous colleague, a charming faculty member and above all, a sterling human being. Cirisha was special to all of us. And our condolences go out to the family—husband Aditya Raisinghania and father Mr Narayanan—both of whom are with us today. Their grief is unparalleled. May God give them the courage to withstand the trauma.' Antonio's speech was a moving one. Many in the audience could be seen wiping a tear or two.

Aditya and Narayanan were sitting in the front row, flanked by Cardoza on one side and Deahl on the other. Narayanan had his hand on Aditya's shoulder, trying to console him. Aditya kept breaking down.

The memorial for Cirisha ended with Aditya speaking about his wife. His was a passionate and moving speech, which ended with him saying, 'Pending the coroner's inquest, the Boston Police have declared that they will be treating this as a homicide, which makes it even more tragic. Why would anyone want to kill someone who was loved by everyone?'

Aditya collected all of Cirisha's belongings—whatever had been cleared for handover by Lieutenant Windle and his team of detectives—and walked back to his car. As Aditya drove out of the parking lot, Narayanan spoke. 'When will they allow us to perform the last rites?'

'I spoke with the chief of MIT Police an hour back. The toxicology tests will take a bit longer. Another forty-eight hours is what he said. Only after that will they hand over her body and allow us to perform the last rites. Since they are treating this as a homicide, they need to investigate all possible angles.' There was a prolonged silence after that, only to be broken by the persistent ring of Aditya's phone.

'Good afternoon, Mr Raisinghania. Calling from Cambridge Partners. Please be on the line.'

'Mr Raisinghania. Hello!' A mature voice came on the line.

'Good afternoon.'

'This is Etienne Lucier. Remember, I met you at the office of Cambridge Partners last week?'

'Yes, I do. How can I forget?'

'I heard about the tragic death of your wife. Please accept my heartfelt condolences.'

'You don't mean that, do you? You wanted her out of the way.'

'Oh no, Mr Raisinghania. We wouldn't want her out of the way. We were just requesting for a small change in approach. That's all. In fact, I was wondering if we could meet sometime this evening. Same place.'

'I will confirm.'

'Sure, Mr Raisinghania. I will wait for your confirmation.' And the caller hung up.

'Who was it?' asked Narayanan.

'Someone from Cambridge Partners. The guys who I met for a job last week. They want to meet.'

'What for?'

'I don't know. We will soon find out.'

'Will you go to meet them?'

Aditya thought for a moment. 'Yes, I will.'

'Why would you want to do that?'

'Dad, Cirisha was killed. The cops believe so. I want to know if there is any link between Cambridge Partners and Cirisha's death. If I go, I might just be able to confirm my suspicion. You don't stress yourself, Dad. I will also be going to the duPont Center for a game of fencing after the meeting at Cambridge Partners. I'll probably be late getting back.'

Aditya was in a pensive mood. Cirisha's death had shaken him. The fact that Cirisha's last thought of him was that of a deceitful, unscrupulous and morally degenerate person was gnawing at him. He would never have the chance to correct that impression. He would have to live with this regret all his life.

57

7th June 2008, evening

Boston

Lucier was waiting in the lobby when Aditya walked in. It was seven in the evening, well past regular work hours, and most of the people in the building had left. 'Welcome, Mr Raisinghania. It's good to see you again. The circumstances are very unfortunate.'

Aditya didn't bother to say anything in response. He was fuming. It showed in the way he was breathing. Heavy and fast.

Lucier led him to the top floor where they had met the previous week. The bar was open. Bottles of the finest of single malts were on display. 'Can I get you something to drink?'

'No, thanks.' Aditya waved his offer away.

'Thanks for coming, Mr Raisinghania.'

'What is it that you want from me? That couldn't wait for a few days more?'

'I know what you are going through.' He walked towards the bar, poured a drink for himself and turned to face Aditya. 'Mr Raisinghania, the board of directors at Cambridge Partners is very impressed with you. In fact, we were that day too. But there were some extraneous factors because of which we couldn't do anything for you.' Aditya rolled his eyes in response, frustration writ large on his face. That didn't have any impact on Lucier. 'If you are still interested, we would like to hire you as a partner in our fund. USD 340,000 per annum, a mortgage at zero interest to cover the house you are staying in, business class travel and a car of your choice. Does that sound attractive, Mr Raisinghania?'

For a moment, Aditya didn't know what to say. He proceeded to get up from his seat. 'Thank you for your offer. I am not in a state wherein I can think properly. Give me a couple of days' time. I will come back to you.'

'Oh, come on!' Lucier extended his left hand, touched him on his shoulder and pushed him back into the seat, albeit gently. 'You are a big man now. In our business, business takes precedence over everything else. Family, grief, joy, occasions, celebrations. In fact, business takes precedence over life itself. You have seen that before, haven't you?'

Aditya had had enough. He got up. He was about to open his mouth when the door opened and the chairman walked in. 'Mr Raisinghania. I see that my friend Lucier is trying to make up for his rude behaviour last week.'

'You assholes!' Aditya bellowed at the top of his voice. 'You threaten me that you will kill my wife and you expect me to work for you?'

The chairman didn't react. 'Mr Raisinghania,' he said coolly, 'in our business, we hire only men, not their families. Men who work in Cambridge Partners come here alone without any baggage. I'm sure you understand that. We are hiring you for your skills. Nalin had recommended you very highly. We had opportunities in India and wanted to see if you would be interested in fronting it for us. If you are not . . .' He paused for effect. 'Thank you for coming.'

Aditya stormed out of the room, making a futile attempt to bang the door shut.

He got into his car and cranked the ignition. He tapped the gear stick, moved it to drive mode and pressed the accelerator. The engine revved up and, within minutes, he was driving back towards Cambridge. The men he met hadn't denied killing Cirisha. Did they have a role to play? He couldn't say. He had mentioned to Lieutenant

Windle about their threat, but didn't know why they had not been investigated. Or maybe they had and he didn't know about it. The traffic cleared up and he was zipping on the turnpike. The rubber rolling on the road made a humming sound which always excited someone like him with a fondness for driving. Flipping the car into cruise mode he picked up his mobile from the seat to his right. There were four missed calls. All from Narayanan. He would get back home and speak to him. Serious conversation was not something he wanted to engage in.

Forty-five minutes later, he turned right at exit 94 and drove up to the gates of MIT. It had become dark by then. The clock on the dashboard was pushing 8.30 p.m. A game of fencing would help, but there was only a slim chance of someone being there for him to engage with. However, deciding to take a chance, he drove up to the duPont Center and parked. He was about to get out when he saw four men entering the ground floor. All of them wore jackets and seemed well dressed. When one of them turned to check on the main door, a piece of glistening metal under his jacket caught Aditya's eye. The men were armed. This worried Aditya. They didn't look like students. Nobody walked into the duPont Center in expensive suits and that too with concealed weapons—it required a fair degree of arrogance and courage. Especially in Massachusetts, where carrying any kind of firearm in public was banned. MIT in particular was even stricter about it. Especially after the Richard fiasco, they had become paranoid about anyone carrying guns on campus. What was the campus security doing? How were these men allowed to come inside?

He decided to leave and turned the car. In no time, he was cruising on the turnpike, heading towards home.

He slowed down as he entered Glen Evelyn Drive. A strange instinct told him that everything was not as it should have been. A perfectly acceptable state of mind for a man who had just lost his wife. As he hit the final hundred-metre stretch, he noticed that the lights were on in all the houses down the street.

Except one.

Where was Narayanan? Why hadn't he switched on the lights? Had he gone out for a walk and not returned yet? He drove up to the garage door which didn't open when he clicked the remote. Was there a problem with the power circuit? He parked the car in the driveway and got off. He walked up to the front porch and, with a spare key, opened the main door to the house and stepped in.

It was dark and everything seemed quieter than usual. There was an eerie edge to that silence, which made him nervous. He switched on the passage light. It didn't come on. So that was the problem. The power supply had been cut. 'Daaad?' he called out. No response.

'Dad? Are you home?' No response. He felt he saw a fleeting shadow move across the room. Maybe he was hallucinating. 'Dad!' he called out again. He had reached the kitchen. It was pitch dark. Holding on to the kitchen counter with one hand for support, he started walking towards the living room. The kitchen counter kept him company for twelve feet and then deserted him. He tapped his pocket for his mobile, but that was warming the car seat. He walked a few feet, something didn't feel right. Something on the carpet was sticking to his shoes. He held on to a doorframe, bent down and touched the sole. It felt gooey. Maybe Narayanan had dropped something, he thought as he walked towards the steps leading to the basement, where the electric room was located.

He rubbed his feet on the wooden flooring to get rid of the sticky substance. Maybe he could restore the electricity once he got to the power room. He took the first step, the second and then the third. On the fourth step, he tripped, fell and hurtled down the twenty-step staircase. And then, as suddenly as he tripped and fell, with almost the same abruptness, he stopped. His feet were in the air, his head was pointing towards the basement and his back was on an incline between two steps. And he hadn't hit the lower floor. He was stuck midway. Something was blocking his free fall. He gathered himself, turned around and sat up on the stairway as he tried to see what had interrupted his fall. Hurriedly, he reached out and touched the object. First he felt hair, then the face and then the torso. He screamed. 'Daaaaaad!'

But the scream was lost in the deafening stillness all around. Aditya reached out to touch the near-lifeless body of Narayanan lying in front of him. He patted his way to the right hand and felt for the pulse. It was missing. Not knowing if he was doing it the right way, he moved his hand up swiftly and brought it close to Narayanan's nostrils. He held it there for a couple of seconds. He couldn't feel his breath. Devastated, he was about to take his hand away, when he felt something warm. A warm gust of air. Narayanan was alive. He was breathing. Feebly, but breathing nevertheless. Aditya stood up and ran. Ran out of the door. Straight to the car. His mobile phone was inside. He pulled it out and called 911.

It took twenty-six minutes for the critically injured Narayanan to be wheeled into the emergency care section of MIT Medical, the medical centre dedicated to the needs of the MIT community. While Narayanan was bleeding profusely, greater damage had been caused by the blow of a blunt object to the right side of his head.

The doctors were of the view that it would take a while for Narayanan to recover. It was their rider that worried Aditya: 'If he recovers.'

Whoever had done this to Narayanan had left the house in a mess. Everything was upside down. Mattresses had been ripped, sofas cut open, drawers pulled out, everything strewn on the floor. They were obviously looking for something. Narayanan must have come in the way and got hit.

58

8th June 2008

Boston

It was the second time that day that Lieutenant Windle had come to meet him. He had come once in the morning to take charge of the crime scene and make sure that his boys were in control of everything. This time, he had come to interrogate Aditya.

'Hmm. So it's Cambridge Partners that you think could be involved.'

'I don't know. They had categorically said that if Cirisha does not back off from poking her nose into the *Staring Down the Barrel*-related research, they will do what they have to. It was a clear threat. I had mentioned this to you a few days back. And then they called me yesterday to meet them. All this happened while I was in their office. Isn't it too much of a coincidence?'

'Yes, it is.'

'They have everything to lose if the research gets retracted. The valuations of gun-manufacturing units will come down dramatically. This will have an impact on their investments. But more importantly, it will be a loss of face and credibility for them in this long battle. And more than any other battle, in this one, he who loses credibility loses everything. Cirisha had told me about Lucier, who had first spoken to Michael Cardoza, soliciting him for this research project. On being turned down, Lucier went to James Deahl. The same Lucier, who is from the NRA, met me at Cambridge Partners both times.'

'What do you think they were looking for?'

'I guess it's the research data. The raw data that Cirisha had in her possession. Those papers could have seriously embarrassed them.'

'Where are the papers now?'

'I don't know. They were with Cirisha. I hunted for the papers whole of yesterday and the day before. They're not here.'

'That's really strange. And by the way, what were you doing when she was on her jog?'

'I was asleep.'

'And you didn't realize she was leaving?'

'No. I was sleeping outside, on the living room couch. She was in the bedroom.'

'On the couch? Was everything all right between the two of you?'

'Yes, lieutenant.'

'Then why on the couch?' Windle asked him and turned towards the couch in the living room. 'It doesn't look particularly comfortable.'

'We had an argument.'

'Hmm . . . I'm listening.'

'It was a regular husband–wife squabble. She was not happy with me losing my job in India,' Aditya lied. He could not think of anything else.

'You know, Mr Aditya Raisinghania . . .' and then he stopped. 'By any chance do you have a short and easy word for that?'

'Adi.'

'OK. By the way, Adi, the world thinks it was a cardiac arrest. An excited, overtired jogger, whose heart stopped pumping. I don't believe it. And that's why I had impressed on the coroner to do a toxicology test. Let's see what it throws up.' He had mentioned this to Aditya earlier. But it was what Windle followed it up with that stunned him. 'She was killed by someone known to her.' It was more the way he said it that surprised Aditya.

'How can you say that?' And suddenly he realized what Lieutenant Windle was implying. His voice dropped to a whisper.

'Are you saying that I am a suspect?' It dawned on him that though Cirisha had died three days ago, Windle had stayed away from interrogating him purely on humanitarian grounds. He was always on the list of suspects.

'That possibility has not been ruled out yet, Adi.' And his face became stern. It scared Aditya to see the transformation. 'Adi, you need to be in town till you are cleared. In case you need to travel either out of this county or even back to India, you need explicit permission. I am just communicating the coroner's order to you.'

'But how can you be so sure that she was killed by someone known to her?' Aditya was beginning to get worried. The moment he asked the question though, he realized that it was a mistake. It would now appear to Windle as though he was trying to cover his tracks.

'Because leading up to the place where we found her body, there were two sets of footprints. We were able to see them because the ground was wet on account of the drizzle. One of them was Cirisha's. The other one we don't know yet.'

'It could have been anyone!'

'That he,' and he paused, 'or she, was known to Cirisha Narayanan is clear, Adi. The footprints were right next to each other for a good half a mile. The span of the steps was large, which means that they were walking next to each other. If someone is jogging, the span is relatively smaller. People tend to take longer steps while walking. If she had any inkling of what was coming her way, she would have broken into a run. Which she didn't. Tell me, Adi, under what circumstance would you walk half a mile with someone who was about to murder you? It can only be if you know the person and don't have the faintest idea that he or she could harm you.'

'But how does the question of my involvement come up?'

'Simple. You had a fight the night before. She was vehemently against something you were doing. Depending on how important it was to you, you could have wanted her dead.'

'Oh, come on.'

'We will see, Adi. We will see.' And he got up. He opened the door, looked outside and said, 'Two officers from Boston Detective Corps will be in the area 24 × 7 for the next few days.' He walked out, letting the door shut on its own.

59

9th June 2008

Boston

'Noooooooo!' squawked Aditya as he crumpled and flung the morning newspaper with all his might. He was livid when he saw the headline on the front page. Red eyes marked his helpless fury.

A little later, when the anger subsided, he picked up the newspaper from the floor, stretched it out and read it again. 'James Deahl's *Staring Down the Barrel* wins Bancroft Prize.' Aditya's sense of frustration and outrage was driving him insane.

He sat down on the living room couch and held his head in his hands. There were tears in his eyes. The newspaper article had reminded him of Cirisha and her struggle. He was reasonably sure that she was murdered in connection with the research that had gone into *Staring Down the Barrel*. But what it was, he couldn't say. His obsession with Cirisha's death made him almost forget about Narayanan, who was still not out of danger. It could take days for him to come out of coma.

Aditya was convinced that the papers they had found in Richard's locker at the duPont Center held the clue to Cirisha's murder and, possibly, his own innocence. The documents were not in the house—he had scoured every nook and corner after Cirisha's death—so the chances of Narayanan's killers having got them were negligible. Where could they have gone? Did the people who killed her get their hands on them? If they did, then why did they ransack his home and attack Narayanan? The papers had to be somewhere out there. Safely tucked away from the men who were after them. Unless . . . it was not the documents they were after.

Lieutenant Windle came calling again that afternoon. The two other detectives who had been patrolling the neighbourhood were with him. They grilled him for over two hours. By the end of it, Aditya was a nervous wreck. He had already told them about everything he knew, including the documents that they had picked up from the duPont Center.

'Adi, our detectives went to Cambridge Partners.'

'What do they have to say?'

'I'll skip the details. Most importantly, they said that they called you to offer a job. They had liked you when they met you the first time. However, they denied any suggestions that they threatened you.'

'They have 22 per cent of their investments in gun-manufacturing units. Don't they have reason to worry? If the anti-gun movement picks up speed, their investments will tank.'

'They don't have any investments in gun-manufacturing companies.'

'Says who?'

'We had someone verify their books.'

'What the hell? This is ridiculous!' screamed Aditya. 'They told me categorically.'

'Unproven,' one of the detectives responded coolly.

'Anyway, Adi, we have informed Mumbai Police through the Indian consulate. I've sought information from them on anything that could be relevant to this case. And just to check, Adi, do you suspect Mr Singh could have been involved?' Windle asked Aditya as he got up from his chair.

'He was baying for Cirisha's blood. She was the cause of all his problems. But I always thought his bark was worse than his bite.' Aditya knew that Shivinder was more worried about his money than taking revenge on Cirisha.

'He was released a few days back.'

'A big mistake.'

'Well, Adi, we have as much reason to disbelieve you, as we have evidence to suspect him. So if he must be in custody, so should you.' Aditya didn't know what to say. He just stared vacantly out of the window.

Windle walked towards the door. 'I have kept the security cover intact for the time being.' Just before he reached the door, in what had become his trademark style, he turned. 'And Adi, one last thing. What would you say if someone were to ask you the motive for travelling to Mexico two weeks ago?'

'Mr Narayanan had some work.'

'At a bank? Greater Boston Global Bank, Adi? A bank whose global headquarters are less than a hundred miles from where you are.'

'That's where he wanted to go. He is old so I just accompanied him there. I don't know what business he transacted there.' Aditya was sweating. He was getting drawn deeper into this. If they got to know that he had gone to GB2 to launder money into the United States of America, they would haul him to federal prison.

'We will find that out. Soon.' And the door shut behind Windle.

That's when Aditya realized that the two officers patrolling the neighbourhood were not meant for his security—they were there for surveillance. He was their prime suspect now. His hands turned cold and he started shivering. Lying down on the stained carpet, he curled himself into a foetal position and clenched his fists. What had he got himself into? He didn't even know when he passed out. Was it severe exhaustion from all the stress of the past few days? The only thing he realized, albeit much later, was that the doorbell was ringing. Repeatedly. He wasn't expecting anyone. He got up. His head was still spinning. He stumbled to the door wondering who it could be.

60

9th June 2008

Boston

Windle's next port of call was MIT. He met Antonio, who summarily dismissed Aditya's suggestion that Cirisha was killed because she was poking her nose into activities related to Deahl's book. 'If what you are saying is true, lieutenant, more than half this country would have been dead by now.'

'So what else could it be?'

'I don't know. But do you suspect anyone?'

'Aditya heads the list. There were some indications of trouble on the domestic front. There is one more angle which we are investigating. But we don't have anything concrete.'

'Hmm . . . That is really sad. She was a great talent.'

'We will soon get to the bottom of this. I need your permission to speak to people who have worked closely with her, her colleagues, supervisors and students. People she could have been in conflict with.'

'Sure, lieutenant. You don't need my approval for that.'

'Just following protocol, sir. Yours is an institute of repute. I'll make sure that I'm accompanied by the chief of MIT Police, or anyone he deputes.'

'Thank you, lieutenant. Please do use your discretion and advise me in case you notice anything which is not the way it should be.'

'Thank you, sir.' Lieutenant Windle stepped out. On reaching

242

his car, he pulled out his phone and dialled a number.

'Can I speak with Simen Munter?' He waited for a few seconds to be put through. 'Hi Simen. Just called to check if there has been any progress.' There was a moment's silence. He was listening to Simen. 'Tomorrow evening. Great, I'll speak to you then. Thank you.' And after a pause when he heard what Simen Munter had to say, he added, 'Sure. The report can follow the day after.'

~

On hearing the bell, Aditya groggily found his way to the door. He drew the curtain apart and looked out. At the door, in full uniform, were the two officers from the Boston Police Department. Aditya stepped back and unlatched the door. And then he saw why they were there.

'This gentleman wants to meet with you.' One of the officers had his hand on his gun, while the other was talking to Aditya.

'Let him in.' Aditya turned and walked into the living room. Shivinder followed him. 'I hope you don't think I murdered Cirisha. If I were involved, I wouldn't be here, Aditya.'

'I don't know if you did. But you made some serious threats to kill her.'

'It was something that I said in the heat of the moment. She was the cause of all my problems. That's what I told Lieutenant Windle when he asked me.'

So Windle had interrogated him. For a moment, Aditya was glad that Windle was pursuing the leads seriously. 'Anyway, that's for the cops to figure out. What brings you here?'

'I may be a criminal, Aditya. I stole from a well-off corporate. But I helped them make money. What is wrong if I made some money on the side too? Does that mean I am a murderer?'

Aditya walked to the other corner of the room and looked out of the glass door into the woods that extended for a hundred feet from his backyard. He had no interest in talking to Shivinder.

'Look at me, Aditya. Didn't you make money in the deals that you struck? You took your cut, right? You were as much a part of what I did, but do you see yourself killing anyone? Can you slash someone's throat in cold blood? You will have to trust me, Aditya. In any case, I am here for another week at best. It all depends on how soon the Mumbai Police files charges against me in response to the FIR. Once they do that, I will be put on the first flight back to Mumbai. Extradited. I came to tell you that. I did not murder Cirisha. My conscience is clear. At least in the case of Cirisha, it is.' And he got up. Aditya continued looking out of the window. 'If there is anything I can do for you, let me know. You know how to reach me. Take care.' And he walked towards the door. The detectives were standing at a distance as a precautionary measure.

He had covered half the distance to the door when Aditya spoke. 'Stay.' After a long pause, he turned around. 'I believe you. Come back in.' Many thoughts churned within his mind at the same time, but he had no option but to trust Shivinder. The only other choice was to fight the battle alone, which was going to be difficult, considering he was a prime suspect. He took a calculated punt.

~

Cardoza was meeting some people in his room when Windle, accompanied by an officer from MIT Police, walked in. Antonio had already called and briefed him.

'Good afternoon, Dr Cardoza. Sorry to have barged in like this. Would you prefer that I wait outside till you finish?'

'It's all right, lieutenant. Juan had just called to tell me that you might be coming. If you could wait, I will join you in a minute.' He opened the door adjoining the small meeting room. 'Please,' he said, ushering Windle into the room and slowly shutting the door behind him.

After a couple of minutes, Cardoza joined Windle in the meeting room.

'Yes, lieutenant. How can I help you?'

'Here we meet again, not in fortunate circumstances.'

'Cirisha was much loved, lieutenant. Isn't it tragic that we have to sit here and ponder over what could have killed her?'

'Yes, Dr Cardoza. In my brief interactions with her, I always thought she was bubbling with energy.'

'Her murder is a real mystery to everyone here.'

'I met her husband.'

'Who? Aditya?'

'Yes. He feels that she was involved in some sleuthing. On *Staring Down the Barrel*. Aditya feels that this could have resulted in her death.'

'There may be some truth there, lieutenant. She had stumbled upon some inconsistencies in the data. Actually, she had access to the raw data which formed the basis of the book. And that apparently had severe contradictions. She shared some of it with me; it had largely to do with data regarding the inmates in your prison, which was fudged. She felt that with the data she had, she could recreate and validate critical parts of *Staring Down the Barrel* and was sure that she could expose the inconsistencies.'

'She had met me with the names of twenty-three inmates who had apparently been interviewed for the research. But many of them were either dead or had been released. She felt that the story in the other prisons could be the same.'

'How did she get hold of this data? If what she said is true, then it could be extremely damaging to the university and James Deahl.'

'Did you ask her?'

'Yes, I did. But she didn't tell me. I was confident that she'd share it with me at a more appropriate time. All she told me was that she wanted to go to Phoenix to investigate this further. But she died before she could go.'

Windle also queried Cardoza on Lucier and his proposal. Cardoza confirmed his interaction with Lucier and his suspicion that Deahl's research was NRA-backed. But there was no concrete evidence to prove this.

Windle spoke to Cardoza for a few more minutes and handed over to him a laundry list of information that he wanted from him.

Cardoza glanced at the piece of paper. The list was long but uncomplicated: attendance records, time of arrival and departure from office along with dates, schedule of meetings, list of people she had met on work in the last week, call records from her office phone, swipe-card records indicating access to the building and a lot more.

'Most of these are in the system. If you give me ten minutes, I'll have someone pull this out for you.'

'Wouldn't mind if I get a cappuccino to go with it.' Windle smiled.

In the next twenty minutes, Cardoza gave Windle almost all the information that he wanted. 'I just need to confirm the list of official meetings that she had. I'll email it to you by the end of the day. The rest of the information that you asked for is here in this folder,' Cardoza said, handing Windle the documents.

'Thanks, Dr Cardoza.' Windle got up to leave. Cardoza gave him his visiting card. 'In case you need anything else, please give me a call, or send me an email.'

'Appreciate that. But before I leave, I wanted to check why you do not have CCTV monitoring in the Academic Block.'

'Not sure. But I think it had something to do with privacy for the faculty. It was a decision made by the provost about four years ago. And no one questioned it.'

'Thanks. Now if you will tell me how to get to Dr Deahl's room . . .'

'The floor above this. Last room on the left.'

'Oh yes. I have been there. One last question, Dr Cardoza.' Cardoza nodded. 'What is your view on gun control?'

'Unequivocally, my answer would be YES. Guns must be banned. Had guns not been available, my colleagues would still be alive. Richard Avendon too would be very much in our midst. I have seen the devastation that guns can cause. I fought in the Vietnam

War and have seen with my own eyes the terrible, terrible damage that guns can inflict. We live in a civilized world, lieutenant. Guns have no place here.'

'Do you own a gun yourself?'

'I can't be a Liberal and own a gun, lieutenant,' Cardoza smiled.

'Thank you, Dr Cardoza, have a great day.' On his way to Deahl's room, Windle glanced through the sheets of paper that Cardoza had given him. He skimmed through Cirisha's record. The last time she had entered the facility was on 4th June—the same day that she had met Windle to discuss the Boston prison inmate data. She was murdered a day later.

~

A desperate Aditya told Shivinder everything he knew about the case. 'I do not know what to do. David Windle knows everything about me. And even you. I think he knows why I went to Mexico with Dad.'

'Our only hope, Aditya, is to find the set of papers that you pulled out from Richard's locker and hand it over to David. Let him see for himself and then make up his mind.'

'He has seen part of it. Cirisha showed him the data pertaining to his prison. But that was only one of the hundreds of other aberrations that she suspected.'

'Where are the papers now?'

61

9th June 2008

Boston

Deahl got up from his chair, walked around his desk to the small round table at the right-hand corner of the room, and picked up a bottle of Dasani water. He cracked open the top and poured half a litre of it down his parched throat. Turning towards Windle, who was patiently watching his antics, he asked, 'So, Lieutenant Windle, you want to know how well I knew the deceased?'

'Yes, please.'

'There are a number of deceased around here. I presume you are referring to Ms Narayanan.'

Lieutenant Windle was trying hard to control his annoyance at Deahl's cockiness. 'Cirisha Narayanan. This meeting is about her.'

'Very good research faculty, she was truly committed to her work.'

'Then why would anyone kill her?'

'It's tragic. But who am I to say? Everyone around is speculating. Someone says that she didn't have a good relationship with her husband. Which Indian wife would stay away from her husband for this long? It's only recently that he joined her in Boston. Some even speculate that maybe there was a Richard angle to it. She was close to him, which probably didn't go down well with her husband. Everyone will have their own interpretation.'

'Yes. I know. Some even say that she was killed because she

248

had stumbled upon some irregularities in your research, and that spooked the NRA, and together, you eliminated her.'

'Rubbish!' Deahl's face went red. 'There is nothing in the research which is fabricated. You are wrong, lieutenant, and quite frankly, your allegation is very insulting.' Deahl's voice was beginning to shake. He was furious but was trying to control his anger.

'I can understand. People do gossip about these things. It's very easy to rubbish and attribute motives to certain actions. By the way, just to let you know, *Staring Down the Barrel* claims that during the research process, you interviewed twenty-three inmates from my prison. This never happened.'

'Is that so?' Deahl looked concerned. 'I need to investigate this internally. Richard was handling that leg of the research. I am not sure how he managed it or how his team put together that data. I can't validate everything that my team puts together, you see, lieutenant. Now that you say it, I will get it verified.'

Windle moved on. 'When was the last time you met Cirisha?'

'A few days ago. Can't remember the exact date. I had forgotten something in my room and had returned to pick it up. I met her at the elevator. It was late at night and she was the only one there on the second floor. She didn't have any reason to be there and she seemed nervous. That was the last I spoke to her, I think.'

'Did you ever get the feeling that she was trying to accuse you of deliberately misleading the public into believing in your philosophy of gun rights for all?'

'Half the country says that my research is reassuring, while the other half claims that the research is rubbish. Who do you believe? Take your pick, lieutenant.'

'You didn't answer my question.'

'No. I didn't think so,' he replied curtly.

'What is your role in Cambridge Partners, the Boston-based hedge fund?'

'Is this some kind of interrogation? If it is, I would appreciate it if you could give me sufficient notice, so that I can request my lawyer to join me in these discussions. It's better to be prepared. You never know what will get misinterpreted. Thank you, Lieutenant Windle.' And Deahl got up from his chair.

On the way back, a not-so-happy Windle made a phone call. 'Is this the *New York Times*? May I speak to Christopher Jenkins?' The call went on for fifteen minutes, after which Windle hung up.

62

10th June 2008

Boston

Aditya was at home that evening. Shivinder was worried about the money in his GB2 account in Geneva. Aditya used his Mexican connections and transferred all the cash lying in GB2 Geneva to Enrique Nieto's account in GB2 Mexico. A corresponding credit appeared in the San Diego account of Enrique, which was controlled by Aditya. The money was now safe. They still did not have full control over the money—the collections from the franchisee security deposits—lying in GB2 in Mumbai.

Aditya spent the rest of the day trying to patch up parts of the house that had been torn apart during the assault on Narayanan. The doors had been restored and security alarms installed. But the inside of the house was still a mess.

That afternoon, too, the detectives from Windle's team spent over three hours with him. It had become a routine for them. This time, Shivinder was also around. The detective found it extremely strange that two friends who had turned bitter foes had suddenly found solace in each other's company.

After they left, Shivinder went off to visit the lawyer they planned to hire. This was going to be a longer process than what either of them had ever imagined.

Aditya walked to the garage to pull out some tools from the kit hanging on the wall. His car was parked there. He switched on the lights, walked to the far end beyond the car and plucked a hammer from the wall. He needed it for putting a few nails through the hard wood of the cupboard. He turned back and was crossing the car, when he looked inside casually. A big box was lying in the boot. Carefully, he carried the box into the house, wondering how he had forgotten to remove it after he brought it back from MIT on the day of Cirisha's memorial.

Memories of that day flashed before him as he cut open the box.

At the top were several files—work permits, visa papers, income statements and so on. A photoframe with a wedding photo of the two of them was next. Awards, mementoes and stationery formed the next few layers. There was a picture of the entire team. He recognized a few of them from community dinners. There was also a strip of medicine. Like her mother, Cirisha too was diabetic and needed regular medication.

At the bottom of the pile were a few plastic folders with papers in them. He pulled them out. In one of them was the printout of the email which Cirisha had intended to hand over to Windle—Richard's cryptic email. He had seen the email earlier when they were trying to crack open the lockers at the fencing facility. Back then, Cirisha had SMSed the image to him. It didn't prevent him from clicking a picture of the email with his iPhone again. This email was the root cause of Cirisha's involvement in this mire, he thought.

There was nothing else of significance in the box. He packed everything back in it, taped it up and dumped it in Cirisha's study. As he turned back, Cirisha's pretty face beckoned him. It was lying on the floor, sandwiched between the study table and the wall. A red band around the photograph made it easier for him to pick it up. He looked at it for a while. The white plastic around her photo had browned. It was a long while back that she had got it made. The photo was almost a decade old. Not much had changed. He reached for it and picked it up. Bringing Cirisha's MIT identity card up to his lips, he kissed it, looked at it adoringly and kept it back on the table. She was not going to come back.

63

11th June 2008

Boston

When Deahl drove into the MIT parking lot, it was fuller than what he had seen over the years. On a regular day, there would be about eight to ten cars. However, that day there were over twenty-five cars parked. His intuition was telling him that there could be trouble today. When he got closer to the Academic Block, he could see what the problem was. He continued walking. Flashbulbs started going off, almost in unison. When they saw him, the journalists standing outside the Academic Block started running in his direction. They had been waiting for him since morning.

'There has been some talk going around that the data, which is the basis of *Staring Down the Barrel*, is doctored. What do you have to say about that?' They all had the same question.

'Rubbish!' Blood rushed to his cheeks. He was furious. 'What are you talking about? I have no clue,' Deahl snapped. It was a bad start to the day.

'Is the inmate data incorrect?' someone screamed. So that's where it came from. That asshole David Windle had leaked the information to the press.

'Your allegations are ridiculous and undeserving of a response.' He continued walking and entered the Academic Block. The door shut behind him; the journalists couldn't get in and were left outside holding their mics and video cameras. Deahl first called the security in-charge of the block and gave him a dressing down for having allowed the press into the campus. He then called Windle. 'Who the hell authorized you to talk to the press?'

'Pardon me?'

'How did the press get wind of the issue we discussed yesterday? How could you tell them?'

'Must I remind you, Dr Deahl, I take instructions from the American government, not you or your university or your sponsors. Have a good day, Dr Deahl.' And he slammed the phone down.

Christopher Jenkins had spread the word and in a matter of hours, the whole media circle knew about the controversy surrounding *Staring Down the Barrel*. The NRA was upset by the turn of events. Lucier called Deahl and advised him to hold a press conference and address all the questions. Deahl grudgingly agreed.

64

11th June 2008

Boston

Around the same time, not so far away, Aditya had just woken up. He made himself a cup of coffee and sat by the window reminiscing about the past. The last twelve months had been pure hell. First it was his job, then his wife, then his father-in-law and now, he faced the prospect of being convicted for his wife's murder. 'Whoever said you pay for your sins in your next life was wrong. Here I am paying for my sins in this life itself,' he thought. As his eyes panned the outside of the house, he saw his overflowing mailbox. Cirisha was always the one who cleared it. He had to get used to doing things on his own now. He staggered to his feet, walked up to the mailbox and began pulling out what looked like junk mail. Credit card offers, a few newspapers and discount coupons.

There was also a rejection letter from Cambridge Partners. They had displayed amazing alacrity in sending him that. They presumably wanted to document the reason why they had met him. The very sight of it got him agitated. He swung around and in one sweeping motion of his hand, began pushing all the mail furiously into the garbage bin sitting right next to the mailbox. As he turned around to head back into the house, he saw from the corner of his eye, a yellow paper sticking out of the bin. In a flash, he picked it up and stared at it in surprise. Thank God Cirisha was not around, else she would have given him grief over this!

Back inside, Aditya was keeping himself busy, trying to get the house back in shape. His mind kept oscillating between thoughts of Cirisha, Narayanan, GB2, his job, his career and his life back in India. He remembered how Cirisha had pinched his ears hard when she had found out that he had bribed a traffic constable on being caught for jumping a red light. Her absence was beginning to turn into a ghost-like presence.

He walked to the table, picked up the yellow speeding ticket and looked at it. 'You could have got me in trouble,' he said. His eyes skimmed over the ticket from top to bottom subconsciously.

And that's when he saw it.

It struck him like a lightning bolt. The colour drained from his cheeks. He read it again. Then for the second time. And then again and again. It was not a speeding ticket that he had been handed. It was in Cirisha's name. But more importantly, it was for the car that she used to drive. He looked at the date. It was the same day that she died.

Time of offence: an hour and a half before her body was found.

65

11th June 2008

Boston

Aditya stiffened a little the moment he heard the voice over the phone. 'Lieutenant? Aditya here. I need to talk to you.'

'Tell me. I am a bit tied up. So please keep it short.'

'The day she was killed, Cirisha had gone to MIT.'

'What?'

'Yes.'

'But MIT is in a different direction. Boston Public Garden is to the east of Glen Evelyn Drive, whereas MIT is a fair distance to the west. And she was in her jogging gear.'

'Yes. I know. But that day, in the morning, she was spotted close to the institute, driving at a very high speed.'

'By whom?'

'The traffic cameras. The pilot cameras that the traffic department has installed at the 93rd entry into the northbound carriageway of the Massachusetts Turnpike.' Windle knew that the 93rd entry into the turnpike, northbound, was on the road leading to the turnpike from MIT. Anyone getting on to the highway from the 93rd entry was in all likelihood coming from MIT.

'Have you seen the feed? How did you get it? Are you sure?'

'I haven't seen the feed, lieutenant. However, I have a speeding ticket. The overspeeding was recorded by the speed guns an hour and a half before she was found at Boston Public Garden. And she was going at 120 miles an hour in a place where the speed limit is 80. I can't imagine her driving so fast, lieutenant. Unless she was really stressed or worried, she would never do something like this.'

Shivinder walked in just as Aditya was finishing the last leg of his conversation with Windle.

'Let me check and get back. I have the access records for the Academic Block. Let me call you back.' He hung up.

Aditya saw the confused look on Shivinder's face and told him about the ticket.

'MIT? Why would she go there that early in the morning?'

'I don't know. It surprises me even more because she was in any case planning to go there later that afternoon on her way to the airport. She was to take a flight to Phoenix.'

'What time did she leave?' Shivinder was curious.

'Dad saw her leave around five in the morning. He saw her stop by the door to his room. The keys are hung there, you see.'

Shivinder started thinking. 'Unless she went there to . . . check on something about those papers.'

'That is, assuming she took the papers to the university,' Aditya argued.

'They were not with her when she was found. Either she hid them or someone took them from her.'

'Correct. There are only three possibilities. The papers are here at home, they have been kept somewhere safe by Cirisha, or someone has taken them from her. There can't be a fourth option, right?'

'Very unlikely.'

'They're not at home. I have scanned every nook and corner. In fact I hunted for the papers even the day she died and the day after. If her murderer had the papers, they wouldn't have assaulted Dad. So it's clear that they didn't find them on Cirisha, if the papers were what they were after.'

'Which only means she has kept it somewhere in the university,' Shivinder reasoned.

The phone rang. Aditya picked it up on the third ring. 'Aditya.'

'Lieutenant Windle.'

'Yes, lieutenant.'

'I checked on what you just told me. The traffic department has a record and a visual of someone driving the car away from the university and getting on to the turnpike. The images captured by the traffic video are too grainy to make out the driver's face.'

'OK. So she did go to the university.'

'But strangely, her access card shows no activity. She hadn't used her access card to get into the building.'

'She couldn't have. It's here. At home.'

'At home?'

'Yes, lieutenant. I just saw it a while ago. And it was not something that came with her personal belongings, which the university returned to us. It was very much here. At home. All along.'

'Then how did she get in?' Then after a ten-second pause, he added, 'Let me check the activity on the Academic Block access control on the morning of 5th June. I have the data with me. Let me call you back.' And he hung up.

Aditya turned towards Shivinder. 'She did go to the university. But why? If she wanted to keep the papers, Shivinder, she could have kept them there in the afternoon too. Why at five in the morning?'

'The only reason I can think of is that she wanted to do something there without being seen.'

'To hide something?'

'Maybe,' Shivinder agreed. 'Do you really think she would have hidden the papers on campus itself? So that they are safe?' When Shivinder said this, Aditya's eyes went round in anticipation. He clenched his right fist and punched it into his left. 'Yes. Yes! Yes! Yes! As I said, that's what would have happened. She would have taken the papers and hidden them somewhere. I haven't seen it since the night before the incident.'

'But where? Aditya, if you were to hide them on campus, where would you hide them?' After a long pause, he added, 'Which is the safest possible place in the institute?'

'Same place where we found it?' When Aditya said this, very matter-of-factly, he himself was stunned. Aditya looked as if a hundred-ton container was about to collapse on his head. He slowly opened his mouth and whispered, 'The locker, Shivinder. The locker.' He turned and looked at him, a victorious look in his eyes. 'She went to Richard's locker and hid the papers there. And she wanted to do it before the campus got crowded. She was worried if the papers were safe here at home. So she wanted to hide them in the locker before the men came in. Remember, it was a men's locker. That explains why she went there so early.'

The phone rang. It was Windle again. 'Can you come and see me right away with the traffic ticket and Cirisha's identity card? By the way, Cirisha did not enter the Academic Block that morning. But I found something strange, paranormal almost. Richard Avendon entered the block at 5.10 a.m. and exited at 8.05 a.m.'

Aditya was stunned beyond belief. It took some time and a hand on his shoulder, that of Shivinder, for him to close his mouth and resume normal breathing.

'And you know what's surprising?' Windle continued, 'Between 5.10 and 8.05 a.m. he has exited and entered again twice. Exited at 7.01 a.m. entered again at 7.14 a.m., exited at 7.29 a.m., entered again at 7.39 a.m., and exited finally at 8.05 a.m. What do you make of this?'

'Richard Avendon. Cirisha had Richard's access card. Instead of her own access card, she took Richard's by mistake when she went to the campus.' Aditya whispered into the phone. 'I am coming there, lieutenant.'

66

11th June 2008

MIT, Boston

The executive committee of the university met again that afternoon to take a final call on who was to succeed Meier as the provost. In the previous meeting they had annulled Deahl's suspension.

The shortlist was now down to three candidates. The fourth had expressed a lack of interest in taking up the role. Probably the fact that he was up against two bigwigs had influenced his decision. Of the remaining three, the third seemed to be a candidate put up to the committee to make up the numbers. It was mandated by statute that there had to be at least four final candidates. The battle was down to two people—James Deahl and Michael Cardoza.

Both had their godfathers in the executive committee. When their names came up for discussion, the debate expectedly was a heated one. The two of them had furiously lobbied for the post. The desperation was the same on both sides.

67

11th June 2008

Boston

The same afternoon, Shivinder sneaked into the locker room of the duPont Center unnoticed. Aditya had given him his fencing ID card to flash in case anyone checked. Security at the duPont Center was virtually non-existent. To make it easier for Shivinder, Aditya had sketched out the exact location of the locker. Shivinder didn't encounter any trouble in finding it. On specific instructions from Aditya, he had carried a backpack along.

When Shivinder entered the locker room, there were three people inside. He went straight to Richard's locker but didn't attempt to open it. He could feel his heart pounding. He loitered around till the last of the three guys left the locker room.

After making sure that he was alone, he keyed in the code to open it. By the time the locker made a low hissing noise and cranked open, his shirt was wet with perspiration. He looked inside. There was a pile of papers inside the locker. Carefully, he pulled out the entire lot and shoved it into his backpack. His palm swept the floor of the locker to make sure he had taken out everything. He groped around for a couple of seconds. His hand hit something. It was a pendrive. He shut the locker, slipped the pendrive into the side pocket of his backpack, and was out of there in a jiffy. Keeping his head down, covering it with a hoody, he walked out of the locker room to the parking lot. Once he was in the safe confines of the car, he took the papers out of the backpack and inspected them.

He called Aditya.

'Aditya, where are you?'

'I'm with Lieutenant Windle. Did you find anything in the locker?'

'Yes, I did, Aditya. The papers were there. There was a pendrive too.'

'Pendrive? That's new. It wasn't there the last time.'

'There is one. It has Richard's name inscribed on it. Looks like one of those gifts that you receive in conferences. Maybe you guys missed it the last time. It was deep inside the locker and is very small.'

'Wonderful. Get it here quickly. Now we will show these fuckers.' Aditya could hardly contain his excitement before he realized that he was in Windle's office.

'But tell me,' Shivinder interrupted his celebration, 'were these papers supposed to be originals?'

'Why do you ask?'

'Because all I have here are photocopies.'

'Strange. The ones we saw that night were originals. All filled in ink. I saw ticks and crosses in blue and red on those sheets.'

'Strange.'

'It's OK. Get back home. We'll figure out what we do next.'

The moment Shivinder disconnected the line, his phone rang again. It went silent before he could answer it. In thirty seconds, it started ringing again. Shivinder reached out to respond.

Aditya turned to Windle and explained his conversation with Shivinder.

'Cirisha probably had the original papers when she drove to Boston Public Garden. That's where she was murdered. And the papers were stolen from the car. That explains why we found the keys in the car.'

'But if the person who took away the papers from her got what he wanted, why did he have to ransack my house and murderously assault Dad?' Aditya's mind was working at a furious pace.

'Maybe he wanted the photocopies.' Windle's eyes rolled up as if he was thinking. He lifted his right hand, shook it as if to crystallize his thoughts and then pointed a finger at Aditya. 'The pendrive. The killers were looking for the pendrive.'

'But why?'

'I don't know. We will find out once we see what's in there. You go home and wait for me. I will join you there within the hour,' Windle instructed.

Aditya reached home and sat there waiting for Shivinder to come in with the papers. Why was he taking so much time? Two hours passed. Shivinder had not returned. He dialled Shivinder's number a few times. No one picked up. A look of fear passed across his face. Streams of sweat meandered from his forehead along the wrinkles and started flowing into his eyes. Instinctively his hand went up and rubbed his eyes. He walked to the washroom, splashed some water on his face and looked into the mirror. There was only one thing he could see in his eyes. Fear.

There was a knock on the door followed by the doorbell. He ran to the door; it was Windle. He let him in and walked back to his living room. Windle walked behind him without a word.

'Shivinder has not returned, lieutenant. I should not have trusted that guy. He has taken everything and cut a deal with the NRA. Or whoever. He played me, lieutenant. He played me.' Aditya was furious. 'Instead of listening to him about how someone might spot me on campus, I should have gone to the locker myself.'

'Well, in which case, we wouldn't be having this conversation because you would be dead.'

Aditya's face turned pale. His mouth opened to say something. But no words came out. 'When? How?'

'On his way back an eighteen-wheel trailer truck knocked his car over. He died on the spot, even before anyone could pull him out of the badly mangled vehicle. The skid marks indicate that it was a trailer that killed him but we haven't been able to trace it yet.'

Aditya's eyes were focused on the floor. After a minute he looked up. 'What about the papers?'

'We didn't find them on him.'

'No! No! This can't be true. This just can't be true!' Aditya held his head in his hands and started howling. Windle walked up to Aditya and awkwardly placed a hand on his shoulder, trying to comfort him. He didn't know what to say. Aditya looked up towards Windle. Fear in his eyes. 'Am I next, lieutenant? Do you think they will come for me next?'

'Don't worry, Adi. We are there to make sure that they do not succeed in any misadventure. Leave it to us. You relax.' Windle made a feeble attempt at reassuring Aditya. In an hour, he left, leaving behind the two detectives to keep watch.

~

By the time the executive committee meeting ended that evening, history had been created. For the first time ever, the executive committee had not been able to come to a decision on who the next provost should be. It was split right down the middle. For the first time ever, the casting vote of the president would be brought into play to decide who the provost was going to be. The committee meeting was adjourned until the next day. Antonio needed time to think about who his choice was going to be.

68

11th June 2008, night

Boston

Sleep had deserted Aditya. Cirisha died believing that the man she had chosen as her life partner had stabbed her in the back. The guilt gnawed at him constantly, leading him to the edge of a nervous breakdown.

He was tossing around in bed waiting for the night to end, hoping that the new day would bring something bright and positive. An hour past midnight, his phone rang. He was wide awake. On the third ring, he answered the call, wondering who it might be.

'Hello.'

'Hi Mr Raisinghania. It's David.'

'Oh.' He didn't recognize the voice. The line was unclear. 'Yes, lieutenant.'

'I just called to confirm if everything is all right. I spoke to my officers a while ago. I have instructed them to be vigilant. You don't worry, Mr Raisinghania. Have a good night. We are there to make sure you are safe.'

'Thanks for checking, lieutenant. I was trying to catch some sleep. Maybe I will be able to think clearly with a fresh mind. I'll talk to you in the morning. Goodnight.'

Windle had never called at such a late hour. Did that mean the cops were worried he might be in danger? Was there reason to be?

Numerous thoughts ran through his mind the moment he put the phone down.

He walked over to the window. Through the crack between the curtains he peered outside. A police patrol car was stationed about fifty metres away. Two officers were standing near the bonnet, chatting. Every thirty seconds one of them would look around cautiously. They were vigilant. Aditya didn't move from the spot. His eyes were focused, though his mind wandered. He was strangely uncomfortable. There was something more than what met the eye. He thought about the incidents of the last few days. Cirisha, the documents, the hospitalization of Narayanan, the duPont Center, Shivinder joining him, volunteering help, the photocopies in the locker, the pendrive and then the accident. The events kept playing in front of him like a video on endless loop. There had to be something somewhere, which would tell him what those guys were after. Knowing that was the only way he would survive.

He went into Cirisha's study. Something there might give him a clue. Maybe. Maybe not. In any case, he didn't have anything better to do. He had no option but to keep trying.

Once more, he went through the contents of the box that had come from the university. The folder marked 'David Windle' was still there. Apart from that, nothing in the box interested him. He looked up. Cirisha's ID card was hanging from the soft board above her table. He looked at it and then at the box. He plucked the ID card and kissed it softly. 'I've made many mistakes but loving you wasn't one of them, Ciri. I don't know how to prove this to you. I am sorry,' he stammered as a continuous stream of tears began to flow. 'I am sorry, my love, that I hurt you. If you are listening to me, I really mean it. I love you, baby.' He kissed Cirisha's picture on the ID card once again.

At that very instant he heard a car pull up somewhere close by. Instinctively, he walked back to the window, ID card in hand. A black SUV had stopped near the two officers. The front window on the passenger side was rolled down. One of the officers had walked up to the SUV. It looked like someone was seeking directions. At 2 a.m., and when most cars were fitted with GPS devices? It surprised him. Standing there behind the curtains, he had a hunch that the SUV meant trouble.

The officer returned to his patrol vehicle. The SUV window rolled up again. Aditya couldn't see anything inside the car. The SUV didn't move from its position. Its engine was on, he could make out from the parking lights. They were probably waiting for someone. Aditya was wide awake now. Three minutes passed. One of the officers again went towards the SUV. The window went down again. It was a short conversation this time. The rear door of the SUV opened and the officer went in. Aditya's heart was racing. Did the officer know those guys? Windle hadn't mentioned any additional cover being sent for him. And the car didn't look like a patrol van either.

And that's when it struck him. The phone call. It was not Windle. The man on the phone had sounded like Windle, but it was someone else. Hadn't he called him Mr Raisinghania? Windle would never call him that. It was too much of a tongue-twister for him. For Windle, it was always Adi. Or at best Aditya. He panicked. Was it Cirisha's murderers who had called to check if their next victim was at home?

That's when he saw the officer who had got into the SUV getting out, envelope in hand. Had he been paid off? The officer with the envelope then walked towards his colleague and within a minute, both of them got into the patrol car and drove away.

'Run!' something inside him screamed. He scrammed from the window. Hurriedly, he put on his shoes. Not even waiting to tie his shoelaces, he bolted towards the back door. Six steps and he was at the door. He was about to open it, when he stopped. He remembered something. He ran back to his room, opened his cupboard and from the third drawer from the bottom, pulled out a double-action Colt Python with a 4-inch barrel.

Pausing for a moment, he checked if it was loaded. It was. The discussion he had had with Cirisha a few years back, when he had forced her to buy it despite her discomfort with guns, raced through his mind.

He tucked it into his trouser pocket, picked up his jacket from the bed and tumbled through the house, snatching his backpack lying on a lounge chair on the way.

In the distance he heard the click of the SUV door.

Time was running out.

He sprinted to the back door and yanked it open. It surprised him, albeit for a couple of seconds, that the alarm didn't go off. The intruders had disconnected it: it was programmed to go off if the door was opened between 11 p.m. and 5 a.m.

He jumped into the backyard, climbed over the fence and ran into the woods behind the house. Standing about a hundred yards away, under the cover of darkness, he could see the house lights come on. Three men were in his living room, and one person was running up and down, as if he was looking for someone. Surely they had come for him. He looked up and thanked God. And then, he turned and ran. For the next fifteen minutes he kept running till he reached the highway. For a moment, he considered going to the Boston Police station. But he decided against it. The officers at his front door seemed to be hand in glove with the intruders. He crossed the road, dodging oncoming traffic. It was easy, for the traffic at that time was thin. Only container trucks passed on that road during the early-morning hours and you could hear them rumble as they barrelled down the street.

He waved down a passing truck and hitched a ride till the 94th exit, a couple of miles from the entrance to the university. It cost him thirty dollars. He walked up to a roadside motel. He needed to be safe for the night, hoping that the next day would bring some cheer. His close escape got him thinking—maybe his luck was finally turning.

69

12th June 2008

Boston

Aditya was fully awake when the first rays of the sun signalled the dawn of a new day. He had hardly slept a wink. A quick shower followed by a breakfast of French toast and sausages in the room got him ready for the long day ahead.

He had got his clothes washed and ironed at the motel launderette. Dressing quickly, he sat on his bed, fully alert, until the clock in the room beeped eight times. Time to go. He called the university front desk. 'Can you please put me through to Michael Cardoza?'

'He isn't in yet, sir.'

'Can I speak to his assistant?'

'Who, Louisa?'

'Yes, please.' Aditya knew Louisa. He had met her a few times.

'Good morning. Dr Cardoza's office.'

'Hi Louisa. Aditya. Cirisha's husband.'

'Hey. How are you? I couldn't speak to you that day. The president and the others had hijacked you. I had planned to come and meet you once you were more settled.'

'Thanks, Louisa. I wanted to meet Michael.'

'He won't be in till late afternoon. He has been summoned to the executive committee meeting.'

'Executive committee meeting? Sounds like a very important

forum. Hope all is well.' Aditya had no clue what an executive committee meeting meant for those in academia. He was just fishing for information.

'The word on the street is that he is getting the provost's job. He's been summoned for that, I guess. But that's a bit later. He has some other work to attend to in the interim.'

'Oh wow! Congratulations! You will become the provost's assistant. Even more powerful.' And he faked a chuckle.

'Haha! Thanks.' And after a second's pause, she added, 'How can I help you, Aditya?'

'I was missing Cirisha, Louisa. How heartless does one need to be to murder someone like her? There is no limit to human cruelty.'

'They are still treating it like a murder? The cops?'

'Yes. At least till the time the toxicology tests are out, they have no choice. I am really hoping that they get to the bottom of this soon.'

'I know, Aditya. It must be really difficult for you. We are all there for you, love.' Aditya felt horrible to be doing this to Louisa. He was lying to an unsuspecting soul.

'I was wondering if I could come and take some pictures at Cirisha's workstation. She has spent close to a decade there. I wanted to take back some memories.'

'Sure, Aditya. When do you want to come over?'

'Can I come now?'

'Sure. Come over. I am in office. I can show you around.'

'I'll be there in thirty minutes.'

'Great, I'll see you soon.'

'Could you please let the guards know? So that they let me in without any trouble.' Aditya didn't have his duPont Center identity card. He had given it to Shivinder.

Aditya waited for another ten minutes, and then he was on his way to the university. It was about a mile away and took him a little over fifteen minutes to get there. The guards at the gate recognized him and didn't bother to stop him. He walked straight to the Academic Block. Louisa met him at the entrance. She gave him a warm hug and led him inside to the first floor. Aditya walked with her through the corridor till she stopped and turned towards him. A sad smile appeared on her face. 'Cirisha's room,' she said, pointing to the door on the right. 'Give me a minute.' And she walked to the far end of the corridor. In no time, she was back with a bunch of keys.

Aditya looked at her surprised. He brought his hand up to the access control module on the door and mocked a swipe, raising his eyebrows. Louisa smiled. 'Long story. One of Cirisha's colleagues, who shares this room, lost her ID card a few months back. The replacement card took some time in coming. She was finding it difficult to access her workstation. So a couple of months back, the access control to this room was disabled. We use only keys now for this room.' She smiled, opened the door and led him in.

'This is where Cirisha spent the last six or seven years,' she said, pointing to a workstation. Aditya looked around. There were two other workstations in that room. 'This is where part of Michael's team sat. Cirisha and two others.'

'They will be coming in now?'

'Both of them are travelling on work. In fact, they were not here for Cirisha's memorial either. I spoke to one of them yesterday. She was very upset that she could not make it. They have been away for over three weeks and are not expected back for another week.'

Aditya scanned the room. Three workstations, each with an iMac. There were individual lockers for each workstation. In one corner was a round table with three seats, which probably served as a place for small meetings, a Xerox photocopier, a small refrigerator and a flat-panel TV, which played university videos. 'Can I sit here for five minutes? And take a few pictures?' His voice was barely a whisper now.

Louisa patted him on the back. 'Sure. Take your time. I will be at my workstation. Down the alley, the last room to the left. Come over once you are done.'

Aditya looked around the room. He had orchestrated the visit to the university for two reasons. One, he wanted time to think. Even though he had kept his mobile phone switched off the whole night, he knew the motel was a stopgap safe house. He had switched it on once in the morning to call Louisa. But that would have been enough for those chasing him to figure out where he was. He could have called from the motel lines, but didn't. With hindsight, he realized it was stupid of him. Two, he wanted to examine Cirisha's room, just to make sure that there was nothing she would have wanted him to know. If she had had any inkling of her impending death, she might have left a clue.

The cupboards were empty. The drawers drew a blank. The computer refused to come up. He didn't have the login ID and password to Cirisha's account. He stood up and looked around. Helplessly. Hopelessly. There was nothing on the wall, just a solitary painting, apart from the TV, to break the monotony. A lounge chair stood guard next to the entrance.

His vision wandered over the two other workstations and that's when he saw it. Nestled in the space between the third workstation and the wall. Though he had seen it earlier, it hadn't registered. Taking a few steps he went closer. The machine looked old, but well maintained. Admiring it, he felt the contours, as if trying to assess its features. There was a sticker on its front with detailed user instructions. It was a monster of a photocopier. That model had not hit India yet. He had read about it, though. Quickly he got down to work.

Surveying the sides of the machine, he intently looked for a niche. A slot which, when nudged, would open up the back of the machine. He squatted behind it and patted every inch, trying to find the hollow part which would most likely contain the wedge. He found it right at the bottom. He had to remove one screw to get there. It was easy. The steel foot-scale did the job. He had found it on Cirisha's colleague's table. The screw opened up the panel, behind which he found the toolkit. Once he had the toolkit, the rest was easy. Using it, he took apart the back panel. He clearly hadn't forgotten the skills he had acquired as a sales and maintenance engineer for Xerox in India before he joined the banking industry.

He kept digging. A few more layers and he was inside the machine. In front of him were several circuit boards, all fitted into their slots. Carefully he took them all out. He knew he would not be able to put them back in order. To do that, he would need time. And that was a scarce commodity.

Whosoever tried to use the machine next, would call the maintenance personnel who would take another forty-eight hours to respond. In any case, Cirisha's colleagues who shared the room had been out for three weeks and weren't expected any time soon. By the time they would realize that someone had tampered with the Xerox machine, the job would hopefully be done.

Behind the space occupied by the circuit boards was a large black box. On it was written '100 GB, Seagate (for Xerox)'. He snapped it out of the slot, pulled the wire connecting it to the rest of the board and placed it next to him. It was about five times the size of his mobile phone.

Reassembling the machine took all of three minutes. All he did was stuff everything inside and cover it up with the back panel.

He reached out for the telephone lying on the workstation of Cirisha's colleague, right next to the Xerox machine. While trying to dial a number, his sweaty fingers slipped and pressed the redial button. He quickly disconnected and dialled Windle's number. Even before Windle's phone could ring, he hung up. He was a bit unsure of Windle. The phone call the night before and the events after that had shaken him up. He picked up the hard disk, dropped it into his bag and quietly made his way to the door.

His hand was on the handle and he was about to pull the door open when the phone rang. Aditya froze. It was the phone next to the Xerox machine. Who could be calling at that time? That early in the morning. He was in two minds. His eyes wandered to the Xerox machine next to the phone. 'Shit!' he exclaimed. He had left two circuit boards lying on the floor. While taking them out, he had carefully kept them behind him and in his hurry to finish, he had forgotten to stuff them back in.

If he let the phone ring and left the room, Louisa might hear it and walk in. She would then surely see that something had been tampered with. That helped him decide: he walked back to the phone and picked it up.

'Good morning.'

'Who is this?' He had heard that voice before.

'Sir, I am from . . .' and he hesitated. What should he say? His eyes searched around for clues. Then he saw the name. Sterling Automation. He stammered a bit but recovered fast enough. 'I am from Sterling Automation. Here to fix the photocopier. There was a complaint.' The label on the back of the machine was the inspiration.

'Sure. Someone called me from this number.' The voice sounded familiar. But he couldn't place it.

'Mistake, sir. I was calling my office and would have pressed the wrong button. My sincere apologies.'

'That's OK.'

'I'm sorry, sir.'

'It's fine. Thanks.' He was about to hang up when he heard a noise in the background. 'Who is it . . .?' When he heard the name just before the click, he knew why the voice had sounded familiar. He clicked a few buttons on the phone. From the redial list he noted down the number, just in case he needed it later. Hurriedly he took the two circuit boards and dumped them inside the dustbin. He bent down next to the Xerox machine, noted something down and walked out. Cirisha's access card came in handy. Thank God for administrative inefficiencies. Just as with Richard's card, Cirisha's access ID card was still active.

He walked straight out of the Academic Block.

The shuttle to the Cambridge area was just leaving from a spot fifty metres from the Academic Block. He got into the shuttle and took a seat at the rear end. The hoody came up and he drew it tight over his head.

In thirty minutes the bus reached Cambridge. He got out. He knew he had a two- to three-hour lead over his pursuers. As the bus was leaving the university, he had seen a black SUV enter the gates. It looked like the one that was parked outside his house the night before. He couldn't say for sure. Maybe he was hallucinating. But thus far all his hunches had been right.

70

12th June 2008

North End, Boston

North End, one of the oldest residential neighbourhoods in Boston, was a place initially inhabited by the original settlers. Waves of the Irish followed, only to be joined by the Portuguese and the Jewish. Throughout the twentieth century, the Italians had been the dominant immigrant community. No surprise, then, that the area was dotted with Italian restaurants.

Aditya got off the bus at a busy intersection. Clutching the backpack in his hand, he hastened through the hustle and bustle of a midday crowd that was stepping in and out of restaurants. He walked for about fifteen minutes till he reached Pavers Mansion, a quaint three-storeyed, brick-walled building. He stopped outside the building which was to his left and looked at the address he had hurriedly scribbled on a note. He was at the right place. He walked in. There was no elevator so he sprinted up the stairs to the top floor.

A plump lady at the reception desk smiled at him. He smiled back. 'What can I do for you?' The place smelt of fish. It was lunchtime.

'I hope I am not intruding during your lunch hour. I can wait.' He knew that this was a sure way of winning over the lady.

'Not at all. I just finished mine,' she replied.

'I'm coming from MIT,' and he flashed Cirisha's ID card covering her photo. 'We are in a bit of a jam. We have to submit a research

277

paper day after tomorrow. We had photocopied all the research data and sent it to the sponsors. The person carrying both the originals and the copied documents had an accident. You would have heard of the terrible accident on the Massachusetts Turnpike yesterday afternoon. That's the one. While our associate is safe, most of the papers were lost under the wheels of the fast-moving cars on the highway.' Aditya saw that the receptionist's badge had her name: Merissa. She looked on with puppy eyes as Aditya fed her his story.

'Thankfully, all the papers were photocopied on one machine. I pulled out the hard disk from the photocopier hoping that you would be able to retrieve the data for me.'

'You said MIT, didn't you?'

'Yes. MIT.'

'We used to service their machines until a few months ago. They've changed their service providers now.'

'Oh my God. So are you saying you can't help?'

'I'm afraid you will have to go to your existing service providers. We will have to charge you if you want us to do anything. They might even do it for free.'

'Oh, you go ahead and charge us. We are running against time. If you are able to help me, I will definitely put in a word that you were there for us when we had an emergency and we should not have moved to another service provider. In any case, MIT isn't very happy with Sterling Automation.'

Merissa smiled. 'Let me see the hard disk.' The moment she asked him, he knew the job was done. Merissa opened the door behind her and went inside. She came back in five minutes. 'We will do it as an exception. It will be six hundred dollars. And we will print out all the pages for you. It will take us about half an hour to decrypt the data and then we should be able to print it out. You got lucky. Your photocopier was configured to save an image of every paper photocopied or printed on it.'

'Thanks a ton, Merissa! You have no idea what this means to me.'

Aditya waited at the reception while the service personnel

decrypted the hard disk. He had retained an interest in his previous profession and had kept track of the developments in the photocopier space. Sometime in 2002, the industry had made a giant leap, developing photocopiers with embedded hard disk drives which stored a digital image of every document copied or printed on it. Though some organizations had taken cognizance of it and put in certain data security and privacy measures, most companies hadn't thought of it. When he pulled out the hard disk drive, he was hoping MIT was not one of those institutions that had taken such measures and disabled this feature. His wish had come true.

After the phone call, Aditya had carefully examined the sticker of the maintenance firm on the photocopier and figured out that there was something beneath it. He had peeled off the sticker, only to find that it was stuck on top of the address of the previous service providers. He had thought of taking the hard disk to Sterling Automation at first, but expecting that the previous maintenance agency would be happier to be of assistance—keen as they would be to win the relationship back—he had taken a chance and come here.

While waiting at the reception he scanned a few magazines. There were a few old newspapers but they bored him. He fiddled with his iPhone. There were a few pictures of Cirisha: memories of their honeymoon came rushing back to him. He flipped through the pictures one by one till he arrived at the last one. He zoomed in on the image and read the email again—the email which Richard had sent Cirisha. The cryptic email. He read it again. And again. Trying to make sense of it. The image he had on his phone was of the second message. The one in which Richard had said that it was 'sent by mistake'. In the image he could also see the beginning of Cirisha's complaint about Shivinder's Dharavi factory to Richard. Cirisha had sent this image to Aditya's phone when they were both trying to crack open Richard's locker.

'Sir.' Aditya's string of thoughts was interrupted. It was Merissa. 'Do you want any other information to be printed out?'

'As in?'

'The file size, the time it was printed, the file name . . . Obviously there wouldn't be any file names for the photocopied files, but they would be there for the files whose printouts were fired from the computers.'

'That will be lovely. Thank you.'

'Sir.' Merissa nodded and went inside to give instructions, while Aditya went back to his phone.

He went over it line by line, word by word, letter by letter. He didn't want to miss anything in the email. He flipped the image and looked at the top of the page. And that's where he saw something.

The first mail containing the cryptic words was from Richard's MIT email ID. But the second mail was different. While it was from Richard's MIT email ID and was sent to Cirisha's ID, there was a small variance. A minor addition, which would not have caught a casual observer's eye. But Aditya wasn't one; instead, he was trying to spot contradictions everywhere. While sending the second email to Cirisha, Richard had also copied himself in on his personal Gmail address. Why would someone do that? Was that a normal thing to do if the first email was genuinely a mistake?

When you are information starved, any additional bit of it seems like a gold mine. Aditya's mind started working at a furious pace. 'If I were to send a message to someone by mistake, I would just forward the message to the same person and tell him that I had sent the message erroneously. Worst case, I would do a "reply all" and send it back to the same group, stating it was an error. I'd definitely not add another email ID to it,' he said to himself. 'There has to be a message in it. Surely Richard didn't add the second email ID without reason.'

'Sir, it will take another forty-five minutes,' Merissa's voice broke his trance.

'Is there an internet café nearby? Might as well do some work while I wait.'

'There is. Not the best of places, but functional. Adjacent to the third building to the right is a small lane. If you go down the lane, you will find a café on your right. It might be a little shady-looking but it is safe.'

It took him three minutes to walk down to the address Merissa had given him. There was no one else in the café at that time. He took the cabin towards the end with just a wall behind him.

He settled down on the chair and looked at the watch. He was expected back at Merissa's in thirty-five minutes. Not knowing where to begin, he googled the two cryptic codes but not the locker code. Google threw up nothing of significance. He tried various permutations and combinations. Nothing helped. He didn't know what to do. Just to give his mind a break, he logged into his email. Nothing of significance there either. After he left GB2, his email traffic had come down tremendously. No one felt the need to be in touch with him.

He logged off. The screen in front of him was the Gmail home screen. It asked for an ID and password. He was staring at the screen blankly when a brainwave struck. He looked at the image on his phone. Richard's personal email address was a Gmail ID. He keyed in the ID. From the same image he keyed in one of the codes, the third one from Richard's email. He moved the mouse to bring the cursor to the 'sign in' button and clicked. His breathing became heavy as he waited for the hourglass cursor to disappear.

71

12th June 2008

MIT, Boston

At the executive committee meeting, president Antonio's decisive casting vote went in favour of Cardoza. Deahl's book, *Staring Down the Barrel*, though not completely in violation of the university laws, was against their spirit.

'A provost is someone who has to have an impeccable track record. No one should be able to point a finger at his conduct. A provost is expected to take tricky decisions regarding the running of the institute, research, grants and so on and if there is a history to the provost's conduct, the same may hinder his ability to deliver on the job,' Antonio had said while announcing his decision to the group.

Cardoza was ecstatic. It was a dream come true. Wasn't this the reason why he had given the best years of his life to the institute?

'Thank you, Juan. I will do my best.'

The vice president of the HR team stepped up to the two of them. 'There is some paperwork to be completed, Dr Cardoza. If you would come up to our office tomorrow, we will do the needful. We plan to announce your appointment next week. A day before Gordon Meier relinquishes charge. Please keep it low-key. As a rule, no press interviews, no TV appointments till such time that the university releases the news officially.' Cardoza nodded. He was willing to wait. The job was his in any case.

It was a big blow to Deahl. The same Deahl who had held America spellbound with his book. Despite being unhappy, he accepted the verdict of the committee graciously, at least on the face of it.

72

12th June 2008

Internet café, Boston

After what seemed like an interminable wait, the words 'logging in richardavendon@gmail.com' appeared on the screen and then his inbox came into view. So the email ID and the password were bang on. Cirisha was right. Richard had not sent the password to her by mistake. There was a purpose to his email. The only way to know what it was, was to get into the inbox.

Richard's inbox too was just like him. Perfectly organized. Appropriately named folders made it easy for him. Aditya read through a few emails. Nothing out of the ordinary there. He spotted the email with the cryptic message.

He clicked on the draft email folder. All the emails in the folder were written on the same day—the day that he sent the email with the passwords to Cirisha.

He opened the draft email folder and read through. The first two lines of the email that he opened confirmed Aditya's fears. The trail that he was following was no red herring. Slowly and steadily, with fear in his heart and excitement in his head, Aditya read the first message in its entirety. He couldn't have imagined this in his wildest dreams. Sitting in that small 3-foot by 4-foot cabin, he was sweating. How much of this did Cirisha know?

Email one

Ahmed Siddiqui wanted to place fresh evidence in front of the panel to deny me my tenure. My worst fears came true that day. Despite my best efforts they found out about my relationship. Someone from the institute had complained to the provost about my liaison with Xerxes Abidjan. Xerxes was a student in the final term, though not in my department. I met him during his fencing classes. He sought me out to help him with his footwork.

As you know, the institute rules prohibit any kind of relationship between a student and faculty.

Only God knows that my conscience is clear and that I did not use my position of authority to get him to submit to my whims. We felt for each other. We had a relationship which was beyond any logic, any explanation. But I guess it did not go down well with some students. When I look back, someone could have felt aggrieved because I rated Xerxes higher and included him in the fencing team which participated in the inter-university men's fencing challenge held at Boston University. He deserved his place in the team purely on merit.

A clandestine investigation was launched. It did not have the institution's sanction. I know the rules. Any such investigation into any dalliance between a student and a faculty member needs a sign-off from the president, Juan Antonio, which is, almost always, not given. The normal practice is that the parties concerned are ticked off and they decide—institute or relationship. If someone had confronted us, we would have explained. Xerxes and I had decided that he would seek admission at Boston University at the end of the term so that we could be together without any worries.

Ahmed, who was in charge of the investigation, had someone trail me and gather evidence. I guess this was done because they were worried that in case the issue got discussed without evidence, James would use his influence and scuttle it.

A private detective would wait for hours below the Academic Block and trail me everywhere I went. They thought I wouldn't notice, but I am not an idiot. I guessed that something was wrong. I finally figured it out when I saw the same person walk into my interview and hand over a brown envelope to Ahmed. I didn't know what the contents of the envelope were, but realized that it had something to do with me. Pepped by the evidence, Ahmed wanted to nail me that day. Thankfully, James convinced everyone not to discuss the issue.

Twenty minutes after the interview, Michael called me. He was very disturbed. Apparently, Ahmed had dropped the envelope by mistake and while picking it up, Michael saw what it contained. He told me that Ahmed had foolproof evidence, largely photographic in nature, about my relationship with someone (he didn't know Xerxes as he had not met him). When I confessed to him about Xerxes, he confirmed the university's stance on it. It was what he told me next that got me paranoid. He said that if word got out, it could signal the end of my academic career not only in MIT but also across universities in the USA. A blacklisted academician is never hired by any university.

I didn't slog for a decade to give it all up. That's when I made up my mind. I went after Ahmed. James, who was to drop me till the metro station, dropped me off instead at the Massachusetts Turnpike about a mile from the university. I got down and waited for Ahmed to pass by. I requested him for a lift. An unsuspecting Ahmed allowed me to get into the car. When we were on a lonely stretch of road, flanked by woods on both sides, I took out the paperknife and stabbed him many, many times. He kept screaming and I kept stabbing till he could scream no more. I cleaned myself up. Cleaned the spot of anything that could be traced back to me. It was easy because I was wearing the fencing sabre glove. I made sure that the brown envelope was in my custody. By the time Ahmed's body was discovered, I was back home in the arms of Xerxes. I wish there had been another way, but I had no other option.

Aditya read the email thrice over. Richard? The one who killed Ahmed Siddiqui was Richard! And all along they thought Richard was the cleanest of the lot. How wrong they had been. And because it was a clandestine operation initiated by Siddiqui, no one knew about it, before or after the murder. And Richard was never investigated as a suspect.

Email two

Aditya looked at his watch. He was expected in the photocopier shop in fifteen minutes. But he didn't fret too much about it. It was just that he didn't want them to spend too much time looking at what they were printing out for him. But he couldn't stop himself from reading the next email.

Ahmed Siddiqui's killing played on my mind for a long, long time. Ending someone's life changed me in ways that I couldn't comprehend. It impacted me. I started getting distracted. I would stay at my workstation for hours together. Not talk to anyone. James noticed this change in me. He asked me to take some time off. I didn't want to. The year was crucial for me. If I didn't get my promotion soon, I would never get it. I have just turned forty.

Forty-five days after Ahmed's death, I got a call from Michael. He asked me to meet him. He said it was in connection with my tenure reconsideration. Just to make sure that no one saw us, I met him in his office at 9 p.m. Late at night. The Academic Block was normally deserted at that time. When I walked in, he was alone. Cirisha, you were back in India at that time. There was no one on that floor.

So Richard had wanted Cirisha to read this email. Either he had intended to send it to her or he had hoped that Cirisha would be able to decipher his cryptic message.

That day, Michael told me that the committee had upheld the earlier decision on my tenure. I would have to wait for one more year before I could be considered for my tenure again. I broke down. It was a big shock for me. He told me that my affair with Xerxes was one of the reasons, though he said he would never put it down in writing for it would impact my future in academia. He advised that I shouldn't create an issue about it, since it would harm my interests, more so because it involved my relationship with a student. His contention was that in case I did a song and dance, and James backed it, then there was a remote possibility that the committee's decision might get reversed. However, if that were to happen, the relationship between Xerxes and me would come into the public domain. And that would get me sacked. The institute rules were very clear in this regard. Even if I forced my way to a tenure, it would be short-lived. I was extremely upset. My mind, which was already burdened by the impulsive killing of Ahmed, couldn't take one more failure. I lost control. Michael helped me calm down. He made me sit down on his lounge chair and offered me a drink. I badly needed one. Michael was very understanding towards me and even dropped me home. I was touched by his actions that day.

Aditya was surprised at Cardoza's gesture. Everyone knew that Cardoza hated Deahl to the core. The feeling was mutual. Yet he made sure that one of Deahl's team members was taken care of at a difficult time. He was happy that Cirisha had been in Cardoza's team and not Deahl's.

At that very moment a pop-up appeared on his screen. 'You have two minutes of internet usage left. Do you wish to continue?'

73

12th June 2008, same time

MIT, Boston

Windle's car screeched to a halt in front of the office of the MIT chief of police. He got down from the car and walked straight into the cabin of Chief Nelius. They shook hands. The warmth was missing. At one point of time, they had been very close to each other, working for the same boss in the New York City Police Department. However, over time they had fallen apart. Career advancement and professional rivalry had played the villain here too. Nelius was cold but professional in his dealings with Windle.

'What can I do for you, lieutenant?'

'The forensic report of the campus firing has come in, chief.'

'I thought it came a long time ago. Didn't it?'

'No. Based on the depositions of Gordon Meier and Michael Cardoza, and the fact that Richard Avendon owned the weapon, the coroner, Simen Munter, and the jury felt that forensic investigation might not be required. As per Massachusetts state law, if the victim is over forty years of age and there is no reason to suspect foul play, the coroner can waive the requirement for an inquest. This was an open-and-shut case. We had seized the murder weapon and also captured the site data. We had no reason to pursue it further.'

'Yes. It was an open-and-shut case, I remember. That's why the coroner had waived the need for an inquest and an investigation by a forensic pathologist,' Nelius declared nonchalantly.

'Well, not if you were to go by what I have here.'

'Is that right? Who approved the reopening?'

'Based on certain additional information that we had, and subsequent to Cirisha Narayanan's death, we approached the coroner, who gave his sanction for the investigation.'

'It would have been nicer, though, had I been kept in the loop. We were handling the initial leg of the investigation, weren't we, lieutenant?' There was a look of frustration in his eyes. Much to Windle's relief, Nelius did not dwell on the point. 'Now that it has been done, what does it say? Does it confirm what we all know or are there any surprises?'

'Surprises! You need to read this, chief, before we talk any further.' He pulled out a file from the bunch of papers he was carrying and handed it over.

Nelius began reading it. Years in law enforcement had taught him to maintain a poker face when surprised or shocked, but this time his eyes gave his changing mood away.

Nelius looked up. 'Holy shit! You can't be serious about this!'

'That's why I came to you first. To figure out what we should do next.'

'This is terrible. We need to talk to the president.'

74

12th June 2008

Internet café, Boston

Aditya hurriedly pressed the 'yes' button. His internet access was extended by thirty minutes. He continued reading Richard's email.

That was just the beginning. Michael Cardoza's interactions with me began to increase. He would talk to me almost every day. Call me to his workplace when no one was around and talk about all and sundry.

It was around this time that James took on the project on the Second Amendment. Irrespective of what name he calls the project by, it was a gun control vs gun rights research, with a presupposed result. Michael was very upset that James had taken up something that he had declined. The attention that James was receiving probably disturbed him more.

My relationship with James started going through a turbulent phase. He was not happy with my work. I was the only person in his team who questioned his principles. He wanted the team to get him the research data, manipulated in the manner that the sponsors wanted. Everyone else obliged. I didn't. We were going through an intense data-gathering phase.

As a part of the data-accumulation process, we wanted to interview felons and understand if they would have committed the crimes had guns not been available. I fixed up meetings, took permissions from the law enforcers to interview prison inmates, even went ahead and interviewed them in three state prisons—Vermont, Florida and Phoenix. The data from these interviews suggested something which was very different from the result that James wanted. He was not happy about it. Rather than tweak his research results, he calmly took me out of the data-gathering process, and put Caroline and Philip in charge. They were two associates completely in awe of him. He could play them like a puppeteer.

They went through the process of data gathering. The papers came to me for my analysis. They couldn't have done it any other way, else it would have attracted attention. When I saw the data, I was surprised. The names of felons who were interviewed in Boston differed from the names I had picked during my interaction with the Boston Police Department. This got me curious. I asked around. That's when I figured out that while they were doing the interviews in most of the prisons, the responses were being fudged and altered in our offices. James was preparing a backup paper in case someone questioned his survey or wanted to tally it with the raw data. So along with Caroline and Philip, he created the entire data. James even got the research for the three centres where I had done the prison interviews done again. When I saw it, I put my foot down. I refused to change the findings for the three centres that I had researched. James was unhappy but he didn't say anything. But when Staring Down the Barrel came out, I was surprised. James had manipulated the data for Vermont, Florida and Phoenix too and brought it in line with what the research demanded. I confronted Caroline and Philip and asked them for the research papers for these three centres. They only smiled in response. Didn't say a word. It was then that I actually realized the extent to which the data had been compromised.

Michael's conduct on the other hand was very statesmanlike. He told me how his morals and values had prevented him from taking up the research. My respect for him only grew. We were very comfortable with each other. No one knew about this. Not even you.

The day James knocked me off the data-gathering responsibility, I was very upset. I shared my frustration with Michael. He lent a sympathetic ear. And then, on the pretext of helping me relax, he came up to me, stood behind the lounge chair and comforted me by massaging my shoulders. There was a long period of silence. That's when he said, 'You have seen worse times, Richard. This is nothing compared to the trauma you went through when you killed Ahmed.'

I turned towards him as if I had been stung by something.

'You should not have killed Ahmed. He was a good friend of mine.' When he said this, I didn't know how to react. Michael had a weird look in his eyes. Couldn't make out if it was anger or something else. 'I know everything about you, Richard,' he said. 'You and Xerxes. You and Ahmed.'

I looked at him in desperation. I was exposed. If anyone else got to know of this, I would be dead meat.

'Don't worry, Richard,' Michael reassured me. 'Ahmed's is a closed story. When the chief of MIT Police met me the day after the accident, I did not tell him that I saw you taking a lift from Ahmed and getting into his car that evening after the tenure interview. I told him that it could have been a regular case of carjacking. Or maybe passion killing. Because Ahmed was a colourful man, you see. Interesting tastes.' And he smiled. It was then that it struck me. It was not anger that I saw in his eyes. It was something more. It was lust. He wanted me.

'If you are with me, Richard, no one can deny you your tenure next year. I will make sure it happens,' he said and his hands slid down my shirt. My body responded to his touch. He saw it as a green signal. That was the first time we made out. In his cabin. On the lounge chair, at 9.30 at night.

After that Michael was quite helpful. He once asked me if I had ever experienced holding a gun in my hand. Till that day, I had never ever held a gun. He felt that since I was doing research for the NRA, I must experience this feeling. He was, for some strange

reason, also worried about my safety. He was of the view that the
NRA might suddenly turn against me if it found out about my
attitude towards James's research. Michael took me to a gun dealer
he knew in Riverdale, forty miles from Chicago. We had gone there
for a Social Psychology conference. James couldn't go and had sent
me in his place. I was surprised at Michael's contacts. The dealer
took some identity documents and said that he would deliver it
within the week. I don't know if the gun was ever delivered. I
reminded Michael a few times. He said he would speak to the gun
dealer and follow it up but that never happened.

My relationship with Michael stayed in the closet. Michael had
a family to take care of. He also had a reputation to protect. I had
a boss from whom I had to hide this fact.

Once Michael got what he wanted, he started avoiding all
discussions regarding my tenure. Maybe I was becoming a bit of a
pest. James too was no different. Non-committal.

Whenever I would raise the issue of my tenure with either
of them, they would brush it off. I was getting restless at their
indifference. Neither of them was serious about my tenure. James
kept promising, while Michael kept reassuring. They kept saying
that it would happen in due course. I figured the best way out of
this was to make sure that I had their Achilles' heels in my control.
I clandestinely took pictures of Michael and me. I just wanted
insurance for a rainy day. In any case, he was getting what he
wanted from me.

The day I told Michael about this, he was furious. He screamed
at me, even slapped me. It pained, but I didn't react. And finally
when he settled down, he asked me if I trusted him. I told him that
I didn't. From that day on, Michael became more careful in his
dealings with me.

And then James's book came out. I could make out that Michael
didn't like the attention that James was getting. I had already
mentioned to him that the research had been fudged to suit the
end result. When Michael got to know that I had the raw data

with me, he asked for a copy. He wanted to use me in his game of upmanship against James. The data would have helped him prove that James was a spineless academician paid for by the NRA.

I never gave those papers to Michael. I was not an idiot. The day I would give them to him, my value, as far as Michael was concerned, would evaporate.

The next round of applications for tenure appointments was invited. I applied. Michael promised to make sure that my appointment went through. Well, he didn't have a choice. James for the first time threw his hands up. He had enough problems of his own to deal with at that time. Staring Down the Barrel was becoming big. It needed his time and attention. I was upset. After all, it was not for nothing that I tolerated him and his idiosyncrasies for close to a decade. I have told him that if he doesn't help me out this time and make sure that my tenure goes through, I will make public the raw research data that I have in my custody. It is a matter of life and death. It took a lot of courage to do that. Failure to get tenure this time will mean me getting the boot from MIT.

Last night, I was with Michael. His wife was out of town. When I was in bed with Michael, his phone rang. The phone was on my side of the bed. It was from James. Michael never ever spoke to James unless forced to, even when they came face-to-face. Why would James call him at 1 a.m.? It set me thinking. Michael brushed off my question and stepped out to the washroom. I knew he was hiding something. Before he could come back, I called Xerxes's internet phone from Michael's landline and let it stay connected. And then when he returned, I headed to the washroom to clean up. As expected, Michael quickly called James. I managed to record Michael's side of the conversation on Xerxes's answering machine.

When I heard the conversation later, I could figure out that these two monsters—Michael and James—had got together to fix me. Both know about the photos and the raw data in my custody. I am in a very difficult situation and don't know what to do.

I am not giving myself too much importance, but James needs

the research data back from me and Michael needs the pictures. These guys will go to any extent to protect their reputations and careers. I am scared. And that's why I am writing this email, that too from a computer I clandestinely managed to get access to by sweet-talking a salesgirl at BestBuy. I am sure my office emails, office telephone, computers and even mobile phones will be under surveillance. I just hope no one gets to see this but you, just in case something happens to me. You have the passwords. I hope you understand the implicit message in my previous email. I am also leaving the raw research data gathered by James's team and copies of the images of me and Michael in my locker, number C-37, in the duPont Center. I don't know what will happen to me, but you take care.

In case all goes well in the tenure, obviously you may not be reading this. For then, all that I have done and compromised will have been worth the effort. But I am worried. Worried for myself. I am stuck between two biggies who will do anything to protect their careers, their families and their reputation.

After his clear-headed investigations that got him to this point, logic deserted Aditya once again. His mind went numb. It could only mean one thing. Richard did not take his own life. He was killed. Cirisha found out, she was silenced. Narayanan came in the way of their search and was almost eliminated. And poor Shivinder tried to help Aditya and got killed.

There was only one way out of this for him.

75

12th June 2008

MIT, Boston

Antonio was not in his office when Chief Nelius and Lieutenant Windle walked in. The two of them made themselves comfortable in the conference room adjoining the president's cabin. They began discussing the forensic report. 'It's very clear, chief. The gun from which shots were fired was bought in Richard's name. It's a licensed weapon bought from a gun store in Riverdale.'

'So the weapon is his, the fingerprints on it are his. The DNA traces all point to Richard as the perpetrator of the crime.'

'Yes. But as you saw in the forensic report, he was not the one who fired the gun. The gun was placed in his hand. Had he fired the shots, there would have been residue under his fingernails. Residual explosive waste.'

'The blood on the scene and on his fingers had muddied the fingernails and we couldn't make that out on visual examination. So all of you, including the coroner, were quick to assume the sequence of events,' Nelius argued.

'The more critical point to be noted is that the panellists were seated on the podium and Richard was sitting in front of them. The bullets too seem to have come from the front. From the point where Richard was seated.'

'Yes. Richard's gun, bullets fired from the point where Richard was sitting . . . Everything points to the fact that Richard killed everyone.'

'True. The last piece of evidence that the forensic report now lays out clears the air. Doesn't it?'

'I saw that. It's too damning.'

'Chief, Richard had been shot from close quarters. The gun had been held to his head and fired. So everyone assumed suicide.' Windle pulled out his gun and held it to his head. 'Look. If I were to shoot myself in the temple, the bullet would enter here'—and he pointed to the right temple. 'And would normally exit here'—he moved his right hand to his left temple. 'When you have a gun in your hand and shoot yourself, the gun normally has a small tilt upwards and hence the trajectory of the bullet would either be horizontal or marginally upwards. The exit point of the bullet would always be at a level higher than the entry point. At best at the same level.'

'That's obvious.'

'Strangely, in the case of Richard, the bullet entered through his right temple and exited below the ear on his left. The difference in height at the bullet's entry and exit points is two and a half inches. And this can only happen if someone else fired the bullet at the seated victim.'

'Or if Richard was standing and the person who fired the bullet was much taller than him,' Nelius interrupted.

'Yes. That's right. Michael Cardoza is six foot three, while Richard was a little over five feet. Michael most likely fired at a seated Richard. Standing or sitting . . . it doesn't matter. What's of importance is the fact that Richard did not kill himself. Someone else did. And that someone else can only be Michael Cardoza. We of course have to figure out why he did that. What was the motive? This, to me, defies all logic. The trajectory of the lone bullet which missed its mark and hit the board points to the fact that the gun was held by someone standing and the gun level was over five feet above the floor, at the barest minimum. It is most likely that the gun was fired by someone more than six feet tall.'

'We should not have waived the forensic investigation at that time. We took them at their face value. And since Michael Cardoza too was injured, we assumed he was speaking the truth. What a game he played!' Nelius lamented.

And at that very instant, Windle's phone rang.

'Lieutenant, it's me. Aditya.'

'I'm very busy, Aditya. Can this wait?'

'It can't. It's crucial. I called to tell you that Michael Cardoza and James Deahl have a role to play in the killing of Richard and the three other faculty members, and may have a hand in the killings of Cirisha and Shivinder, and the assault on Narayanan.' Aditya then told him the entire story that he had uncovered in the emails.

'Where are you now? I'm coming to get you.'

'No, don't. I will head to the institute. You come there if possible. I don't want to be out in the open.'

'I am already there. In Antonio's cabin. You want me to send a police car to pick you up?'

'No. I will be there in an hour.' And he hung up.

76

12th June 2008, evening

Boston

It was at 6 p.m. that the president returned from his meetings. He walked into his room only to be told by his secretary that he had visitors. He didn't know Windle well, but he knew enough to understand that if the chief of MIT Police had been waiting for him that long, it had to be serious.

'Good evening, gentlemen. What can I do for you?' Obviously something was wrong.

'We have come here to take your permission,' said the chief.

'Permission for what?'

Finding the chief hesitant, Windle took the initiative.

'To detain Michael Cardoza.'

Antonio didn't react. Windle assumed that he hadn't really understood what was happening.

'You might want to take a look at this. There could be another big name involved too. But we will wait till we have enough evidence against him.' Windle handed over the forensic report to Antonio, who looked at it and handed it back. 'It might be better if you explain it to me.'

After the chief narrated the sequence of events, Antonio, in a feeble voice asked, 'Who else is involved?' It was as if someone had pulled the carpet from under his feet.

'We believe James Deahl was the mastermind of the entire act and had a motive to kill Cirisha and the others,' Aditya said as he walked in. The president recognized him and Windle offered to explain, 'I knew he was coming. I requested your secretary to allow him to come in.'

Aditya continued from where he had left off. 'James was as much involved in the conspiracy as Michael was. They were partners in crime. Two of your most fierce and competitive members of the academia came together to silence someone who had them by the scruff of their necks. They proved to the world that if two academic powerhouses come together, their combined ambition and intellect make them unstoppable.'

'Aditya,' Antonio began. 'I understand your grief at losing someone close to you. But we cannot put down a senior member of our faculty just because you strongly feel so.'

'It's not about what I feel, sir. Let me show you what I have. May I request you for access to a computer? I can show you what I mean.'

Antonio led Aditya to his computer and logged in. Aditya sat down on Antonio's seat, swung towards the computer and started working his way around. In forty-five seconds he was ready. 'Here we go.' Everyone looked at him and gathered around the computer. He clicked something on the screen and a hiss came up on the computer speakers. Aditya cranked up the audio.

The noise of a toilet flush could now be heard in the president's room. It came from his computer speakers. Antonio looked at Windle, who shrugged his shoulders.

A door opened and closed in the distance. Antonio turned towards Aditya and the computer. That's where the sound came from.

The hiss continued. Then someone spoke.

'*I need to use the washroom. Will be back in a minute.*'

'*Hmm,*' someone responded.

And then the silence returned. There was no sound for a while until a whisper could be heard. Aditya increased the speaker volume a bit more.

'*What happened? Why did you call now? This late at night?*'

A pause.

'*Tell me quickly. Richard is here but is out of the room now.*'

A longer pause.

'*I'm trying my best to get the research papers from him.*'

Silence.

'*He is not telling me where they are. The bastard even has the photos.*'

No noise.

'*What did he tell Cirisha?*'

Silence.

'*Hmm . . . Richard will prove to be a pain, James.*'

A pause. The only noise audible was the hiss.

'*It's with me. Got it last month itself. Picked it up from Riverdale.*'

Silence.

'*How? How did I get it? I told you. He had given a letter authorizing the gun to be handed over to me.*'

Silence.

'*No, no. I don't need any help from your NRA contacts to get it delivered. It's done.*'

A long pause.

'*I don't understand.*'

Silence.

'*You want me to do it during the interview?*'

Silence, interspersed with heavy breathing.

'*I understand that's our best chance of getting him out of the way. But what if it goes wrong?*'

Silence again.

'*Bullshit!*' The voice went up and, suddenly, realizing that it would be heard, dropped to a whisper. '*I don't think I am ready to do it yet.*'

The sound of a door opening interrupted the pause.

'*OK, I will talk later. He is coming out.*'

There was a lengthy pause. And then someone else's voice came on the line.

'*I'm going to get myself something to eat. What about you?*'

'*Nothing. Tell me what you want. I will get it from the kitchen. You may not be able to find it, Richard.*'

'*Cool.*'

And then the line went silent. It was the end of the conversation.

'What the hell was that?' The president was shocked at what he had just heard. He recognized the voice.

'That's the conversation between Michael Cardoza and James Deahl a few days before Richard's tenure interview. That's only Michael's side of the conversation, though. You can make out that he was talking to James. The person who came in at the end was Richard.'

'And how did you get it?' Antonio didn't know what to believe any more.

'Richard was in a physical relationship with Michael. Emotional too? I can't say. That night he was with Michael when Michael got a call from James. It was at 1 a.m. Richard heard Michael's phone ring and was surprised to see that the call was from James at that time of the night. Michael and James wouldn't speak to each other even if they were alone in a room. He suspected something fishy. When Michael went to the washroom to clean up after a session in bed, Richard dialled Xerxes's telephone number, knowing very well that Xerxes was somewhere in eastern Africa at the time. The call went to Xerxes's answering machine. Xerxes was a tech geek. His CallWave answering machine was wired to email the voice message to his preconfigured inbox. Richard left the call on and went to the washroom when Michael came out. The moment the bathroom door clicked shut, Michael returned James's call. At 1.25 a.m., Michael's side of the conversation got recorded on Xerxes's answering machine, which Xerxes received as an email attachment in his inbox. He forwarded the message to Richard with a simple message from his side: "*WTF?*"'

'No. This can't be true.' It was Antonio. He couldn't believe what he was hearing.

'Why would Richard call from Michael's line and that too to Xerxes, knowing fully well that Xerxes would freak out on hearing such a message? Though there was nothing which would suggest a relationship between Michael and Richard in that conversation, the timing of the message would be enough to get him concerned.' Windle's investigative mind was at work.

'Richard suspected that he was under surveillance. Had he called Xerxes's line from his mobile and left it on, he ran the risk of it being intercepted. He was scared. He probably wouldn't have wanted them to know that he suspected Michael and James had joined hands. Since the call went from Michael's landline, it didn't get intercepted. If we check Michael's call records for this date, we will be able to confirm both these calls—from the mobile to James and from the landline to Xerxes.'

'How do you know all this?'

Aditya turned the screen towards them to show the two emails in Richard's draft folder. The email from Xerxes with the attached conversation was in Richard's inbox. 'See the link at the bottom of the email connecting to the CallWave homepage. It gives you details of how this answering machine works. I read that up on my way here.'

He then narrated everything that Richard had mentioned in his emails. Everything from Siddiqui's murder, to the details of Deahl's misdeeds in the research, to Cardoza's successful attempt at seducing him, to his confession of trying to arm-twist the two of them to give him his tenure.

'So, when cornered, Cardoza and Deahl conspired to get rid of Richard. The day of his interview, Cardoza took advantage of the isolated section and shot Richard and the three panellists dead. The forensic report is very clear in this regard,' Nelius added.

'The three other faculty were excellent cover for Cardoza. Everything logically pointed towards Richard and everyone assumed that it was a frustrated Richard who was the perpetrator of the carnage. A detailed investigation at that time would have revealed more, but we got carried away,' Windle admitted.

'Also, one must not forget that Michael was great with guns because of his experience in Vietnam but he made a big song and dance about his anti-gun stand because of the death and destruction that he saw first-hand at war. It suited us to believe that the carnage was the result of the failed career ambitions of a frustrated academician. We were blinded by all the sympathy,' a crestfallen Antonio confessed.

'James wiped out the data from Richard's iMac. He knew Richard was not coming back. I am guessing that James and Michael would have assumed that the pictures and the research data would be traced if they were in Richard's computer.' Aditya continued the revelation.

'Office records show that he had entered his office that morning around the time that the computer was wiped clean. Hence the assumption that since Richard had planned to kill everyone, he wiped out all the data from his iMac seems quite rational. Doesn't it, lieutenant?' Nelius stepped into the conversation.

'No, he didn't,' Aditya countered. 'I cannot prove this. But that morning, Cirisha met him as she was entering the block. He threw his card at her, requesting her to swipe it and sign him in. Cirisha told me this. He didn't even get to his workstation that day.'

'Wait,' Windle stepped in. He opened his file and looked at a few papers. 'The day he was killed, at the time he was swiped in, there were only two other people who had come in. Cirisha and James Deahl. In fact, the next swipe in was only after forty-five minutes and that was Louisa. No one else. Cirisha was on a lower floor. On the morning of the carnage, James was the only person on the second floor. So it has to be James who cleaned out Richard's computer.'

'Cirisha got stuck in the scheme of things because she figured out that the Boston prison data was fudged. Michael played her on till he realized that she was getting too close for comfort about the raw data.' When Aditya said this, Windle looked around. Antonio had a blank look on his face. Quickly, he brought him up to speed with the research data saga.

'But that still doesn't explain why she was killed and who killed her. She didn't know about the images either.'

'It was Michael.' Aditya was firm in his response. There was no doubt in his mind.

'How can you be so sure?'

'Lieutenant Windle, the day Cirisha died, she entered the building at 5.10 a.m. That's what your records show, right?'

'Yes. For the first time that morning, she entered at 5.10 a.m. Presumably using Richard Avendon's access card.'

'Yes. She photocopied all the papers, around a thousand of them, on the high-speed Xerox photocopier from 5.14 a.m. to 6.50 a.m.' He reached into his backpack and pulled out a hefty bundle of papers. 'Here'—he extended the pages towards Windle and continued—'these are the papers she photocopied. I extracted them from the hard disk. The time of printing is embedded at the bottom right-hand corner. The date is 5th June, 05:10 hours onwards. The last photocopy is around 06:53 hours.'

'Hard disk?' When Antonio asked him this question, Aditya requested that they continue their discussion in Cirisha's room. By then, Meier had joined them. The five of them in two cars headed to the Academic Block, which was hardly half a mile away. En route, Antonio brought Meier up to speed with the developments.

'We nearly made him the provost, Juan,' Meier lamented.

Once they were in Cirisha's room, Aditya walked up to the Xerox machine, tapped it and continued. 'The Xerox machine that you have here is an advanced one. It has a built-in hard disk. An impression of everything that gets copied or printed on this machine gets embedded on the hard disk. This is the default option. One can manually modify it, but nobody does. Strangely, 80 per cent of photocopier users are not even aware of the risks this poses. I was hoping that MIT didn't fall into the balance 20 per cent when I chanced upon this machine in the morning today. I got lucky. MIT hadn't changed the default configuration.' Seeing the amazed faces around him, he explained that he used to be a Xerox engineer at the very start of his career.

'So these were the papers Shivinder found in the duPont Center locker,' Windle remarked.

'Yes, copies of those. Only Cirisha knew about the locker apart from me and the photocopies were found in the locker by Shivinder. So she must have kept them there. When she exited the Academic Block the first time, she would have headed to the duPont Center to Richard's locker.'

Windle took a deep breath and quickly explained to Antonio and the others who Shivinder was, then turned towards Aditya and said, 'Let's move on. I am still wondering why she entered the Academic Block twice after. At 7.14 and 7.39 a.m.'

'Lieutenant,' Aditya said, 'remember what Shivinder told us? Apart from the photocopies, he found a USB drive in the locker.'

'Yes.'

'When Cirisha and I took the papers out of the locker, we didn't see the pendrive. Perhaps we didn't check the locker carefully enough. When Cirisha went there again to keep the photocopies, she would have found the USB drive and, curious to know what it contained, she would have come back to the Academic Block.'

'That is an assumption,' Nelius interrupted him.

'Yes. It's an educated guess. A guess corroborated by the fact that at 7.14 a.m. she re-entered the Academic Block. At 7.22 a.m. she printed these six images from the removable drive on her iMac . . . the pendrive.' Aditya handed over six sheets to Windle. 'Look at the bottom right-hand corner. It has the file name. It says /Volumes/Richardavendon/Michael one, Michael two and so on. Which can only mean that it got printed from a pendrive, named as Richardavendon.'

The expression on Antonio's face changed completely when he saw the pictures. Meier's hand went up and covered his mouth. 'Oh my God!' he exclaimed. 'Jesus Christ!'

'These were the pictures which Richard had taken of himself and Michael in bed. Remember, in the email I showed you just now, Richard says that he has left the pictures in a pendrive in the duPont Center locker. These could only have come from there.'

Antonio looked up. 'Who all have seen this? Apart from the people who are dead, it's me, now all of you and, of course, Michael Cardoza.'

'You think Michael has seen this?' Nelius interjected again.

'Yes, he has. When Cirisha came back and saw these pictures, she printed a copy of these because she wanted to confront Michael with the images. She adored Michael. If there was anyone in academia who could have been God, it was Michael Cardoza. She had that much faith in him. I know she would have been devastated at this. She then called Michael.'

'We had checked her mobile call records and even scanned her workstation extension for calls made. Neither indicated that she had called anyone that morning. We can recheck that,' Windle said.

'That may not be necessary, lieutenant,' Aditya said as he walked to the Xerox machine. He picked up the phone on Cirisha's colleague's workstation, the one adjacent to the Xerox machine. With his left hand he pressed a button and started reading out from the instrument display.

'Redial 1: dated this morning at 9.42 a.m. To Lieutenant Windle. I made this call. Disconnected before it could go through because I was not sure of what to do.' He looked down towards the phone and pressed the button with the word 'next'.

'Redial 2: dated this morning at 9.41 a.m. To . . .' and he stopped. He drew a deep breath and continued, 'It was me. While trying to call Lieutenant Windle, I had pressed redial by mistake. By the time I could figure out a way to cancel the call, it connected. Thankfully, I disconnected before anyone answered the call.' Carefully avoiding naming whom the redial had led to, he pressed the 'next' button again.

'Redial 3: dated 5th June, 7.26 a.m.' He pressed the speaker phone button.

The phone went into dial mode and started ringing. After four rings the phone was picked up. 'Hello.' Antonio's eyes went round, he looked at Meier. 'Hello.' The voice crackled on the speaker phone. 'Hello. Michael Cardoza. Hello . . . Can you hear me?'

Aditya disconnected the call. 'She called him from the phone closest to the Xerox machine. The last of the printouts was printed at 7.25 in the morning. She picked up the printouts, was shocked by the images and, in an unstable frame of mind, called Michael. We only checked her extension and her mobile number for calls made. I figured out that Michael was involved in some manner when this morning I erroneously pressed the redial button while trying to call you and the call went to Michael. I hung up. Michael thought he had missed a call and called back. I fabricated a cock and bull story that I was a service executive for the Xerox machine and disconnected the line. Before the line went off, a lady asked, "Who was it, Michael?" That's when I realized it was Michael and that he had been called from this line earlier. Just out of curiosity I checked. Michael had been called on the morning of the day Cirisha died. I had no clue why she called him, till I saw all this,' Aditya reasoned, pointing towards the documents that Merissa had given him.

'We need to take Michael into custody right away,' Windle looked at Nelius and declared.

'There is one last chapter to the story, lieutenant,' Aditya stopped him.

'At 7.29 a.m. Cirisha exits the Academic Block and heads to the duPont Center. She keeps the pendrive in the locker and comes back to her block. This explains the third entry. For some strange reason the Academic Block does not have CCTVs.'

'Yes, James and Michael had led the crusade against CCTVs in the Academic Block. The only time I had seen them agree on something. In the interest of privacy, we had disconnected the Academic Block CCTVs,' Antonio volunteered.

'The duPont Center is a new building. I had seen the cameras myself. If we check the CCTVs there, we might be able to get a confirmation on what we have thus far assumed.'

'Can you get that done, chief? Now?' When Windle asked him, Nelius quietly walked out of the room and pulled out his phone. The next minute, he was back in the room. 'Fifteen minutes. We will have it here.'

'At 7.46 a.m., Michael Cardoza comes in. Swipe card records show that he came in at that time. He meets Cirisha. Cirisha confronts him. What transpired? No one knows. Only Michael can tell us.'

'Correct.'

'Cirisha exited the building one last time at 8.05 a.m. She must have been extremely disturbed. I am completely sure that she would have threatened to expose Michael. Not because she was against same-sex relationships. She must have realized that Richard left all this for her to see because he was probably being coerced into a relationship by somebody who had used his position to get leverage. In that very combustible state of mind, she must have driven towards Boston Public Garden at a high speed. The speeding ticket, which helped us get to the bottom of this, must have been a result of that. Our trail stops there. We don't know what happened from there on.'

There was a knock on the door and Louisa walked in.

'There's a fax for you, Lieutenant Windle. It's come from the president's office.' She had a curious look on her face.

'Thank you.' Windle stepped forward and took the fax from her. He looked at it intently, eyes screwed up, indicating that he was trying to read something in small font. 'I think we have an answer here. Our trail does not end.'

'Can you please be more specific, lieutenant?' Meier said impatiently.

'This is a list of all vehicles that were snapped for overspeeding by the pilot traffic cameras within five minutes of Cirisha's car being flashed. The car which passes the spot fifteen seconds after Cirisha's is owned by someone called Stephanie.' He looked up and, after a pause, added, 'Stephanie Cardoza.'

'Michael's wife!' Antonio exclaimed. 'Steffie.'

'In all probability driven by Michael himself. Assuming that it was Michael driving it, our story becomes clear from here on. Michael followed Cirisha to the Boston Public Garden. He would probably have tried to explain his point of view. Cirisha, being bullheaded, would have refused to see reason.' Aditya volunteered to complete the story. 'Actually, could there have been a reasonable explanation for what Michael did? And when Cirisha didn't listen to him, at an opportune moment, he must have killed her.'

'The post-mortem report of Cirisha will tell us what happened. Initial reports suspect it to be cardiac arrest.' It was Nelius.

'The toxicology tests which are expected tomorrow will give us a better picture. But what we know as of now is good enough to take Michael Cardoza and James Deahl into custody. We do have an airtight case against Cardoza for the killing of Richard Avendon and the others.'

'If we take him into custody, he will sing like a canary,' Nelius stepped in again. He was upset that something like this had happened under his watch.

'Yes. This also explains the other murders,' Aditya continued. 'From Cirisha's car, Michael finds the raw data and the printout of the images, but not the pendrive. He takes help from James to trace the images. The research papers he got from Cirisha would have given him enough leverage on James and, of course, the sponsors, the NRA.'

'The same pendrive which Cirisha left in the locker, which Shivinder found. When Shivinder got killed, they got what they wanted. The only person who knew far more than what he should have known, was you, Aditya. Which is why they were coming after you.' Windle completed the rest of the story.

Antonio finally picked up the document that Windle had given him and looked at it. He had already signed it. It had one name on it—Michael Cardoza. He pulled out a Mont Blanc from his pocket, wrote down something on the document and handed it over to Windle. 'Please do it in a manner that does not impact the reputation of the university,' he said. Windle looked at the document. The president had added Deahl's name and authorized action against him too.

The same evening, Cardoza was taken into custody from his residence in Watertown, twenty miles from the university. Word spread like wildfire. MIT was agog with stories of how a man who almost became a provost had been arrested for multiple murders.

When Lucier heard about Cardoza's arrest, he called Deahl. 'We could be in a spot of bother here, James.'

'Everything that Michael could have used against us is safely stashed away. The original research papers are with us. Michael had picked them up from Cirisha's car.'

'I know, we traded the pendrive in return for the papers. Nalin had bought it off the sacked Snuggles CEO before he was bumped off. In fact, if Michael decides to sing, we have enough to embarrass him. But that's not the problem, James.'

'What is it that is bothering you, then?'

'Too much of negativity around the whole issue, James. It's suddenly become difficult to deal with it. We should have been careful with the team. In life, it's not bad to be ambitious. It's criminal to have a team which always dreams of personal glory. Desperate for success. When their aspirations are not in sync with what we need from them, it leads to trouble. Richard was the guy who should not have been on your team in the first place. He was a guy ready to sell his soul for his tenure. You failed the first lesson of leadership. You failed to select a team which would have helped you deliver.'

'What do you mean, Lucier? Everything we did had your sanction.'

'Well, that's the way it was and that's the way it will be . . . unfortunately.'

'Pardon me?'

At that very instant there was a knock on the door. 'Someone at the door. Let me call you back.'

'Well, I am holding. We need to complete what we started, James. You attend to the door first.'

Deahl walked up to the door and opened it. 'How may I help you?'

'May we come in and speak?' There were two men in suits. 'We are from the special investigation team.'

'What's it about? And may I see your badges, please?'

~

Late at night when a team of officers from the homicide department of Boston Police landed up at the residence of James Deahl to take him into custody, they found his body sprawled on the living room floor. Blood from his temple had oozed on to the carpet and dried up. He seemed to have shot himself—or perhaps been shot—hours ago.

77

The next few years

Meier remained the provost. Antonio convinced him to continue till the end of his term and called off the selection process. It was a blessing that MIT had not officially announced the appointment of Cardoza as the new provost.

The basic toxicology screening for opiates, cocaine and carbon monoxide came back negative for Cirisha. It had been initially declared that she had died of a cardiac arrest and subsequent seizure on account of excessive running in an agitated state. It had been compounded by her extremely low blood sugar at the time of her death. She had been on medication for chronic diabetes, a hereditary problem, and had not eaten anything in the twelve hours preceding her death. In the circumstances, the cardiac arrest had proved fatal.

However, given the chronology of events leading to her death, Windle had pushed the coroner to agree to a more expansive investigation. A detailed autopsy revealed the possibility of death due to arterial embolism: gas bubbles in the bloodstream, leading to cardiac arrest or stroke. Strangely, in the first autopsy, once cardiac arrest had been established as the reason for the death, a few obvious signs had been missed. Minor indentations—divots just above her left breast, where doctors normally place their stethoscopes to check the heartbeat—had been overlooked. The divots indicated that Cirisha had been injected with something straight into her heart which caused it to stop beating. When the results of the pre-autopsy computed tomography were seen in conjunction with the results of the aspirometer analysis of the air originating from the heart ventricles, it was concluded that Cirisha had died as a result of an injection of 20–30 ml of air directly into the right ventricle of her heart. A clear case of homicide.

How and when the air was injected remained a mystery till the day Cardoza confessed. Getting Cardoza to confess was not easy. As expected, he initially denied everything. However, when confronted with the facts, the recording of the conversation with Deahl, the deposition of the shop owner in Riverdale identifying him as having accompanied Richard and taken delivery of the gun, a CCTV grab of Richard and him outside the gun trade fair in Riverdale, the access control details of the Academic Block and, most importantly, the forensic report of the crime scene, he didn't have much to say. The courts convicted him for the ghastly murders of Richard Avendon, Henry Liddell, Sandy Gustavo and Frederick Lobo, and awarded him a thirty-five-year sentence. He knew that he wouldn't survive long enough to outlive his sentence and was destined to spend the rest of his life in prison. Consequently, he cracked and confessed. His life now is truly Staring Down the Barrel.

Cardoza admitted in his confession before the jury that the day Cirisha was killed, she had called him and blasted him over the phone. An angry and worried Cardoza reached the Academic Block, only to find Cirisha away from her desk. When she returned from the duPont Center—the CCTV feeds confirmed that she had been there—Cirisha had an ugly showdown with him. The possibility of Richard having been exploited by Cardoza and the latter not standing up for the values she thought were integral to life in academia, was too much for her to bear. She even suspected that Cardoza's relationship with Richard could have been one of the reasons for his death. After the confrontation, she left him and headed to the Boston Public Garden in an extremely agitated state of mind. She had perhaps felt that her morning jog would help her get a hold on herself.

Cardoza, who had tried to calm her down initially, followed her there. He tried his best to convince Cirisha, who would have none of it. She threatened to expose Cardoza and tell the world about his dalliance with Richard. Had she carried out her threat, it would have sounded the death knell for Cardoza's career, family and reputation. At the fag end of his academic career, where reputation mattered the most, he could not afford to risk it all. After walking with her around the park for twenty-odd minutes, trying to talk her out of her resolve, Cardoza got lucky. Cirisha, who had had a stressful night and an even worse morning, collapsed. Medics attributed it to low blood sugar. She hadn't had anything to eat the night before. She had left early on the morning of the 5th, probably in the hope of coming back in time for breakfast, which she couldn't.

When he saw her collapse, Cardoza panicked, but he sensed an opportunity almost immediately. An evil thought crossed his mind. He recollected Erica's research on suicides. It had listed air embolism as one of the common means of committing suicide. He ran to his car and pulled out the syringes and large needles that he had got for Champ, his ailing Dobermann. He rushed back to where Cirisha lay and, with a three-and-a-half-inch needle, he pumped in air directly into her chest. The three and a half inches were enough to penetrate her skin and muscle cover, and reach deep into her right ventricle. He repeated the procedure thrice, just to make sure he had pushed in enough air to make it fatal. He waited for ten minutes. By that time the gas bubbles had blocked the pulmonary valve. It prevented low-oxygen blood from moving into the lungs through the pulmonary artery to replenish their oxygen levels before flowing into the left ventricle and from there to the rest of the body. The cardiac arrest that resulted was so massive that Cirisha had no hope of survival.

After making sure that Cirisha was dead, he quietly walked away from the scene, only to resurface at her house in the next couple of hours to offer his condolences to an unsuspecting Aditya.

Deahl's death and *Staring Down the Barrel* became highly discussed issues across America. Many felt that for a man who strongly advocated the use of guns and misused his position to lend credibility to a false cause, the manner in which he met his end was nothing but natural justice. The NRA was quick to dissociate itself from the research and stated that linking them to the fabricated data was politically motivated. It denied that its representative had ever met Michael Cardoza or James Deahl and lay low for a while till things cooled down. Lucier decided to visit his ancestral home and took off on a long vacation to a quaint French village in Aix-en-Provence. The FBI could not find a shred of evidence linking anyone remotely close to him to the killing of Deahl.

The Bancroft Prize to *Staring Down the Barrel* was rescinded. In the general interest of the nation, the publishers withdrew unsold copies of the book from the market and pulped them.

Windle confessed to a guilt-ridden Aditya one day that without him, they would never have been able to solve one of the most complex cases in Massachusetts. It didn't matter much to Aditya: the pain of living with the knowledge that his wife's last impression of him was that of an unscrupulous and morally bankrupt banker was still gnawing at him. The only way he could make it up to Cirisha was to give up his ill-gotten wealth and live life the way she would have wanted him to. He gave himself up to law enforcers. For having cooperated with them, he was let off with a lesser sentence of four years in jail, almost all of it on account of laundering money from Mexico into the United States of America. Over time, Aditya became a federal informer. Narayanan, who had by then recovered, was acquitted on the basis of Aditya's confession.

Before giving himself up, Aditya had transferred back to Coimbatore the money that Narayanan owed to investors in his emu farms. Once the courts cleared him, Narayanan returned to India and paid back every rupee. Thankfully, the money was sufficient to pay back the invested amounts along with a reasonable interest. The authorities in India, however, booked Narayanan and he is being tried for money laundering offences in Coimbatore.

The money ripped from Snuggles Inc.—the millions Shivinder had transferred into his account with GB2, Geneva—was returned to Snuggles Inc. to compensate for the losses incurred in their India business on account of Shivinder's and Aditya's wayward ways. In return, Snuggles dropped the case against Jigar Shah. As a goodwill gesture, they even offered to replace, free of cost, the shoes of suspect quality that customers had bought from the stores that Shivinder had fraudulently opened.

Nalin Sud, the behind-the-scenes operator and suave investment banker—the one who set up Aditya's meeting with Cambridge Partners, the one who struck a deal with Shivinder and collected the pendrive and photocopies from him before he was eliminated—remained free for some time. The world at large was oblivious to his involvement with the NRA, Cambridge Partners, Aditya or the gun movement.

However, everything changed the day Aditya confessed to the authorities in the US about the modus operandi in the Step Up Shoes fraud. He implicated Nalin as the mastermind of the scam and also led them to uncover his unexplained dealings with the NRA and Cambridge Partners. Wasn't he the one who had put Aditya in touch with Cambridge Partners in the first place?

In a face-saving measure, GB2 launched an internal investigation into Nalin's business dealings. That's when the skeletons came tumbling out of the closet. GB2 Private Bank had invested heavily through a complex, structured investment paper in gun-manufacturing units at the behest of and as a front for Cambridge Partners, many of those transactions not passing the muster as fair and legal deals.

Lucier had not lied when he had mentioned to Aditya that they had a 22 per cent investment in gun-manufacturing units. When Windle's team had investigated, they couldn't establish it because it was all on the books of GB2, with Chinese walls between GB2 and Cambridge Partners preventing anyone from linking the two. However, when the economic offences team from the FBI and the bank's internal control team reconnoitred in detail, it was just a matter of time before these transactions showed up.

Today Nalin is facing serious charges of forgery, fraud and embezzlement. When convicted, which he is sure to be, he stares at the possibility of a compounded jail term of over forty-two years.

Aditya more than paid for his sins. He had lost his wife. His banking career was over. The trauma he went through in 2008 was unparalleled. However, when he walked out of jail in end-2012, he was a reformed man. Windle, who by then had moved on to an influential position in the economic offences team in New York, offered him a job there. It was not something that would tickle the senses of a hotshot investment banker, but Aditya had moved on. Not wanting to return to the world of investment banking which had taken away everything that he loved, he dedicated his life to the prevention of economic crime. How long his resolve will last is difficult to say, but as of now, he is doing a great job.

The Democrats came to power in 2008 and again in 2012. But they did nothing to stem the easy availability of guns. Gun control still remains one of the most passionately debated subjects in modern-day America, with the Second Amendment probably being the most discussed topic. But that's how it stays—a perennial discussion.

~

6th June 2013: A gunman armed with an assault rifle kills six people on the streets of Santa Monica, before being gunned down by the police in a college library. The incident reignites the debate on gun rights vs gun control. Nothing has changed since the time Lucier met Cardoza for the research on gun crime in 2006. The game continues, only the players have changed.